INDIAN SUMMERS

INDIAN SUMMERS

Eric L. Gansworth

Michigan State University
East Lansing

All Michigan State University Press books are produced on paper which meets the require-
ments of American National Standard of Information Sciences—Permanence of paper for
printed materials ANSI Z39.48-1984.

Michigan State University Press
East Lansing, Michigan 48823-5202

02 01 00 99 98 1 2 3 4 5

Library of Congress Cataloging-in-Publication Data

Gansworth, Eric L.
        Indian Summers / Eric L. Gansworth
            p. cm.—(Native American Series)
        ISBN 0-97103-479-5 (alk. paper)
            1. Indians of North America—New York (State)—Fiction. 2. Tuscarora Indians—
Fiction. I. Title II. Series: Native American series (East Lansing, Mich.)
        PS3557.A519615   1998
        813'.54—dc21   98-14999
                                                                                        CIP

The following chapters have appeared in slightly different form in the following places:
"Getting Used to It," in *Iroquois Voices, Iroquois Visions* (Bright Hill); "The Ballad of Plastic
Fred," in *Growing Up Native American* (Morrow); "As the Crow Flies," (part of "Independence
Day") in *Quartet* (just buffalo literary center); "The Rawleigh Man," in *Blue Dawn, Red Earth*
(Doubleday Anchor).

Cover painting: Eric Gansworth
Cover painting photography: Catherine Linder

Michigan State University Press Native American Series

Native American Series Editor: **Clifford E. Trafzer**

for the Bumblebee,
without whom I could not grow

Contents

AUTHOR'S NOTE

To have finally arrived at this point still seems unimaginable. As much as I have contemplated this page over the years, the thought of actually having to write it felt so remote that I never realized how formidable an opponent it might actually be. So many people have had a hand (at least) in this coming about, it seems impossible that I won't forget someone along the way. If this has happened, my apologies.

Most significantly, I would like to thank Larry Plant, ever-present, for constant support and for allowing me the belief that this was even remotely possible, especially through my period of writing "Stephen King/Indian Stories" (big creepy monsters and all), for offering criticism, even knowing the cost of my stubbornness, and for being willing to read chapters "just one more time." To Bob Baxter, friend, teacher, reader—thank you for the years, for the ghost machine and for passing on the responsibility that comes with listening. Thank you to my family, whose remarkable survival techniques, blending humor with even our most tragic moments, telling stories through endless summer nights, taught me how to endure.

I would like also to thank those people I've met along the way whose experiences far exceeded mine, and who were encouraging to yet another beginner. Thank you, Diane Glancy, Joy Harjo, and Maurice Kenny, for welcoming me so warmly to the ranks. Patricia Riley, thank you for allowing me the honor of having my first publication in such amazing company. Thank you to Bertha Rogers, Robert Bensen, and Deborah Ott for also seeing my work worthy of publication. Thank you to Will Schwalbe, for continued belief and interest, and consistent support. Thank you also to Aviva Goode, whose suggestions and discussions helped shape this work from the initial naive plan into a feasible form. Thank you especially to Cliff Trafzer, who has been there from the start all the way up to this point, and whose voice coming down the line was, from the very beginning, that of an old friend, welcoming me home.

I would also like to acknowledge my second cousin Ted C. Williams, whose book *The Reservation* showed me that our stories are as worthy of telling as any other. Similarly, while actual locations and historic events are part of this work's backdrop, this is a work of fiction. Names, characters, places, and incidents either are products of my imagination or have been used fictitiously. Any resemblance to actual events or locales or persons, living or dead, is entirely coincidental.

Prologue

ᗧᗧᗧ

WAKEFULNESS

"**H**ey. Bug." Sy Jimison cracked his eyes open, responding to the name he'd gone by for well over fifty years, spoken in a voice he recognized as belonging to one of his nephews.

"What are you doing here?" he asked, rolling over in the bed to check the clock glowing on his night stand. "It's not even five. Christ, even I don't get up this early." Nearly forty years of living without electricity had developed a dependency on the sun in him, an attachment to its cycles, though he recently began lamenting the winter nights he had gone to bed shortly after five in the evening, sometimes throwing out his visiting nieces and nephews as the shadows filled his house. He wondered if he shouldn't have just given up the kerosene he carefully rationed in his lamp use. He craved the warm glow and sharp odor now. The blue edge of fluorescence in this building bothered him, its unnatural hum, a constant reminder that he no longer lived at home.

"Sorry. Guess I just wasn't paying attention. So, how you feeling? They treating you all right in here?" Floyd Page leaned against the guard rail on the unoccupied bed a few feet away.

"Well, I can't complain. Won't do me any good, anyways." Sy didn't bother asking how his nephew had gotten past the nurses' station. He knew that visiting hours became much more flexible once the residents grew closer to the end of their terms as "terminals." The old jock who had recently abandoned the next bed had family swirling about him behind the closed curtain at all hours the week before he'd died, hoping to be there at that special moment, to remember it with fondness and sorrow.

1

"Good, good. So, tell me a story."

"What kind of . . . here, crank this bed, so I can see you better." The younger man did this as Sy wriggled his way up on the pillows. "Okay. Good. Now, what kind of story?"

"I want to know about the dike."

"What about it? Shit, you probably been up there a lot more than me. Fact, I'd guarantee that. Christ, I ain't been up there in, must be almost twenty years. Pour me some of that water, will you?"

"No. I mean, you know, before the dike. You lived there, didn't you?" Floyd clarified, handing Sy the plastic tumbler.

"Me and a bunch of other folks. Boy, that was a time." Sy nodded and sipped from the water. "Okay, I'll tell you, but we gotta talk about something else, first. You know, the house is going to Hank." He watched his nephew closely. Sy's only son, Hank, had not lived among the family since before Floyd had been born, over thirty years before. Actually, it had been in the time of the dike that Hank and his mother had left the reservation for good.

"Look, Bug. Don't talk like that. Come on."

"You know this here bed is my last home as much as I do. Now shut up and listen. You boys all had each other, growing up. He didn't have none of that, but that wasn't his fault. His ma decided to leave. That wasn't him. He loved it at home, too. I can tell you that. So, you boys treat him like you would anyone else from home. That's what I want to tell you. You hear?" Floyd nodded. "Okay, pretty dood. Now, the dike. Let's see. Around about the nineteen-fifties, in the middle of the summer, sometime. . . . What you got there?"

"Uh . . . a notebook. I been having some troubles remembering stuff, lately, so I thought, you know, I might write it down."

"Oh, jeez. You don't need to write nothing down. Everyone remembers this shit. Just ask 'em."

"I'm here asking, Uncle Bug." Floyd sat back, his pen resting on the brand new spiral notebook, waiting to begin.

"Okay, so around about the nineteen-fifties, in the middle of the spring . . ."

"I thought you said it was in the middle of the summer."

"I thought you were having troubles remembering." The two men laughed and Floyd poured his uncle another cup of water.

"The when never matters. It's the what. So, whenever the hell it was. . . ."

〰
〰

"Chewant, Bug." Sy Jimison cracked his eyes open a little. His sister, Nora Page, swept into the room, as she always did, straightening up with a mixture of precision and annoyance. The morning paper and a fresh glass of water sat on his tray table, framing the exact width of his breakfast tray, awaiting its arrival.

"It must be a day for Pages," he said, sitting up in his bed. "Floydie was here, oh early, early this morning. What's the matter?" His sister's stare halted him. He wondered if he looked closer to death than he expected. No one had let him see a mirror for a couple of weeks, but his withering fingers and arms told the truth of his cancer.

"Floyd's been missing for almost a week. No one has seen him," she said, picking up the telephone in his room and dialing. "Damn! Innis and them must have left their shop already. Well," she said, hanging up the phone, "at least we know he's alive."

Chapter One

_{ᗰᗰ}

GETTING USED TO IT

FLOYD PAGE

Some of the most curious things happen on the reservation. Last summer, one morning about six o'clock, my mom heard this horrible crunching noise out on her front lawn. She went out to see that there was a pretty new Trans Am sitting in our bushline, the engine revving and the tires digging deep grooves in her lawn. She walked up and saw that the driver was some nicely dressed white kid, no more than seventeen, she suspected. She said he looked like he came from Lewiston, the snobby village just below the reservation.

He had just jumped our driveway, ripped through our lawn and uprooted the remains of a dead cherry tree before landing in the bushes. He tried rocking the car for a while, but finally got out and began kicking it, making big dents in the doors.

"Hey there," my mom said as he caught a breather from his kickfest; it was the first time he noticed her. "You okay?" she asked as he stared blankly at her.

"You got any loose joints you'd be willing to sell? Just a couple?" he asked my sixty-eight year old mother.

"Go on in my house and call someone about getting your car out from my bushes," she said, tugging on the collar of his Izod shirt. She told me this story later in the day, and when I asked her why she didn't have him arrested, she shook her head.

"Who're they gonna believe," she asked, "some rich kid from Lewiston, or some old Indian woman?" As I nodded my head, she added: "Besides, I been wanting for the longest time to get rid of that damn cherry tree stump anyways."

Another thing that happened, just recently, was that a body had been found down near the dike. It was a girl, they thought probably in her twenties. She'd been found by some hunter, curled up in the weeds with her dress pulled up over her head. I felt, when I heard the news, that the dike would be changed forever.

My mom's house is pretty close, walking distance, to the dike, or "the reservoir," as the state calls it. So on summer mornings, from the front porch, we caught glimpses of most reservation kids. They'd be piled sometimes twelve to a car, on the roof, on the hood, in the open trunks and anywhere they could fit, all on their way to the dike.

The reservoir was at the end of our road. In fact, our road used to continue on, but where houses and roads and woods and fields had thrived, there now stood this giant rectangular structure, made of boulders and topsoil, and filled with river water. It stood about four or five stories high. The steep walls of it angled in a little bit, but other than that, it was flat and unnatural.

A lot of people didn't like the reservoir too much at first. Most reservation families had lost land when the government felt it would be more convenient to uproot Indian families and homes than white ones. The state had decided they needed a reservoir to harness the Niagara Falls and use its natural water power to their advantage.

It seems they picked the land they thought was going to be easiest to take. They had two other equally good choices. But they knew white people could be touchy about their land and, in the past, Indians had been so good about giving up theirs without much noise. So I guess it was a historical thing.

They took it, even though most people on the reservation didn't want it to happen. There were a lot of protests and fights with construction workers, but nothing big came of them. We never could figure this out. The Chiefs' Council seemed to be powerless over what happened to our land. We didn't know that, even as we continued our fights and protests, they sold the land out from under us. They never said anything.

We were supposed to get something for it, but most of us got very little. The state offered an amount and we were obligated to take it. Though I do know that certain people on the reservation suddenly had nice houses, houses with running water in them. Showers, sinks, even flush toilets. Water magic, must have been.

That decision had been made before I was born. As far back as I can remember, we've been going swimming in the dike. In fact, I didn't even know it was called a reservoir. And when I first heard people using that term, I had no idea they were talking about our swimming pool. As far as I had known, it was always called the dike.

Once you were up top, there was this nice, level stone road to drive around on. It was what made up the top of the dike, and it went all the way around. We couldn't get all the way around, though. Just before you got to where the power plant was, the whole dike had a huge barbed wire fence blocking the way.

The dike had been there since the fifties, and by the time I came along in the sixties, it had become just another part of the reservation for most everybody. So we used to drive over there all the time. Just drive up the dike road and sit on the hood, watching the sunset, or watching someone fishing.

All the bigger kids didn't ride in the car up the dike. They wanted to get let off at the corner of our road and the dike. That way, they could climb straight up it, and that was pretty steep. But people had been doing it for a long time. A well worn path went straight up the side of it at our corner. That path almost looked like it was a continuation of our road, just not as wide as the road itself.

Usually my sister Kay was the one who took us up to the dike to watch the waves. Sometimes we would first go down to Jugg's store and get creamsicles, or if we were really lucky, Jugg might have some of those rare blue popsicles in his freezer case. We all knew the waves were caused by water intake or release for the power plant, but their smooth dance against the rocks was still something to see. And it kind of sounded like what we believed an ocean would sound like, if we ever got to see one for real.

At first, my mom didn't even listen when everyone was saying this. She hated the dike, because we'd lost so much land to it, and so she refused to go up there. She changed her mind really quick, though, when she heard The Bug had gone up there. She wasn't going to let her pain-in-the-ass brother with a wooden leg know something she didn't know. So she did come up with us that one time. That was one of the shortest visits to the top of the dike that I ever had.

We drove up, got out and sat on the hood and waited for the sky to start changing colors. Lucky for her, the clouds happened to be right that day. Sometimes there weren't any, and without clouds, you don't get any sun beams shooting down. But they were there that day, and the beams broke through right on schedule.

My mom studied them long enough to be able to say she had seen what a dike sunset looked like. She had looked, gotten back in the car, and was ready to leave in about fifteen seconds. I hadn't even gotten half my blue popsicle eaten.

This wasn't like one of our usual sunsets. When Kay took us, we stayed up there until almost dark. We even had to put the headlights on as we drove down the dike road, in case anyone might be coming up it. Then Kay would drive over to the path, to pick up the older kids. They not only liked to go up the path, they also liked to climb down it.

I didn't know, at the time, which was harder, and was later surprised to find out going down was much more difficult. It was easier to fall and lose your balance heading down. And if you weren't careful, you'd pick up too much speed going down the steep hill and then just crash and roll the rest of the way down.

In those early trips to the dike, my cousin Ace and I had to stay on the gravel road. We didn't get to go swimming, or to even touch the water. The water was kind of hard to get to and you needed more balance than either of us had. And Kay knew that; with two little kids hanging on to her, she couldn't navigate around the boulder piles and gravel that led to the water. So she stayed up top with us and some of her friends came up to see us for a while. And then they'd leave and others would come up.

Things changed; they always do. Kay eventually got married and left the house and we started going to the dike by ourselves. The state tried to discourage us from going there, too. They didn't like the idea of us being so close to their power plant; they told us it was against the law to be on top of their reservoir. We told them we didn't go to the reservoir. We went to the dike.

The state didn't think that was too funny. They took a little of the golf course that had sprung up on the white side of the dike and built themselves a new road. When that was done, they bulldozed the reservation dike road, so we couldn't use it. So we parked on the regular road and walked up the dike.

The first swim I ever had in it was when I was about ten. I had walked down with my cousins Ace and Innis. Jugg's store had been closed for a few years by then, so we had been walking to the next closest store. That was the Red and White that was just off the edge of the reservation.

It was also right near the dike. "You guys wanna climb up the dike?" Innis asked on the walk home, as we swigged from our bottles of Pepsi past the dike. We took him up on it and carried our bottles to the top, using the straight up path, the big kids' path.

We got to the top and I stood up straight, looking out over the water. I was just about to chug the last of my bottle when Innis began climbing down the boulder side. Ace and I looked at each other and followed him a couple of seconds later.

"Let's go swimming," Innis said, as we caught up to him near the water's edge. I looked at the two of them, and then myself, and mentioned to Innis that none of us were wearing shorts. He started laughing and dropped his pants. He slipped them off from around his ankles and as he stood up, he snapped the waist band of the pair of Fruit of the Looms he was wearing. "You got guds on, don't ya?" he asked, pulling his T-shirt off.

Before I could even nod, he jumped in the water, his skinny body slicing the water like the rich brown eels we are. Ace and I looked at each other while Innis was under the water. Neither one of us wanted to go first, but finally he took off his shirt and then I took mine off. We were both in the water a couple minutes later, not even caring that someone might see us in our underwear. We didn't know this was the common dike swim suit.

After we finished swimming, we sat on the rocks and dried in the sun, like a bunch of lizards. We had been dry a long time, but our guds were still wet. I asked Innis what we were supposed to do about this. He was the expert, after all.

He took the last swallow from his Pepsi bottle, stood up and turned his back to us. He peeled the wet shorts from his body and after wringing them out, he threw them on the flat surface of a boulder. They splatted as water drained down the rock. He grabbed his jeans and pulled them on. He whipped his shorts on the rocks a few more times, leaving Rorschach underwear blot designs to fade on the rocks, and eventually wrapped them around his left hand. He turned around and put on his T-shirt. "Simple as that," he said. I went behind the boulder to change back into my jeans.

Dike swimming became a major part of my summers from then on. And as I got older, I got less uptight about swimming in my underwear. In fact, if we were swimming at night, we usually didn't bother wearing any.

We'd been swimming up there for over thirty years when that body had been found this summer. The dike was probably one of the last things that girl saw. I figured this was going to be like the last time they found a body on the reservation that wasn't one of us; I knew what to expect. That was a few years ago. Someone had found the body down by one of the reservation borders, the one that edges Myers' Lake State Park. With that one, they never caught the killer, but for a while, we all got some pretty chilly looks whenever we were off the reservation. Chillier than usual. A lot of people from off the reservation said what a shame it was; the girl had almost escaped.

A few weeks ago, I was sitting at this bar with this buddy of mine from off the res. "So, you got any idea who killed that girl?" he asked. I thought of the kids who sit at home now, maybe smoking their own loose joints, who knows. They're not swimming at the dike anymore. That girl's ghost lingers in the area. I asked him why he thought I might know.

"Well, you guys are all pretty tight, ain't ya? Smoke signals and all?" he answered.

By this time, I had almost gotten used to this response. For years, people have stolen cars and after stripping them, have abandoned them on the reservation. Outsiders have a tendency to want to do their dirty work on our lands. We always got the blame there, and it appeared we inherited whatever happened in what remained of our boundaries. It occurred to me that if I couldn't convince outside people there was no logic in us stealing cars and bringing them back to our houses to strip and burn, I sure wasn't going to be able to convince them that we didn't bring dead bodies to our favorite places.

I didn't say anything.

Chapter Two

ARTIFACTS

LATE JUNE

Innis Natcha loosened the scorching work boots and pulled them from his swollen feet. His limp and wet socks peeled back easily as he wrenched the boots, and he removed them from where they dangled listlessly at his toes. He set them on one of the larger boulders near the top of the reservoir. Examining fresh walk-blisters on his Achilles' tendon, he sat among the boulders on the interior side and caught his breath. The steep walk up the outer grassy five story high wall winded him more easily now that he'd turned thirty. He slid his feet into the water to rest as he removed his shirt. The water was always high at sunset, so only a few yards spanned the area between the place where he sat and the perimeter road, which topped the reservoir. As he shucked his pants off, he realized this would probably be his first swim without his cousin Floyd in well over eight years, maybe as long as ten.

He dived in, cutting the stored water with his smooth, muscular body. He searched in the soft green water for the boulder with his cousin's blood on it, but he knew it was farther out, where their family land had once been. The two had been out here on a Saturday morning, three weeks before, the end of an all night two-fold party. They'd been celebrating the beginning of summer, and mourning the end of a part of their lives. They'd had the sense that their city cousin, Hank Jimison, was soon to move into their midst. They had surely lost their uncle, The Bug, and his house as their second home. It had seemed only appropriate to end the party with a swim in the dike.

11

The water had been as sharp as a razor blade bath, but they could only tell with some vague and faraway sense. Dew had still coated the rocks and boulders when they'd arrived, and they'd waited for the sun to meander over the reservoir's east wall and burn off the dampness before they'd jumped into the winking and low water.

"Over there," Innis had said that morning, pointing to a general area over the water, as the sun warmed their backs. "I told you it'd be low enough. We can do it." He had lain his clothes on the rocks and eased in. Even through his dense night insulation, the cold had slipped in, and he cursed his own idea, by the time his balls reached the frigid surface.

"Wuss! Like this, man!" Floyd had shouted from atop a boulder. He'd dived straight in before Innis could shout any objection. Floyd had disappeared below the shifting fluid surface, and Innis began a long string of bitching until he saw the red tinting the frothing waves. He'd awkwardly stumbled over more boulders until he'd reached a drop-off and sunk below the surface himself. He'd found Floyd in a few seconds, his mouth gaping open, the dull filtered light gleaming mellowly off of his teeth, a vague bloody halo circling his head as Innis reached out to grab him.

They'd surfaced and Innis shouted to his slightly younger cousin as he'd dragged the unconscious man to the interior wall. Floyd finally woke as Innis slapped him gently. "Cut the shit, man," he'd said, blinking and rubbing the back of his head. "Guess I won't be doing that again," he'd continued, bringing his hand back around, blood swirling with the water still on his skin, tracing through the creases. He'd gently probed the gash with his fingers and, having grabbed his pants, spoke. "I guess I better have that looked at. There's an area of my hard head that ain't so hard, anymore."

They'd driven to the hospital, where the Emergency Room personnel had forced Floyd to stay a day for observation. His head had been stitched up. The skull hadn't been fractured, and x-rays hadn't really revealed anything, but the stay was standard procedure for questionable head injuries. "D'you get the rocks?" he'd asked Innis, after the doctor had left.

Innis hadn't, and now he was back in the dike, swimming out to the area of their family's old homestead, where waves lighted and danced over his family's history. This act, a voiding, often helped Innis clear his mind. Being as young as he was, he didn't have an image of the potential to miss.

That part of his history would be under water, forever, washed clean by the state. This blackness forced thoughts of everything else out, leaving the dark void below him, of plants never to be grown and houses never to be built. Then he would shut his eyes and start over again with whatever needed addressing.

He closed his eyes as he arrived at the spot and held his place, and the thing which washed in, filling the void this time, was his cousin. Floyd had been acting strangely since the accident, but his peculiarities had been pretty minor things, until a week ago.

Innis had been awakened by a noise in the middle of the night. He looked at the digital alarm clock glowing on the table next to his bed. It read a little after four. Innis had awakened slowly and he had even thought he was dreaming at first. The sound droned on and on. It almost seemed to have been there forever, but it couldn't have been. He would have noticed something like this. It was an engine of some sort.

He lay in his crumpled sheets for a while, waiting for the sound to go away or stop. It did neither, and a little while later, he rolled out of bed and threw on some jeans. As Innis stepped out the back door, he knew immediately the noise's origin. He let the door back to its frame gently, hoping not to wake anyone else.

He jumped off the porch and rushed over to Floyd's car, which idled in the driveway. As he got closer, he could see Floyd slouched in the driver's seat, looking intently out the windshield. The Nova's lone headlight shone on Floyd's trailer.

"Where the hell you been, man?" Innis asked when Floyd rolled down the window.

"Just getting home. Me and Alvin were down at The Den. Startin' early this week. What the hell do you care?"

"What!"

"Like you never went out on a Monday night?"

"Monday?" Innis leaned into the cab.

"Monday night or Tuesday morning."

"What?" He repeated.

"Suddenly you don't understand English? Depending on how you wanna look at it. Either Monday night or Tuesday morning." Innis could not see any attempt at deception in Floyd's face, and the man had never been any good at lying.

"You been back to the doctor's, Floyd?" Innis finally asked.

"They didn't find anything, remember?" Floyd climbed out of the car and they both wandered off to their houses. When Innis reached his back porch, he turned around to watch Floyd, making sure he had entered the trailer. Upon the door shutting, Innis turned to grab for his own door. Before he could reach it, though, it met him. Olive, his mother, held it open. He walked in. She had also been awakened.

"Where's he been? Nora's been just worried sick," she said, scooping some coffee into the Mr. Coffee's filter. Neither would get back to sleep, so they started their morning routines a couple hours earlier than usual.

"Don't know, but I don't think he does, either." Innis sat at the table, watching coffee drip down into the glass pot. He explained the interaction, and Olive listened intently. She poured coffee for them both and they sat in silence, and eventually the vague sun tinted the clouds in the eastern sky.

Innis realized he was on his own. He didn't know why, but he suspected it was because he and Floyd had grown up together. They were a couple years apart, but that had never mattered, even way back in school, when it usually matters.

Two hours later, as he waited for his ride to work, he waved Floyd down, who was pulling out of the driveway, also on his way to work. "You goin' out tomorrow after work," he started.

"Wednesday? Probably not."

"Tomorrow's Friday, Floyd. You been missing for over a week."

"Your ass," Floyd said, but not entirely convincingly. "Yeah, I'll be there," he finished.

"Mind if I come?" Floyd shook his head, and Innis continued. "Gotta pick me up at the shop, though. Riding with Ely this week. Won't have a way to get to The Den."

"No problem. Pick you up about five after five, maybe ten after. You know, depending on traffic. Later." Floyd pulled out and Ely, one of Innis's brothers, drove up a minute or so later.

Innis had planned on talking with Floyd about how peculiar he was acting lately. He hadn't identified it as a memory problem yet. After all, it wasn't the first time in history that an Indian had dropped out for a week on a bender. They were always seen by someone, though, either at some bar, or a convenience store, trying to buy beer after hours, or passed out in their car in someone's field, but Floyd had somehow vanished completely for almost a week. Innis had even contemplated talking to Brian Waterson, the reservation medicine man, but he couldn't even tell him at this point, what, in particular, was unusual with Floyd, aside from his ability to disappear. He also still secretly assumed it had something to do with the dike accident.

The talk at the roofers' bar would have at least been able to establish something, he had hoped. But when Floyd hadn't shown, his worry had grown. Unsettling stories about Floyd's continued erratic behavior there from some of the other roofers, who informed him Floyd had disappeared again sometime in the morning, pushed him back out into the sun. The walk from the shop to The Den had been a long and hot one, but he'd continued on, intent only on reaching the dike.

∽
∽

Innis opened his eyes. He heard the familiar sound of tires popping the gravel on the dike's perimeter road. He could see the car way off in the distance, heading his way. Indians weren't officially allowed on or in the reservoir, and Power Authority trucks patrolled the area sometimes, to chase them away. People were rarely caught; they either hid among the rocks in the dike's inner surface, or submerged briefly, allowing the darkness to swallow them.

Innis took a deep breath and disappeared over his family's land. He thrashed, pushing deeper into the cool water, watching his surroundings fade into deeper greens and blacks. Even the familiarity of this could not comfort him in the new loneliness of his swim.

Over the years, they swam in the dike every summer, with about half of the younger folks from the reservation. Today, Innis swam alone. The murdered girl's ghost still lingered for many. They'd be back, some day. Amid the shadowy, deep waves, Innis waited, running out of air. He let a few bubbles escape from his lips and sank lower, trying to reach the granite chunks twenty feet below, which separated him from his family land, a task considerably harder than on the day he and Floyd had attempted it, the day of the accident.

They had decided as the sun rose that morning that they wanted to take history back, and the first step was to each take one of the rocks and keep it with him, forever, to get back in touch with what was theirs, to never forget. But the urgency of Floyd's quest had ended their search in the emergency room, home boulders washed with blood forgotten on the dike's secretive floor.

Innis reached the area, his chest straining with his remaining air. He grabbed two rocks, relatively small ones, but they were enough, and made his way back toward the light.

He reached the surface and gasped a few breaths, trying desperately to keep his grip on the rocks and stay afloat. He blinked his eyes rapidly, trying to clear his vision.

"Hey! Get your ass out of there, now!" he heard. Startled, he dropped the rocks, and he felt their soft impact on his lower legs as they slipped their way back into the cool blackness. He squinted and could see a small figure standing on the perimeter road. Innis had really not anticipated this kind of greeting. He thought for sure that he hadn't been seen, that he'd submerged in time. The patrollers always tried scare tactics, assuming they would work. As the patroller went back to his car, Innis slowly swam back to the interior wall and climbed out onto the boulders, quickly grabbing the jeans from the rumpled pile of sweaty clothes.

"Get out here now, Mister," Floyd yelled at him as he reached the top, sitting on the hood of his Nova and cracking a beer. He reached into a bag he had brought from the car and pulled another beer from it. He threw it down to Innis, who caught it like a pro.

"Pinhead," Innis grunted, joining him on the hood and putting his boots on.

"I saw you when I was driving up Dog Street, so I thought I'd come up and say hi," Floyd said, finishing half of his beer in one long pull from the bottle. "Pretty dood," he said to the sky. "Pretty dood." He smiled into the western sun, lifting a pair of sunglasses to his eyes.

Thinking about the walk from the shop to The Den, and then home to the dike, his aching feet and Floyd's pathetic peace offering, Innis began grinding his teeth. "Forget something?"

"Like what, the chips and dip?"

"You were supposed to pick me up at the shop. Like, almost two hours ago," he said, taking a pull. He frowned at the car. "How'd you get up here, anyway?" he asked Floyd, who still smiled.

"The Dike Road. How else, stupid?" Floyd's smile never faltered. He seemed confident that he had come up The Dike Road. Innis's frown dug more deeply into his forehead. The Dike Road had been bulldozed out of existence by the state, to discourage Indians from driving to the top of the reservoir, twelve years before.

As seven o'clock approached, the sun began setting in Floyd Page's reflective shades.

Chapter Three

ㅅㅅ
ㅅㅅ

MILKWEEDS

FLOYD PAGE

JULY 1, 1992

I got the idea that if I write it all down, it won't be so easy to forget. That's been my big trouble, lately. I don't know where I got that Big Idea from, but we'll see. I never was all that good at writing. I spent, I guess, the last two years of high school in vocational training. But this shouldn't be too hard. It is, after all, my own story. Anyway, I gotta do something.

You know, I even went out to the reservation medicine man, to see if he could help me, and that alone should tell you how desperate I am. But he sent me away. He knew that I didn't really believe, and that must be what he needs. I guess you can't have everything. He didn't just send me away empty handed, though. He gave me something, and told me that if I knew what to do with it, it might help me, but I'll get to that in a minute.

It started out after this accident I had, swimming in the dike, cracking my head on the rocks hidden below the waters. You wouldn't notice it at first. They were real small things, like missing appointments and the such. I just passed these off as my own carelessness and, well, you know, "Indian Time." We haven't exactly been known for our punctuality. So I was able to get away with that for a while. But after and away, some real dumb things would happen.

Like one day last month, I was sitting there, watching this program on the tv, and right smack in the middle of it, I realized I was watching a soap opera. Now I don't have anything really big against soap operas or anything

19

like that, except that they're so fake. Most everything on the tube is. But the thing of it is, soap operas are only on during the week, and during the day.

Get it? I was supposed to be at work, and here I was sitting on my couch, watching tv, and in my underwear, no less. I hadn't even gotten dressed yet. A cup of coffee sat on the table next to me and when I touched it, it was stone cold. The clock on top of the tv said it was quarter to one. So I jumped up and grabbed some clothes that were laying on the floor and threw them on.

I broke all kinds of speed limits (and didn't get caught), flying to the work site, and when I got there, no one else was there, at least no one from our crew was there. The people who worked at that company's building were going about their business, but that was it. Well really, there was something else, too. A brand new roof perched on that building, like a bird on its nest.

The last I could recall, we had only gotten about a third of the roof completed. But there, looking me straight in the eye was a brand spanking new roof, the shingle-sand gleaming and winking at me in the afternoon sun. It later turned out that we had already moved on to the University roofs the week before.

I went home and sat with the tv off, not really knowing what to do. I called old Judy Waterson, to see if she would read my tea leaves, but she said that she only did it for family members. She was always kind of funny that way, you know? Like she didn't even mention that her son Brian had taken over Hillman's medicine after the old man went over the falls. I mean, everyone knows anyway, but you'd think she could at least have said something out of courtesy, or some shit like that.

Well, actually, maybe I didn't call her, right off. Yeah, I think that was later. First I went the way you'd think made sense. The summer hangs high right now, as it almost always does the first week of July. Not only does that mean it was beautiful roofing weather, but also that our season is in full swing. And that means that I still have company health insurance. So I went back to my doctor's.

After I handed over my co-payment, and sat on one of those fierce uncomfortable padded tables, the doctor came in and told me within a couple minutes that he didn't know what I had. He starts ordering up a bunch of tests, all of which have to be done during the day. I told him I couldn't take that much time off. Then he only ordered, get this, the "Essential Five." So I went for the Essential Five. I would highly recommend avoiding them, if I could remember what they were called.

I go back in and, guess what I hear after the co-payment? The accident seemed to have caused some sort of "memory problem." Beyond that, they couldn't tell me. These things are tricky. Basically what they told me was that all those pain-in-the-ass tests came up with was a big zero. I guess it's comforting to know that I don't have some huge brain tumor or something like that, but that still doesn't help me and my missing days. They wanted more tests, but I never went back.

At work, they always make someone be my partner now, you know, to keep an eye on me. And this sucks, because now I can't ever be the one who goes back to the main building for supplies. I mean, it's great that I'm still working. Really, they could have just fired me. But the supply job is the best. It's always only one person who does this, and so they're not gonna send two people, me and my guardian, giving up two workers, when they can send just one. We always used to take rotation turns for this duty, because, obviously, it involves a break from all that ass-busting work on the roofs. So now, me and my partner always get passed over for this, and I'm sure my partner ain't too happy with this arrangement.

In fact, that's who it was, Bob Hacker—"the Hack," we call him—my new partner, who suggested I might go and see Brian Waterson. No, that's not right. It was my cousin Innis, who lives next door. He's not even a roofer. He's a carpenter. But he's been hanging around with us roofers, lately. He and I always hang around, but he's even been coming to The Den, the roofer bar, where we go at least every Friday.

I don't know how he and Brian Waterson know each other. They don't really hang out in the same circles. That Brian went to college, and actually finished, and now works down at the newspaper. Yeah, I know, what's a medicine man doing working at a newspaper, but I guess working the medicines don't pay all that well. Come to think of it, he didn't charge me nothing when I went down to see him.

He used to live in the city, right near the paper and all, but now he lives back here on the reservation. Moved into Hillman's old house, in fact, what

21

with taking the business over, and all that. When I went over there, stuff dangled neatly from all over the ceiling beams. Hooks hung in an orderly way on the beams. Really, they were nails, but he was using them as hooks.

Anyway, they were all over the place. All this stuff was drying on them. I recognized some of the plants as the same ones that grew around my trailer, and some others I had never seen before. I guess he had uses for them I didn't. It was kind of weird to think that a milkweed would be considered by anyone to be a medicine. It's, you know, a weed. But there it was, hanging from a hook like any of the other medicines.

We used to have lots of wars with them. And in a lot of different ways, too. We used them with our plastic Indian tribe, as "pods." We saw *Invasion of the Body Snatchers* on tv and Innis thought that the milkweeds would look just like those big pods in the movie to our Indians. We even hacked one of our Indians up and inserted the body and head section into a milkweed, so it would look like it was growing inside the pod.

Other times, my cousins, sometimes even the older ones, like Stan and Ely, and I used the sticky milk inside the pods as war paint when we speared old bicycle tire rims, pretending they were buffalo. We divided into two teams, and rubbed the milkweed on our faces in certain designs we had seen on tv Indians, one type for each team, so we'd know who scored the point.

Two people stood at the ends of the line of the rest of us. When we all agreed that we were ready, the kid at one end picked up an old bicycle rim, lifted it over his head and threw it straight out in front of him. As the rim landed on its edge, it rolled through the line of us, and we stood ready.

We were lined up on either side, and each one of us was armed with a spear. These spears were the broken remains of old lacrosse sticks and hockey sticks. The hockey sticks were often the best, because they usually had the split shard of a plastic end still on them, which worked as a great spearhead.

We played by a point system, based on your hit. If you missed or if your spear went through the spokes but didn't stop the rim, you didn't get any points. But if you broke off a couple of spokes, you got one point. And if you were able to take the rim down with your shot, you got two points.

The thing everyone tried for, though, was the five pointer. To get this, you had to down the rim by spearing it right in the axle, the buffalo's heart.

This didn't happen very often, but I saw it a few times. On almost every one of those occasions, it was Ely or Stan, the big kids, who had downed the rickety buffalo.

The milkweeds kept track of your points. However many you got in a passing, someone from your team broke open a milkweed and added a sticky version of your team's design. That was how it was supposed to be, but since Stan could draw better than any of us, he pretty much took over the point design making for both teams.

When all the beat-up rims we had were bent to the point that they wouldn't roll any more, or didn't have any more spokes, the game was over, and your warpaint designs were counted. Whatever team had the most, won the game.

Sometimes, we didn't play such complicated games with the milkweeds. Instead, we just whipped them at each other, hoping that their green lumpy skin would break open and the victim would be splattered with the white milkweed blood.

And as I stared at the milkweed up on the hook, Brian Waterson reached up and took some of it down, and held it out to me. I looked at it and took it, because it seemed that was obviously what he wanted me to do.

I touched the milk pod and it pressed in with the light pressure of my fingers. The pod sprung back into its natural shape when I took my finger off. My fingers stuck to each other with the milk I had squeezed out. Fresh produce. I sniffed my sticky fingers, and the sharp, yet pleasant odor filled my nostrils. Same old milkweed, all right.

"Here, you take this," he said. "If you know what to do with it, and I feel you do, it might just help you." He never refused to tell me what to do, but he then put water on for tea, and only set out one cup. I took my milkweed and said goodbye.

So I brought the damn thing home and pounded a nail in my living room wall to hang the milkweed on. I don't like to pound nails in my wall too often, as it causes all kinds of problems. You know how it is when you live in a trailer, or I guess they call them mobile homes now. But you know, the walls are just made of paneling and studs, not too sturdy. And whenever you pound a nail in, even if you are able to find a support stud, the whole trailer shakes like an earthquake.

Any time I pounded, something, somewhere in the trailer, fell. One time, I broke this lacrosse trophy Al from work had given me. I never played lacrosse, but I usually went to the games, because the bar parties afterwards were always some of the best parties I ever went to. You know those trophies, just like bowling trophies. Only instead of the little bowling person on top, they got a tiny metal man standing there holding a lacrosse stick. Al had glued a little plastic beer bottle into the lacrosse stick's pocket. The team gave it to me at a party after the championship, one year. Honorary beer-drinking team mascot.

But you never know what's gonna happen, and that old hammer of mine does some funny things. I began to take its advice after that trophy thing. When the trophy fell, the little statue man broke in such a way that it reminded me of my uncle, and he deserved to have a statue more than I did. He was the best damn blues guitar player I ever met, not that I've met too many.

"Here, Bug, I brought something over for you," I said, walking into his house one day. I handed him the trophy. I had glued a toy guitar onto the little lacrosse player.

"Oh, nyah-wheh," he said, taking it and hobbling over to this plywood shelf he had put up at some point. "Well, let's see. What can I play, make sure I earn this trophy?" he said, sitting back in his big chair and strapping on the guitar. I imagine the trophy's still over there. I think we had some great times over there, at my uncle's house. Some, I remember perfect, but I wonder how many stories I've already lost to my problem.

And it's not just that I forget things either. I was sitting there the other day, doing some reminiscing about being out horseback riding, but I could only remember a little, like the blanket slipping and it being hard to ride.

"Hey, remember where was it that we went horseback riding, anyway?" I asked my cousin Innis when he came over that night.

"We never did any horseback riding," he said, grabbing a cold one from the fridge.

"Oh, come on. You know, when the blanket kept slipping, and we didn't have any saddles . . ."

"Well, you got that right. We didn't have any saddles, 'cause we didn't have any horses." I described it some more and he eventually started looking at me funny.

24

"That was that old movie. One of them ones with Fred Howkowski in it," he said, laughing. "When's the last time you saw the Cavalry?"

"Well. I don't remember any Cavalry," I protested.

"Then go rent it, and you'll see them. Besides, we couldn't possibly have even afforded horses." He finished the argument.

So that's why I wanted to hang up my milkweed as soon as I got home. When I walked into the trailer, the way the sun was shining in, a perfect bar of light stood on the wall and I could feel that was what I was supposed to do with my milkweed, hang it in the light. I tapped on the wall there and, yes indeed, a stud rested behind the sunlight. I got the hammer out of my tool belt and pounded the nail in.

As I expected, the whole damn place shook. Something fell in the hallway closet with a kind of jangly sound, music almost. As soon as I got the nail in its place, I headed for the closet, taking whatever the hammer had to offer.

So I tried to slide the sliding door, but it only moved a few inches. Whatever had fallen had wedged in the door tracks. I laid down in the hallway and slid my arm in as far as it would go. I grabbed onto some sharp metal thing that was, as I had guessed, stuck in the tracks. As I yanked the contraption out, some sharp circular part sliced my finger. I slid the door open and pulled out the object.

It was this damn gadget an old friend of mine had given me a long time ago. The piece that had cut me was only part of it. The rest was still up on the shelf.

I took the box down and brought it into the living room. People give me a lot of weird junk, probably because I usually find a place for it. They like these things, but don't have anywhere for them. Instead of throwing them out, I get them.

But this one was something else. Even I didn't know what to do with it. My friend, Bob Hacker, included an explanation when he gave it to me. He said it was a "ghost machine." He didn't know what its official name was, but that was what his aunt called it, and her husband had gotten it from some far off place.

It was made up of these sharp metal pieces, circles and tubes and one piece was made up of half moons all pierced at the tips and joined by a rod.

I looked at the directions. A hoop was supposed to circle the moons in their centers at equal spaces, making up a globe of the moons, with the rod extending out from the center of one end. The directions were all written in some other language I couldn't read. But there was a picture with the directions, showing you what it was supposed to look like when you were done putting it together.

Right now though, the piece I held onto was all just these half moons, hanging around together. The ghost machine had never been put together. Bob's family had lived with it for nearly fifty years, but when he passed it on to me, the ghost machine was still in the original packaging. It seemed that they didn't know what to do with it either, but I think maybe they were afraid it would really work.

In Bob's note, he told me that the ghost machine was supposed to encourage the ghosts of your relatives to come and visit. It was supposed to spin in the breeze and make a nice noise for them to listen to, perhaps so they wouldn't be lonely anymore. Seemed like a nice idea, if they were friendly ghosts. My guess is that Bob and his family didn't trust their old relatives. This is just a guess, but it never was built.

So I set the box on the table, took the lid off and saw that some of the pieces still lay in the wrapping paper they had crossed the ocean in. I set the pieces out on the table and started putting the machine together. You know, I hadn't pissed off any of my dead relatives, as far as I knew. But the table was too small for all of the pieces and the instructions. So I picked up a couple of the larger pieces, two identical wheels with slanted blades for spokes, and put them on the couch.

But sitting on the couch was my milkweed. I hurried up and grabbed it to put it up on the wall, the light almost gone from the spot. Not that I expected the sun to sit still for me, but it seemed like I had to get the milkweed up there before the light disappeared entirely. As I reached up to hang the milkweed, I felt a breeze come through, real nice, waving the tiny hairs on my arms. I stopped for just a second.

You guessed it. My hammer was telling me the ghost machine should go up there, so I put the milkweed up first, figuring the two could share the space. I didn't think they'd mind. I straightened out the milkweed and went back to my new project. I started putting it together, a real breeze, no rocket science needed there.

But, wouldn't you know, I came to a stopping block. All these years this thing has been around, shifting around in that box and no one noticed there was a god damn piece missing, and an important piece at that. The two blade wheels couldn't be hooked up. The axlerod was missing, and it wasn't like I could call the company either. So I sat for a little while and had a beer.

The sun wasn't stopping for nothing. Just as the light was about to pass out of the milkweed, though, I got a terrific idea. I took the milkweed down and wove the long stem through one blade wheel's axle, with the pod at the center, and then sent it through the tube base of the machine and out the other end to the second wheel. The second stem I wove with the first into the second wheel, so there was a pod at the axle of each wheel.

They weren't all that symmetrical, but they worked. The machine moved just the way I imagined it should when the next stray breeze jumped in the window. Sounds kind of stupid, huh? Well, when stupid's all you got, it ain't all that bad.

But the ghost machine doesn't sound so stupid. It makes a quiet little whistling sound. I'm kind of hoping that the milkweed will do something in there. The ghosts of when I was a kid would be pretty damn welcome about now. Maybe that's why Brian gave it to me.

I guess I believe after all. Because, you know, as that ghost machine spins in the breeze, I can just about hear those old gleaming and battered bike-tire buffalo squawking their stampede through the unoiled hinges, returning from the land of the dead. I'm hoping my aim is a little better these days, and that I'll be able to find my way to the heart.

Chapter Four

∿∿

THE SCENT OF SKUNK

FLOYD PAGE

JULY 2, 1992

I was just sitting here at my table, listening to my ghost machine and looking at my notebook, and thinking I was finding my way home, when something jumped in the window, floating through the ghost machine's wheels and making itself known, strong and clear. It was sharp and right on target. That was the scent of skunk, and though that's a funny smell to be glad of, I was glad of it just now. It's coming by when we need it, about right on time.

My Auntie Selina, my mom's sister who lives in Vegas, will be making her way home really soon. The first time she came back was one summer after she'd been living there about three years. Uncle Lou came with her but, you know, he was never as friendly as she was, always having other things to do when they lived here or seeming to always be on the edge of having something to do.

When their daughter Eileen got married, after the Justice of the Peace ceremony, we all went over to the Old Gym, which is this community building near the center of the reservation, where Eileen's reception was being held. The bunch of us kids weren't too interested in hanging around with all these grown ups in their best duds, so we mostly stayed outside.

The Old Gym had outside lights installed on it that had the big hoods on them, giving out a lot of light, even on really dark nights. We played a bunch of kids' games out there, you know, the usuals, Freeze Tag, Hide and Seek, telling ghost stories—we weren't too original. And we all felt kind of funny, anyway.

It wasn't just because we were in those stupid dress clothes that made us look like tiny grown ups. Uncle Lou stood in the doorway most of the night. A lot of the people came outside to smoke, because you weren't supposed to smoke in the Old Gym. After they had a cigarette, they always went right back in, but Uncle Lou just stood there, his big dark brush-cutted head blocking out some of the light, the tiny bristles on the top of his head standing straight up and shining. And the weird thing was, he didn't even smoke.

As we ran around, sometimes I would catch a glimpse of his face under the hooded lights. The face he made reminded me of the face people make when there is a fly or mosquito buzzing around and no matter how many different ways they try to kill the bug, they just can't quite get it. And they know it, so they give up and just make that face at the flies. I half expected to see him whip a fly swatter out at any given second. I didn't want to be around when he did. I'd rather hear about it from the victim.

When I asked my mom why Eileen didn't get married down at the Baptist Church, she told me to go out and play. Years later, out of nowhere, she answered me. We were watching some movie on her big colored tv, about some nun secretly having a baby, and my mom started up in the middle of a commercial.

"The reason Eileen didn't get married in the church was because her father wouldn't let her. His own daughter! She was going to have a baby, just like that nun on the tv," she said, and quieted down when the movie started back up. She missed the point of the movie, but I finally got my answer. At the time, I hadn't really known what the big deal was, but I thought that if anyone in my family would have gotten married down at the Baptist Church, it would have been one of Selina and Lou's kids.

They always went down there, every Sunday, drinking the Welch's grape juice in styrofoam cups and eating the little piece of Wonder Bread that someone always cut up fresh that morning. They always dressed up, too.

I didn't know anyone else who had as many ties as Lou did. And they were all different colors, too. He even had a couple of turquoise tie clasps, but mostly he had some gold ones that had his initials engraved on them in swirly letters. He only wore the turquoise ones once or twice a year, when they went down to the Old Gym for Community Fair or maybe the Christmas Bazaar.

When they came home from Vegas that first time, I was nine years old. As we picked them up that night at the airport, Lou was wearing one of those

30

turquoise clasps. I think it was a thunderbird, good luck for flying, or something. Normally, it would have been far past my bedtime, but this was one of those special occasions, and besides school was out for the summer.

I had ridden to the airport with some of my cousins in the back seat of Auntie Olive's big brown, fake-wood panelled station wagon, in the far end of the wagon—the end which always looks backwards. We brought along our plastic Indian tribe and had new caves and cliffs for them to be fighting on in the folds and cracks of the station wagon's vinyl upholstery.

After we picked Selina and Lou up at the airport, they'd probably be riding in my mom's car, and though I hadn't told anyone, I intended on switching cars.

"Hey, watch this," we tirelessly repeated to one another, holding our plastic warriors up to the car windows, backlighting them like movie Indians, in the fleeting streetlights.

We shouted greetings and waved furiously at stop lights to the others in my mom's car, behind us, as if we'd never see them again. They waved back every time. We picked up speed in our waving when the light turned green and they fell away as Auntie Olive pounded on the gas, squealing out at every stop light.

As we watched their plane come in from the airport observation area, my cousins and I nagged, jumping around and looking for an exit to head out there. My mother silently pointed to the big accordian tunnel stretching out from the building to meet the airplane door. Our eyes followed the tunnel to the receiving area door, which swung open and a lot of tired looking people wandered out, looking rumpled, as if they had been squeezed out of the tunnel like toothpaste. Their skin was greasy and the fluorescent lights in the receiving area made them appear green.

"Where's Selina?" we shouted, having all taken up the habit of repeating the last thing one of us said. It looked like all the people who were getting off had done so, and Selina and Lou were not among them. They finally came through the door, Lou first, and then Selina, leaning on a cane. The cane wasn't like the sort I had seen in movies or on tv, with the curved head of some animal on top and a pad on the end that touched the floor.

Selina's cane gleamed in the fluorescent lights. It was made of brilliantly shiny metal, the same kind the desks' legs at school were made of. At the top, the cane bent slightly forward and then bent back sharply pointing at her. A handle grip covered the end, just like the ones on our bicycles, but no bright plastic tassels hung from hers. Racing tassels, I think they're called.

The cane's primary tube stopped about three inches from where it touched the floor. It ended in this cap with holes cut into it, kind of like a fire hydrant. Sprouting out of these holes were four identical stubby legs that spread out in the four directions.

But the weirdest thing about Selina's cane was that she had it at all. She hadn't had one when they left. I knew people got old and all, but . . . it appeared that Vegas had been a waste of time, after all.

At home on the res, they had a pretty nice house. They even had a china cabinet, though I never knew at the time why it was called that. There wasn't a Chinese thing about it, in or out.

But in the cabinet, they had this great ceramic mouse sitting on top of a big piece of cheese, and when you lifted the cheese off the platter, a small mountain of cool blue Michigan Mints lay underneath it. That was the first thing we did when we got to Selina's—go for the mouse.

After we grabbed a handful, we always headed upstairs. Tiny spaces existed behind the doors in both of her upstairs rooms, where—since my cousins and I were pretty small then—we could easily fit, and tell ghost stories. They receded into the house's eaves. If we closed the cupboard doors which led to these spaces, it would be really dark, no matter what time of day it was.

If it got too scary, all we had to do was sit and listen, and soon we'd be able to hear our mothers, the three sisters, laughing down at the dining room table. We'd know they were drinking tea and sometimes lifting the mouse up to get a Michigan Mint or two before moving on to the next story one of them was telling. We'd know that we were safe, and we could confidently tell our next story about the dead baby's ghost, or Tallman, who walked the roads at night, peeking into upstairs bedroom windows.

"Let's get the pots and the gloves," Auntie Selina would say at other times, when she and I were there alone. Wild strawberries, raspberies and blackcaps grew behind the house. Both the blackcaps and the raspberries grew on stalks covered with thousands of tiny thorns that could snag fingers, tender or calloused, with no problem. Unlike picking the raspberries, though, we usually had to grab onto the stalks to pull the blackcaps from their stems.

"Here, let's try these," Selina would say during blackcap season, rifling through the box of gloves she kept under her staircase. As she dug through them, she was sure to find a pair that would almost fit me.

"Auntie Sel, don't you remember my special pair?" I'd say, and she'd pull them from her apron pocket. We had bought them at Neisner's the winter before, anticipating the coming spring.

"Here, you oversee. Make sure I'm doing this right," she'd say, lifting me up to sit on her kitchen counter while she made blackcap pies with the berries we'd picked. Other times, we just sat at her picnic table and ate the berries right from the saucepan, until there weren't any more. "Now, don't you tell Uncle Lou that we picked any, or he'll be wondering what happened to them," she'd say as we rinsed the pan clean of evidence.

As I got older, if Selina were watching me, the games we played changed. "Here, you go down and see how fast you can fill the pan, and I'll stay up here and time you," she said those times, pulling her metal lawn chair to the edge of the hill as I raced down it with the urgency of my task.

"Take this and see if you can fill it. Let's see how strong you are," she said at other times, handing me a bucket for pumping water into. The buckets were hard to manage and I usually spilled a quarter of the water out on the way back into her house, but that seemed to be better than nothing. Lou had been the only one who got water when he was home. With her arthritis, Selina couldn't lift the water pail.

"Lou and I are leaving for Las Vegas in a month," she said one day at my mother's house, where she had gathered everyone.

"What! Selina, are you sure? What'll you do out there?" my mother asked.

"What's wrong with home?" Auntie Olive asked, after her.

"Lou's gotten a transfer. It's all done. He's already signed the papers and everything. I know we talked about it last winter, and, well, this position just opened up, and my arthritis isn't getting any better. Lou's checked with the Baptist minister and he said there are some nice missionaries right there who can help us 'til we get settled, and, uh, he starts there a month from today, so we better get packing." She finished this speech with a feathery little laugh which told us this was all news to her, as well, that she was trying to discuss her life in foreign words.

33

They packed up pretty quickly and didn't take much with them. They gave most of it away to their only kid who still lived on the reservation, my cousin Cloo. I don't remember what all he got from them, but I have seen the mouse on the cheese over at his house. I picked it up once when I was visiting him, but there were no Michigan Mints underneath it. Nothing, in fact.

Cloo had found someone to stay in their house, but I didn't know who it was. They might have even been white people, but I'm not really sure. There were quite a few white people living on the reservation in those days. Not like now. Now the only white people who live out here are those who are married to someone from the res, except for the minister. He and his family still live here.

"Ma, let's go pick some berries at Selina's," I said one day, later that summer. "There's gotta be some ripe ones now."

"It's not that they're not ripe . . ." my mother started.

"But that's what you said."

"Well, it's just that . . . well, you see, other folks are living there now, and those berries belong to them." To prove this, my mother drove me by Selina's house, and I saw the strange car in the driveway, and I could just see some kids below the hill, probably picking our berries. It seemed that we had lost all of Selina. We couldn't even visit her house.

They wrote a lot that first year they left. Well, actually, Selina wrote a lot and signed both of their names. Everybody got some kind of letter from her. I was only about six, or maybe just turning seven, so I couldn't read all that well. She sent me a great little package for my birthday that year.

The package was this fold-out set of shiny pictures of all the places in Las Vegas. There were pictures of casinos, and a circus, and the giant cowboy who waves forever, and even a picture of Elvis singing. I didn't like Elvis too much, but the other pictures were great.

After you were done looking at the pictures, you could fold it back up and the pictures became their own envelope. I showed it around to all the other kids, and they agreed that it was pretty cool. But before I showed it around, I had taken out the other part of Selina's gift.

There were four Kennedy half dollars scotch taped to the sky of the last page, four silver suns over the Vegas skyline. In the note that went along with the package, Selina explained that the half dollars were her first winnings in Vegas.

I spent three of them almost immediately on junk. I don't remember what, now, but they were gone pretty fast. But the last one, I kept. I had it up in my socks and underwear drawer. And even when times were tight, and I really wanted to buy something, the half dollar stayed there. Hanging on to it was like keeping a piece of Selina safe at home on the reservation.

~~~

So as we sat in the airport waiting room, watching Selina and Lou come out of the tunnel, I reached into my front pants pocket and felt the Kennedy, warm from being next to my skin. We all headed up to meet them, and the grown ups talked to them as we left the waiting area.

Auntie Olive's two older boys, Stan and Ely, had run ahead to the baggage claim area, so that by the time we got to the airport's front door, they had already collected all of Selina and Lou's suitcases. The suitcases didn't all fit in my mom's trunk, so they stuck some in Auntie Olive's station wagon. I got shifted back to my mom's car, even without using my plan.

I had planned on showing Selina the Kennedy, to let her know that I was keeping her safe at home. I figured if she knew that, she'd want me riding with them, and I'd get to spend more time with her. I sat in the back seat and listened as all the grown ups talked and caught up. Olive had even switched cars, letting Stan drive her car, so she could be here.

My mom, Selina and Lou sat in the front, while Auntie Olive, her husband, my Uncle Frank, my sister Kay and I sat in the back seat. The only reason I really got to switch was because I could sit on Kay's lap. She didn't like this too much. She claimed I had a bony hetch-eh, but that's the way it was.

It was past eleven o'clock, but it was still pretty hot out, hot and sweaty. That was another reason Kay didn't particularly like me being on her lap. So we rode with the windows down all the way home. They talked about all kinds of things but no one mentioned Selina's cane at all.

"Let's take a ride up by the dike," Selina blurted out as we got closer to the reservation. They had never gone up there too much, but as you rode by, you could smell the river water, especially when it was muggy and smells hung low in the air. So we pulled onto the first road to the reservation, Pem Brook. The dike runs right alongside Pem Brook Road.

We could smell the dike even before we got there. The wind flew around in my mom's big Buick and danced in our hair. My mom had strands ripping loose from her bobby pins all over the place, giving her a halo in the moonlight. The dike smelled like it always did to me, but Selina and Lou seemed to find something to really smile about in the night air.

"Ooh, nehts-eh. Smell, pull over, pull over," Selina said excitedly, breathing in deeply. I sniffed the air. She was right. There was no doubt in my mind that a nehts-eh, a skunk, was around. My mom pulled over and almost before she could even come to a complete stop, Selina and Lou were piling out of the car. Selina even forgot her cane for a second.

When it appeared they were going to stay out there a while, the rest of us also got out of the car. We all lined up against the Buick's front end and smelled the air. I never thought skunks smelled as bad as they were supposed to, but at the same time, they were not something I'd go looking to smell, either.

I looked up at Selina and I could see tears gleaming on her cheeks in the moonlight. She turned to her sisters and said, "They don't have any skunks in Henderson. I haven't smelled one since we left home." Off in the distance, we heard someone shoot off a few rounds and it echoed in the night air. Selina listened until the last echo quietly died away, and then she got back in the Buick.

They stayed with us that night, since there were still other people living in their house. Their son Cloo lived just down the road from us, but he had a house full with all his kids. And besides, he was working an odd shift and wouldn't be around as much as he wanted to be.

I got up early the next morning. It was the fourth of July and one of the biggest parties we ever had was about to begin. Everyone brought the usual covered dishes, all trying to outdo one another. Among the adults, the shells and meatballs you ate could be a serious political statement. This one was going to be particularly interesting because it actually wouldn't be just family.

My mom and aunt had taken the liberty of inviting people from the Baptist Church down for the party. Neither of them ever went there, except for weddings and funerals, but Selina and Lou had been regular attenders, so some of those people were asked. You could be sure the dishes would be closely watched this time, to see who ate how much of what. I figured I'd have lots of opportunities to show Auntie Selina the Kennedy, but as often happens, the time slipped away in lost opportunities.

Even after the party, the rest of their week home was very busy, too, visiting and catching up with the whole reservation. And before we knew it, they were packing their bags to leave. My mom wasn't going to let me go to the airport this time. Cloo had actually been able to get his hours switched for one day, so he could go to the airport with them.

I went into my mom's room, where Selina and Lou had slept, and helped Selina pack. We had almost everything packed. Selina sat on the suitcase while I flipped the locks, like in the movies.

She was about to take the suitcases out to the front porch, but I asked her to wait a minute. I dug in my pocket and showed her the Kennedy. She looked at it and knew where it had come from. I told her I had been saving a part of her here at home. She asked me if she could take it with her in trade for something else.

Selina pulled out a big silver dollar and pressed it in my hand. She told me that she didn't win this silver dollar in Vegas, but she won it just the other night, at the bingo hall down the road. It was "silver dollar night."

I slid the silver dollar into my pants pocket and carried her smaller suitcase out to the porch, and then they left.

They haven't been back since, but they'll be here in a few days. We all kind of knew that this was going to be The Bug's last year, so we thought we'd get everybody together for one final time. About six months ago, when we knew for sure how bad The Bug was, we began making arrangements. We knew Auntie Selina would not be able to come in the winter, so we planned the party for the fourth of July.

I'd taken to carrying my silver dollar in my front pants pocket. They stopped making the big silver dollars a while ago, and now only make the small kind that everyone confused with quarters. From years of being rubbed up against the soft cotton of my jeans pockets, the dollar had a glow of its own. It was my homing beacon for Auntie Selina, just like the kind I had seen on *Star Trek*. I figured she could always find her way back home as long as I had it.

When we finalized the arrangements, I got the idea that I could make a necklace out of the dollar. I had the perfect chain, but I needed someone to solder a mount on the dollar so I could attach it. I remembered this silversmith down on Snakeline who was one of Lou's church friends. Lou had introduced me to him at the earlier party. He was the guy who made Lou's turquoise tie clasps. When I explained to him what I wanted, he nodded and said he thought that was a nice idea. He said he'd only charge me five bucks, when he was done.

I waited a few months, but the time was coming close when they'd be home again. I wanted to be wearing the silver dollar when they got off the jetliner. So I went down to Snakeline to talk with the guy.

He couldn't exactly remember what it was I had wanted him to do. So I told him the whole story again, and he started laughing. He had wondered how that silver dollar had gotten into his pocket. He couldn't remember where it had come from, when he found it in his jeans one day.

I asked him what he did with it. He pointed to this big clear plastic margarine tub that was sitting on the workbench. He said he threw it in there. I looked at the tub and could see that it was filled with old style silver dollars.

He said he kept a supply of them in his workshop because he used the eagle images that were on the "tails" side of the coins as bracelet and necklace inlays. They were very popular sellers, he added. He showed me one that was almost complete.

He reached over to the bucket and began digging around in it. He asked me if I knew the year. He was sure he could find one with the same year on it. He began calling off years, like a caller at a bingo game, but I told him to never mind and I left.

Just before my mom was going to leave for the airport, she told me Selina was bringing a wheelchair, so I wouldn't be surprised. Over the years, Selina's arthritis had gotten a lot worse, even out in Vegas.

As I watched my mom pull out of the driveway, I went outside on the front porch. I shoved my hands into my empty pockets and sniffed the air, hoping the scent of skunk would be enough for Auntie Selina to find her way home.

Chapter Five

∿∿
∿∿

GUTS

LATE JULY

I

Janice Freen, known as Jan to her friends, marked off her calendar. She stood—almost to the day—five months from freedom. She would then have her nurse practitioner degree and be on her way. She had been a successful nurse for several years, but now wanted to move on to be of more use in her community. With her Master of Science degree as a nurse practitioner, she would be able to work more effectively in the tribal clinic at home on the Cattaraugus Reservation.

It was four a.m., but she was already up. She'd be taking the final for one of her summer school classes in a few hours and wanted to study a little more. As of ten-thirty a.m., she would be free for a little over a week, until the next module rolled around. She'd head back to Cattaraugus and check on the res, particularly on the old man, Johnny Flatleaf.

Less than a week ago, she'd watched quietly over Johnny, as he lay in his bed, when Brian Waterson came in and sat down. The young medicine man's arrival had awakened Johnny a few minutes before. The old man had guessed the news wasn't going to be good, but that was okay. There hadn't been a medicine man on Cattaraugus who could cure cancer in over fifty years, and even though Waterson was from Tuscarora reservation, about an hour away, his hopes hadn't been too high. And besides, Johnny was in his seventies; he had lived a full life, and his long graying hair and still somewhat muscular body attested to that. Death would be okay. He had given up on a cure; it was really something else he now hoped for. He and Jan had discussed this extensively.

~~
~~

"Here you go, Johnny. It's all I've got. The plants I need for the cancer medicine don't exist anymore, at least not that I could find, but try this. It might quiet your pain some." Brian Waterson held out a cup containing a mixture which resembled tea, but the old man wouldn't take it.

"Nah. I can stand a little pain. It's the other thing that worries me. I don't wanna leave for the next world alone. You find another eel? Know there ain't none 'round here, but how 'bout your area? Any?" Brian was silent for a moment. He knew, and had already told Jan, that of all the clans the Tuscarora people belong to, there weren't too many eels, and of that group, none were traditionals. He didn't think any of them would agree to be participants at a Longhouse funeral.

"One will come. I know it. I can't say when it will happen, but it will." Outside, he had later told Jan that he simply didn't know how he knew this information. He was still pretty new to this way of life and sometimes wished he had not inherited the role. At times, it could be too much for a man in his twenties. He almost felt like he was lying, because he only sensed that another eel would show up from Tuscarora to help escort the last Seneca eel to the other side.

Johnny lay back, closed his eyes, and waited for the coming of the eel. Jan had waited with him and though she was planning on spending more time there, she had a feeling she'd be back on campus before her week was up.

She could see that the roofers would be coming to repair the Nursing building soon and, after asking around, found out that they'd be starting at the beginning of next week. Almost all the roofers who worked on the University were Indians, and skins on campus were such a rare sight that she planned on coming back to Buffalo just to see them. At least she would have someone to talk to at the school.

~~
~~

Jan left class, headed back to her Buffalo apartment and stood at the door for a minute, key in hand. She had come back early from Cattaraugus like she thought she might, but she still had not spoken to the roofers as she had anticipated. Well, she was back here, another opportunity behind her, she might as well go in.

The apartment was sweltering and a heavy, stale cloud of heat seemed to fill the room. She immediately turned on a number of strategically placed fans and opened windows. She opened a two-liter bottle of Pepsi and sat down in the living room, turning the tv on, and began watching some stupid game show. She drank the Pepsi right from the bottle.

She had to return to campus tomorrow, where she knew the roofers would be. She was planning, as she had every day since she had returned, on heading straight over to them on their lunch break and speaking to them. She had seen so many other Indians do this. In fact, it had even happened to her once. She'd been in a K-Mart over in Rochester, a hundred miles away, buying lingerie. She hadn't wanted anyone from Cattaraugus to see her buying any, so she had driven the extra hour to make her purchases. As she held something up at the rack, to see if she wanted to try it on, an older Indian woman had walked past with a girdle and informed her that she didn't want that; it was too slutty—something a white girl would wear.

She had the sense, however, that she would not be that forward, even if the roofers were all skins; she was right. So far, all she had managed was to have a waving relationship with one of them. They'd look at one another, she from the ground, he from the roof, and wave, going in, going out, but that was it.

She got up early the next morning and dressed as stylishly as she could, in clothes entirely unlike those she regularly wore to school. She found her light blouse with the Navajo print on it and wore that with a pair of form-fitting Levi's.

She even drove to the campus with the A/C on, though she knew it used up more gas than she budgeted for the week, so that she wouldn't look all sweaty when she got to the building. As she pulled into the parking lot, she cut it back to "vent," knowing the cold air would last long enough for her to park.

She could see them on top of the Nursing building as she got out of her beat-up old Datsun. It didn't run all that well, and it certainly wasn't pretty, but for the most part, it got her where she wanted to go. They were heading to the access hatch that led down into the main stairwell. It was lunch time. She didn't see her waving roofer and assumed he must already have gone down the hatch. She walked determinedly over to the building, but as she reached the ramp that led up to the door, she sidestepped and headed to the medical library instead.

She justified this by claiming to herself that she was really meaning to go there all along. She wanted to look up some pain treatment strategies for cancer patients. She wanted to ease Johnny Flatleaf's pain in any way she could. She knew that Brian Waterson's medicines were one alternative, but she needed to see what she could do, too. She had known Johnny almost all her life and wanted to help him however she could. In fact, she decided that she would leave for Cattaraugus when she got back to the apartment. It was Friday and she'd have the whole weekend to monitor Johnny.

As she stepped into the library, she looked back and could see the roofers eating at the benches under the trees outside the Nursing building. They'll be there for another half hour, she thought, letting the tinted glass door shut on the sight.

She actually did it, a few minutes later. She turned around in the library and headed back for the Nursing building. She met her waver, Floyd Page, for the first time, in the ground floor hallway of the building. They spoke.

II

Hank Jimison lay awake in his bed at his mother's house. He felt foolish living with her in the city, particularly since he was forty-five years old. He had lived there since his divorce, almost five years ago, but he still felt ridiculous. The thought of moving back to the reservation hadn't occurred to him until his father had gone into the nursing home in Lewiston with incurable cancer a month or so before.

He got up quietly. It was after three in the morning and he didn't want to wake up his mother in the other bedroom. He turned the bureau light on and looked at himself in the mirror. His dark, brick colored skin looked a little drawn around his eyes and mouth. He ran his fingers through his short, cropped hair. It was not the brush cut his father sported, but the similarities could not be mistaken. His barrel chest and hawklike nose seemed to have been lifted right from his father's face. He had gotten his features, if nothing else, from the man his birth certificate confirmed he was linked with.

That really wasn't true. He shut the light off and sat in the dark, knowing he had gotten a number of things from The Bug.

〰〰

The next day, Hank stood in line at Hector's Hardware. He still had not gotten the call he was expecting from Innis Natcha, and was growing a little impatient; he decided that he'd give his cousin a little reminder call this evening. He knew one supply, anyway, he could buy on his own. He had already gotten electrical wire from work, handy, since he was an electrician. But he had to wait on doing the wiring he was planning to.

It was true that he had made an agreement, but Hank knew his way around agreements. He had agreed never to have an affair a few years back, when he was married, but he hadn't felt that particular agreement included just plain sleeping around. In fact, when his wife had caught him with some other woman, he claimed it wasn't an affair. His proof of this was the fact that he didn't even know the woman's name. The woman, a skinny pale thing in her late forties, with bad skin and a really strong overbite, nodded vehemently. The fact that his wife had caught them in his car, in the parking lot of his favorite bar, did not seem to matter to him. Nor did the fact that the woman's face had been buried in Hank's lap at the time.

Hank's wife had not agreed this sort of behavior was not implied in their marriage agreement and left shortly after that. That had been a pretty serious consequence of his loose interpretations, and he was now contemplating another. The beige colored latex interior wallpaint he paid the Hector's Hardware cashier for was a key element in another of his interpretations. He didn't like having to strike deals to get his way, particularly not with his shitheel reservation cousins, and he would show them that he calls all of the shots around here. He thought he'd bring a little city out to those country boys.

III

Innis Natcha stepped into Floyd Page's trailer, as he usually did, and grabbed a Molson from the fridge. He sat down on the couch, moving a couple of magazines from the end table to make room for his beer. He noticed Floyd's modified ghost machine and wondered when that thing had bloomed in the corner of the living room. It seemed to him that Floyd never actually brought objects into the trailer; they just appeared at some point, seeming like they had always been there.

It wasn't like Floyd had an enormous amount of space either. The trailer was on the lower end of the scale, not one of those that had to be split in half for transport. It had been his sister Kay's first trailer, a number of years ago. Innis was surprised it had held up so well, and had lent itself to Floyd's haphazard ideas on decor. The area where the ghost machine hung seemed like it might never even have existed before, almost as if this spot had grown up all around the spinning object.

"So what is that thing, man?" he asked, pointing to the machine. Floyd sat in the space that Innis guessed should have been the dining nook, or niche, or whatever that area was called in the trailer brochures. A table did rest in the space, but Innis couldn't even guess when the last time was that anyone ate there, or ate from a plate, anyway.

Floyd had been almost ignoring Innis, as he often had lately. He obviously knew that Innis had come in, but he didn't stop working on his latest project. He was writing, almost scribbling with urgency in a spiral notebook. It was one of those Mead one subject notebooks, with the dense college rule, and Floyd's sprawling handwriting looked almost neat on the page compressed between the pale blue lines. From where Innis sat, though, he couldn't read a word of it.

Floyd lifted the index finger of his left hand, motioning for his cousin to keep still until he finished. Innis couldn't really recall Floyd ever being so intent on anything that even resembled education, so this motion was enough to keep him quietly sipping his beer and watching the machine turn in the breeze.

"So how's it goin'," Floyd asked eventually, folding the cover of the notebook back, closing it. He set it in the corner of the table, on top of a small pile of others like it.

"Not too bad. How about with you? Been back to the doctor?" Innis asked, leaning back in the couch, getting comfortable. Floyd stepped into the kitchen and grabbed a Molson for himself.

"Ready?" he asked, keeping the refrigerator door open, waiting for his cousin's reply.

"Not yet. A few minutes."

"Fuck that. I ain't getting up again in a few minutes," Floyd returned, setting a new bottle next to the ghost of Innis's old bottle on the end table. He sat back down at the dining room table and shifted his chair to face Innis. He took a long pull from his bottle and leaned back in the chair.

"So have you?" Innis repeated.

"Have I what?"

"Been back . . ."

"No. No, I haven't gone back. Look In, they about said that they didn't know what was wrong. Hell, I can just as well give myself the co-pay and say I don't know what's wrong, you know what I mean? Besides, I'm managing," Floyd interrupted, leaning forward and letting the chair's front legs slam on the old linoleum floor.

"That ain't very logical, you know. They might be able to come up with something, if you let 'em know how things are goin' with you. This way, all they're gonna do is move on to the next patient with the next problem." Innis leaned forward, himself, to make his point.

It wouldn't occur to him until later in the night, a little after two, that Floyd responded to a question that had been asked more than five seconds before. It had been at least a couple minutes between question and answer. He didn't really know what to attribute the progress to, but as he drifted off to sleep, he thought that Brian Waterson might be onto something, after all.

As the two cousins continued their conversation, Innis eventually got back around to pointing again at the machine spinning in the breeze and repeating his initial question.

"Oh that thing," Floyd responded, seeming like he was stalling for time. "Oh, that's just my . . ." he paused, reaching out toward the notebooks on the table, but before he could do more than touch the shiny cover of the top one, he found himself finshing the answer. "That's my ghost machine," he stated confidently.

Throughout the rest of the late afternoon, Innis heard about Floyd's visit with Brian Waterson, the milkweed and finally, the coming of the ghost machine. He didn't quite know what to make of the story. He had suggested Brian as a last resort, when he couldn't think of much else to help Floyd. It was a little hard for him to believe the milkweed had remained appearing as fresh as it had. If what Floyd said was accurate, and he had to admit it probably wasn't, the milkweed had been up in the machine for at least a couple weeks.

"So you think this thing is helping you?" he asked a few minutes after Floyd had finished his story.

"Can't hurt," Floyd replied, walking over to the fridge for another round. "And I think it is working. Of course, I don't think I can really be the best judge of that, you know," he said, handing Innis a new bottle and taking the old one to put in the case of empties under the sink.

"Yeah, I guess," Innis said, standing up and stretching. They had been talking for a while and Innis could see that the late afternoon sun was meandering beyond the trees. "Hey, what time is it, anyway? We're supposed to go over to The Bug's, uh, Hank's. I have to call him after nine to let him know what materials we're gonna need." He stood in the open doorway, enjoying the breeze and waiting for Floyd.

"I ain't going. Shut the door; you're letting the flies out." Floyd leaned back against the kitchen counter, where some dirty glasses and an empty cereal box sat.

"You said you would, along with the rest of us," Innis accused. He had thought he might get this kind of argument from Floyd, but he still wasn't really prepared for any kind of defense of his position. To tell the truth, Innis probably felt more like Floyd did than he wanted to admit. There was something about Hank; actually, they knew virtually nothing about him.

"I forgot," Floyd said simply, taking a drink.

Innis snorted a small laugh, allowing a mixture of emotions to swim around in his buzzing head. Even the fact he only gave the small burst of noise was cause for some sadness. Indians had been told for so long they were "a stoic people," they began to believe it themselves. Innis wasn't really sure of the exact definition of the word stoic, but he had a good enough idea from having seen all of those famous Curtis photos of Indians and the way they were supposed to look and act. They had gotten away from wearing feathers a long time ago, but the only Indian Innis had ever seen cry had been Iron Eyes Cody wandering through landfills in those old anti-pollution ads on the television.

He was fully aware this was one time Floyd actually had remembered something, but was choosing to pretend that he didn't. Floyd was pretending he had forgotten two conversations that had taken place among the cousins at that year's fourth of July party. For the first time in the memories of many of them, Hank had attended. Even he, always out of touch, knew this was going to be the last one for his father. His mother, of course, did not attend. She remained in the city.

Groups of people were spread all over the shade areas on Nora Page's front lawn. Floyd had wired speakers from his trailer, through her back door, and propped them up in her living room windows, so the party would have some tunes. The Grateful Dead were playing through and everybody was singing along with the chorus, agreeing on what a long strange trip it had been.

Even Selina, whose wheelchair was parked in the shade of a large evergreen, was rocking in her seat to the tune. She also was in total agreement. She looked at her brother in his own wheelchair right next to hers. "Wanna race?" she asked him, and he laughed. The Bug's hollow cheeks filled momentarily with the laugh, and then emptied out again, a tide.

"Gosh. It's funny. I've had that damn wooden leg for so long, I had kinda believed that I wasn't too crippled, and now I can't even walk. The damn thing keeps fallin' off. How long you been in one of these?"

"Oh, jeez, almost a year, I figure. You remember I had that cane for the longest time, but then I fell once and the doctors told me I probably wouldn't take another one like that. Legs aint' all they're cracked up to be."

"Gosh, it's good to see you and Lou again. He looks like he's ailing a bit too, huh?" The Bug asked, sipping from a can of non-alcoholic beer.

"Oh, he's managing. Thank God one of us can still move around. I don't know what I'd do . . ." she trailed off.

"Why don't you two come home, anyways. It don't look like that Las Vegas air has helped your arthritis none, you know what I mean? We'll set you back up. Get you back into your old house. We can help you out— that's what family's for."

47

"The bedrooms are upstairs in my old house. I couldn't live there, even if I wanted to. And besides, Nevada is our home now."

"This will always be your home," The Bug said. Nora and Olive pulled up a couple chairs and handed their siblings some of Olive's special pumpkin Bundt cake. The four fell into the conversational rhythms they'd known for the last sixty years, since the time Olive had learned to talk and joined their ranks.

While one conversation about home was ending under one tree, under another tree, further away, a similar conversation began.

"So, I'm planning on moving back into Dad's old place," Hank said to no one in particular. People had commented to one another earlier on how much he was beginning to look like The Bug. At forty-five, he had the same barrel chest and the same sharply contoured face. Floyd, however, denied it anytime someone had suggested it within his earshot. "It's gonna need a lot of work, though. I'll probably have to start from scratch. Puttin' in some new floorboards in the living room," he continued.

"Which room might the living room be?" Ely interrupted, looking straight at Hank. They had a pretty good guess which room that might be.

"Where the pool table is. Anyway, do some wiring, fix the walls, probably tear out most of the insides," he finished, standing up and heading around toward the back of Nora's property, where the outhouse was.

None of this was news to the rest, but it was the first time any of them had actually heard it from Hank directly.

"Damn! That toilet stinks in the summertime. How can you guys stand using it?" Hank said, again to no one in particular.

"You almost welcome the time when you have to put up with the toilet stink," Stan said, examining the peeling label from his bottle of Molson. He was close to being forty and also the closest to being Hank's contemporary, and had taken the role of spokesman for the reservation group.

"What?" Hank replied; he clearly could not see any possible reason for welcoming that particular sensation.

"When you can't smell the shit, it's because it's frozen. And your body don't care how cold it is. When you gotta go, you gotta go. And me, I'd rather have to put up with the stink than hang my ass out in the wind when it's five below and there's snow blowing in on your balls," Ace said. The others laughed in agreement, a couple of them squeezing their legs together in the memories of winter treks to the outhouse. "If you're gonna live out here, you better get used to it."

"What makes you think I'm gonna use that toilet? My house is gonna have plumbing."

"Our houses have plumbing. Just no drainage, no sewage," Floyd contributed.

"Why not?" Hank asked.

"Big bucks, man," Floyd continued, rubbing his fingers together, a wad of imaginary dollar bills between them. "Big bucks we don't have and can't get out here. No mortgages, no home improvement loans on the reservation, but I guess you wouldn't know about that," he finished, not succeeding in keeping the sarcasm from his voice, but locking eyes with Hank anyway.

"Well, I can get a loan; my house is gonna have a toilet," Hank said back.

"Your ma's house for collateral, huh?" Ace asked.

"Anyway, I'm gonna need some help," Hank said, apparently ignoring Ace's question/comment. "You guys interested? I probably can't pay union scale, but I'll do what I can. What d'ya say?" he asked, looking expectantly at his cousins' faces. He had hoped it wouldn't come up like this. He had told Innis earlier he knew they didn't like him for not staying on the reservation, but none of them had ever had that choice to make. And he felt pretty sure they would have chosen to live in a nice house in the city instead of these drafty houses with cold taps and pressure tanks for running water, and even that only having arrived a couple years before.

Previous to the tanks, water had been gotten in pails from the hand pump behind Nora's house, the same pump The Bug used to fill his refrigerator jugs, but this was something Hank never really knew about. He never had to, and the others could sense this; it was something in their nervous systems that usually only buzzed around white people. It was the knowledge that someone in their presence felt superior to them.

Stan was about to lay into him, but as he pulled in a chestful of air, Innis nudged him with his elbow. Stan glanced up and saw their mother had been paying close attention to their conversation, even though she was at least thirty feet away in the middle of an entirely different exchange.

49

"Yeah, I'll help ya," Innis said, while Stan paused, carrying on an eye-dialogue with their mother.

"I'll be there," he eventually said, breaking the contact with Olive Natcha, who continued in her story, nobody else having noticed the silent exchange. The other Natcha brothers joined in, but Floyd stayed conspicuously silent. Later, Innis would wonder in passing if this were one of Floyd's episodes of blanking out, but he didn't suspect that was really the case.

"Floyd," he prompted.

"I'll help you out, and I'll take whatever it is you think is fair, regardless of scale, but on one condition," Floyd stated matter-of-factly.

"What's 'at?"

"Tell you later. Agreed?"

"What! That's crazy," Hank growled.

"Take it or leave it. Yes or no. Simple as that." They knew Hank wasn't going to find a cheaper roofer than a relative, and Floyd was the only roofer in the family. They also knew he was Hank's safest bet, the one roofer least likely to cheat him, and they felt that Hank didn't seem like much of a risk-taker, like he always went with the safest bet. Floyd leaned back far in his plastic lawn chair and waited for a response.

The response had been a yes. The party moved on. Hank had even stayed long into the night, hours after all but the regular die-hards had gone home. He didn't travel into Buffalo with them at three-thirty in the morning, trying to make it to Erie County where the sale of alcohol was extended an hour later than where they lived, but he had made a good enough showing for most of them. As they sat on top of the dike, watching the sun rise, and killing off the second of the three cases they had bought at a convenience store just over the border into North Tonawanda, Stan asked Floyd what his condition was going to be.

"Well, I think he's gonna want to tear down your drawings on the wall," Floyd said, referring to an ambitious series of traditional images Stan had worked on for years on The Bug's spare bedroom walls. "And when he tells us that, I'm gonna inform him my condition is that the drawings stay."

"Why? I mean, I appreciate it and all, but . . ."

"I don't know, man. It's just that . . . they've always been there, and he hasn't. And it's like Ace said, if he's gonna live out here, he better get used

50

to the fact that this ain't the city. He might need those to remind him," Floyd finished.

"A nice case of chapped balls this December'll be plenty enough to remind him would be my guess," Ace said, conjuring up the image he had brought to the surface earlier in the party.

"Well, I just think he's gonna need more before then," Floyd said and burped his conclusion of the Hank issue.

As they watched the sun splitting through the brightly colored ripe dawn clouds, they each wondered how the business of Hank entering their society was going to develop. He wasn't like them at all, had not shared any of their upbringing, the things that made them who they were. He was virtually empty of family experience, at least with their family. None of them knew much about his mother or her family. They only knew of their uncle and his part in their lives.

They all knew the days of The Bug's house were over and couldn't help but feel apprehensive about contributing to that part of their history's demise, but they knew it was going to happen anyway, with or without their help. They had collectively agreed, with a sort of family telepathy, that it would probably be for the best if they were there for the milestone.

〰〰
〰〰

The beginning of that milestone happened three days later, when The Bug quietly died in his bed at the nursing home. Selina and Lou had stayed for the funeral, but left the next day. They had done what they had set out to do. They'd said goodbye. Hank had made his intention known, and Floyd had announced his condition. Now, a little over half a month later, Hank, having agreed, had finally gotten enough of a loan approved to begin the work he'd proposed at the gathering. He didn't want to start anything until he knew it was fully covered. The loan wasn't for enough to get the cesspool dug or anything that complicated, but it was enough to get some of the repairs begun on the house, so when it came time to work on those other details, they would at least have a well-constructed shell to be operating in.

Hank had stopped in at Olive's house one evening a week earlier. Though the reservation cousins had all discussed the work on the house, it had really been the first time any of them had seen Hank since the decision.

He was entirely unaware of Floyd's memory difficulties, but there was only one implication of it that concerned him, anyway. As he and Innis sat in a couple of lawn chairs by an overgrown lilac, he wondered out loud if he were going to have to find someone else to work on the roof.

"No, he's fine. He needs a little supervision. That's what the doctor said we should do, anyway, so one of us will always be there with him, you know, just in case," Innis said, reassuring Hank of their cousin's capabilities, ignoring what an asshole Hank was being, dismissing it as the influence of city life.

"Hey, d'you suppose he maybe forgot about the deal?" Hank asked, raising his eyebrows.

"I haven't," Innis said, standing up and going in the house, letting the screen door slam behind him. He was trying to give Hank as much leeway as he could, but even his patience wore thin sometimes. Hank got the message and walked up to the screen door, yelled in a message that he'd be waiting for the estimate call when they got to it and then drove off back to the city, not waiting for the reply he knew he would not be receiving.

Innis stepped out of the bedroom as soon as he heard Hank's tires popping gravel at the end of the driveway. As he watched the car disappear behind the bushline, he smiled to himself, knowing Hank was already beginning to learn about family.

Now, as he and Floyd actually, physically walked over to the old house, Innis wondered if they really could be a part of dismantling The Bug's domain. He took out a big metal keychain and flipped through the keys and finally found the house key Hank had given him during his last visit. When they reached the back door, Floyd took the lead and jumped up to the platform, not using the steps.

"Just checkin'," he said to Innis after trying the handle. Innis figured this was going to be a battle the entire way. He had finally convinced Floyd to keep his promise by reminding him the drawings were now a part of the equation. He put his boots back on almost immediately once Innis had mentioned them, but actually working with Hank was going to be another matter. Innis almost hoped Hank would stay out of their way while they worked on the house, but he didn't think that was likely.

The door was still locked, as it had been since the day after The Bug's funeral. Floyd stepped aside and Innis inserted the key into the newly installed lock.

As they stepped in, they immediately knew it was already a different place. No smell of steak frying in onion gravy came from the kitchen, as it almost always had before. Even the odor of stale beer and smoke was gone. Instead, the overwhelming scent was that of Clorox.

"Smells like laundry day at The Bug's," Floyd said, reaching up to tug on the heavy nylon cord hanging high from the ceiling. Whenever The Bug had performed his summertime bleaching ritual with his underwear and T-shirts, he'd hung them from this cord to dry in the breeze, filling the room with the acrid chlorine scent which now permeated the room.

"Sure didn't take him long," Floyd continued, looking to his right, where the studs that made up the house's rib cage were fully exposed. While Hank had agreed to leave the walls where Stan's drawings were intact, he had made no such agreement about the other walls, or anything else about the house. This room, formerly the pool room, apparently was the first area to receive Hank's attention.

Occasional fragments of plasterboard hung from stray nails in the studs. He pulled one loose and looked at it.

TI J
AN
A

"Who was this?" he asked Innis, handing the piece of plaster to his cousin. Innis examined it, looked at the place where Floyd had pulled it from, and studied the piece again.

"Mm, not sure. Could be, yeah, it's probably Patti Jo and Ace. Yeah, that's gotta be it," Innis stated with growing confidence as he handed the fragment back to Floyd.

While Stan had gotten the walls in the smaller bedroom, all the other cousins had been able to use the walls in the pool room. Not being nearly as inspired as Stan was, they most often used the wall to inscribe statements of their sexual conquests, or, more often, fantasies. Everyone knew Patti Jo Rokerton would never really have anything to do with Ace, but they all had their own lies on the wall, and so said nothing—not that any of that mattered anymore.

"Jeez, I guess there's no point in getting laid, now," Floyd commented, dropping the piece of plasterboard and kicking it into a garbage heap that was piled in the corner.

"Yeah, like the shit you wrote up here was actually true."

"Every word."

"Uh-huh. How'd you get Fiction Tunny in the sack?" Innis asked, smirking at Floyd.

"Well, okay. That one wasn't true. But Rachel Duke was," Floyd confidently replied.

"Yeah? How'd you pull that off?"

"Just asked her, man. All it takes is guts."

"Guts?" Innis asked, raising his eyebrows.

"Well, I coulda' said 'balls,' but I thought that might be a little obvious," Floyd said, smiling. He seemed like he had been waiting to use that line for an awfully long time.

"Asshole," Innis laughed. "This isn't getting the job done, man. Let's get to it," he said, looking through the studs into the next room. He stepped through a gap between a couple of studs, taking a direct path through the almost empty shell of the house. He stopped in the kitchen, and looked into a large bucket on wheels standing in the center of the kitchen floor.

"Here's where the clean underwear smell is coming from," he said to Floyd who still stood near the back door. Floyd walked into the kitchen, but did not step through the stud gaps. He entered the room as if the walls still existed.

The bucket was full of Clorox and a mop rested in it. The floorboards had lightened where Hank apparently had tried mopping and soaking the floor, but the blood stains remained. Innis pushed the bucket into a corner, assuming Hank would probably try to bleach the red out of the floor again some time.

The Bug's bedroom could be seen clearly from the kitchen. Aside from the room where Stan's drawings were, all the interior walls had been reduced to the studs. In the elongated shadows of the studs caused by the late setting sun, the two cousins stood in a prison of shadows.

"Let's get started, man. The light's gettin' bad," Innis said, taking a tape measure out of his tool box.

"In a minute," Floyd said, stepping into the only remaining room. He moved across the floor, examining a couple of the pictures closely.

"So how'd you know that Hank would want to tear out the whole insides?"

"These walls," Floyd said, sweeping his hands around the few remaining structures, "are not a part of his history. He doesn't care what he's ripping apart. He doesn't think this is where he came from."

"Well, then, how'd you know he'd agree to your deal?" Innis then asked, looking at a deep charcoal drawing of a falseface.

"You know how I got Rachel . . ."

"Balls," Innis interrupted.

"Nope. What'd I say?" Floyd asked, turning to his cousin.

"Guts," Innis corrected.

"That's right. That's the one thing old Hank ain't got. I knew he'd back down. He needs us too bad and he don't know us well enough to know what we might give in on, not that I would've given in anyway. But I could tell, no instinct and no guts to take a risk," Floyd replied, smiling an easy grin.

"We gotta help him get some, and we gotta make him care about where he's come from. And these four walls are the start," he said, tapping a drawing of an eagle dancer spreading his wings.

Chapter Six

∿
∿

THE REAL BUG

FLOYD PAGE

JULY 27, 1992

The Bug's old six-string leaned in the corner of the room, like most of the rest of us, when my cousin Stan pulled the cassette from his pocket. We didn't all lean in that corner, but wherever there was a wall handy, one of us was leaning on it. I had just brought in another beer from the cooler. The fridge didn't keep things too cold, probably because there was no electricity. It's not like there ever had been any, though.

The Bug always had a fridge anyway. Every morning, just after sun-up, he'd cruise over to the hand pump which sprouted from a well just outside my trailer. There, he'd pump away, filling several old white Clorox jugs with the ice cold water. When he'd get back to his house, he'd line the bottom of the fridge with the cold jugs and this method worked for him for as long as he lived there.

If I were home, he'd lift one of his crutches and bang it on the trailer's aluminum side, never waiting for a reply to his wild symphony of fierce noise. He'd just pick up one jug for each hand and hobble back down the path to his house.

Whenever I heard the rattling, I'd throw on a pair of jeans and slip into my moccasins or boots, depending on the season, and go out to grab the other four jugs, heavy sons of bitches that they were. I could see why The Bug couldn't carry them. He never could move too fast after they cut off his leg.

He wasn't all that slow, but he was slow enough for me to catch up to him with no trouble. He could really fly along on that wooden leg, even faster when you added the crutches. But his balance was always a little off. So if I was home, I helped him with the jugs. If it wasn't me, it would be one of my cousins, or maybe even my mom, but that was pretty rare.

She thought that The Bug was a perfect name for her brother. He certainly bugged her, especially after he had first gotten the leg. He used to try to get her to do all kinds of things he really could have done himself. After a while, she claimed he was a nehts-eh, a skunk, that plagued her and wouldn't leave. They may have gotten along before the leg, but I wasn't even born then, so I couldn't say. She saved his life the night of the accident, and claims she's regretted it ever since.

In some ways, my mother was a born liar. She cried at his funeral and that is the only time I ever saw tears from her eyes. Even at the end, when he was in the nursing home, the two of them talked in their same, sort of crabby, way.

"Nora, go into my bank account tomorrow and lemme have a stack of fives, twenty or so," he'd say, and the children who were lined up along the bed, my older cousins' kids, would look expectantly at my mother. As far back as my cousins, my sister, and I could remember, he'd always given us kids something when we'd go to his house. Sometimes it was an enormous mushy molasses cookie, a bee-nana—as he called them—or a five dollar bill.

"You don't have any more money, remember? The nursing home made you sign over all your accounts to them, to pay your bills," my mother said quietly on these occasions, but stressed the word "bills," leaning close to his bed, so as not to announce the truth everyone in the room already knew.

"Bullshit. When I came in here, Christ, I had lots of money. What are you guys, holing it up 'til I die, or what?" he'd say, rising from his pillows and eventually flopping back down, wheezing. In the nursing home, there weren't any molasses cookies, and the bananas were always already peeled and perched on the edge of his tray. He couldn't very well offer anyone a naked banana.

He was stuck with our word, which he hadn't been trusting too much since we moved him to the nursing home. His mistrust even seemed to grow after we took his leg home. He was slowly dissolving from the inside with the bone cancer, and his stump didn't fit in the leg's socket anymore. He fell on it once, trying to walk around, and the nurses really got bent. They could only see him walking around as being more damaging than good, and didn't want him trying again. They told us to take the leg home.

"Here, take this, too," The Bug said as I gathered up the leg and harness from the corner. He held up his six-string. "Can't play the damn thing without m'leg. Need it for balance, even for strumming." I held it up and then set it back down. "Go on. I won't be playing it again unless I get home."

"These folks really like to hear you play, though." He had been playing for the other people in the nursing home, on a fairly regular basis, and I thought other people should get to hear him. He slipped the guitar into its fitted case, closed the lid and flipped the latch.

"Go on, now. I gotta rest."

I leaned the six-string in that corner of his living room when we first brought it back. It made a small noise, kind of like a harp. I went into the bedroom where my mom and my Auntie Olive were sitting on the bed. My other auntie, Selina, had been living in Vegas for years, by then.

"I put the six-string down, in the corner," I said, and they looked up, squinting in the darkening room. I could see them clearly, my eyes honed from years of spending the evenings in kerosene lantern light.

The two of them, however, seemed like night animals caught in daylight. This was The Bug's house and neither of them had spent more than an hour or two here in any given year. It was his place and our place. They looked at the leg, almost as if they expected it to give them some answers. It stood silent in the corner by his dresser, where it always stayed when he was in bed. The scuffed boot and the white hunting sock were wrapped around it like comfortable lovers.

His socks never matched. And I always gave him socks for Christmas. The few pairs always lasted him through the year, because he only used them up one at a time. Walking over to the dresser and pulling the top drawer open, I wondered how long that hunting sock had been on the leg. None of the socks lined neatly in the drawer even remotely resembled that sock. It had probably been on the leg for at least a couple years. It was sundown, and that's why the leg seemed so natural sitting in the corner.

It was a scary thing to my cousins and me when we were kids. We used to tell each other stories about some of us walking around in The Bug's living room and hearing noises in the other room when we knew he was in bed. In the stories, we always turned the corner to find the leg had hopped itself out into his kitchen and was chasing us down to step on our heads. But we always escaped the leg, because it could only hop, and we could outrun it without a doubt.

Of course this was all stupid. None of us ever stayed in the house when The Bug went to bed, when we were kids anyway. He usually went to bed with the sun. He never got around to having electricity installed, so the natural world dictated his waking hours. When we'd grown up, he sometimes shoved off to bed while we were still there, and we'd see his leg, keeping its lonely watch.

On those occasions he did stay up later than the sun, he had some kerosene lanterns to light the house. Though I think he stole the kerosene from my mother's heating tanks—she always claimed he did—I didn't mind. The nights at The Bug's house were the best. When we were kids, my mother and her sister didn't like us going over there at night. They always assumed he was drinking, and he was, but that just made things better. He always had the six-string out when he was drinking. So we made a plan based on the patterns of The Bug's parties.

If someone's car had been over in The Bug's driveway in the afternoon, one of us always watched for the orange glow in the window after the sun went down. If whoever was visiting with him had brought enough beer to last into the night, The Bug broke out the kerosene lanterns. Whichever of us noticed the glow suggested a night-time kickball game, or a snowball fight in winter.

As soon as we were out of the houses, we met up and headed down the back path to The Bug's house. He always greeted us as we piled in the back door. Sometimes whoever was partying with him didn't like kids being around and would say so. They were thrown out pretty fast—so fast, usually, that the beer was still on the table as The Bug shut the door behind them and turned the bar of wood mounted in the door frame that served as a lock.

"Arright! Now we can get on down to business," he'd say, cracking a fresh one and guzzling half in his first slug. "Ahhh! Pretty dood. Pretty dood. So," he'd start, strumming a few chords, waiting for the burp. After it rumbled its way up, he continued. "What do you all wanna hear?" He knew, but he always asked, and then he'd play something else instead. Sometimes it would be "Your Cheatin' Heart," or "Calijah," or other tunes I never learned the names of. We just listened on these numbers.

But eventually he'd get to our song. A couple of years ago, I found out the name of this piece was "Jambalayah." I had always thought it was "Goodbye, Joe." I'm not sure any of us, even The Bug, actually knew the verses. He usually just yodeled through them. We were mostly interested in the chorus. We were all too young to be doing any drinking, but The Bug used to let us do something else, nearly as rebellious for our age.

He always chose one particular version of the chorus for us. And when he got to it, we shouted out with him. "Son of a bitch, we'll all get rich on the bayou," made his windows shake. And at the end of the song, he always gave out a loud war whoop, and if we gave a loud enough one back, he'd start the song over again.

We were always free to do a lot of stuff at The Bug's house that we weren't allowed to do anywhere else. It was swearing, at first, and, as we got older, drinking. I had my first beer at The Bug's house. But it wasn't just things like illegal or bad stuff.

One of the other things I did was draw. I wasn't great, but I could draw people and they actually looked like people. Not like my cousin Ace. Sometimes, if he drew a person, it looked like an accident victim or something. Out of the four boys, Ace Ely, Innis, and Stan, only Stan could draw, and much better than me. But neither Stan, nor I, nor our moms, had money for nice paper and stuff. Stan was a lot older than me, maybe even by twelve years, and he'd been drawing for a long time.

Even before I could draw very well, I always went over and looked at Stan's work, which covered the plasterboard walls in The Bug's spare room. At some point, The Bug had told Stan he could draw on the walls if he didn't have any paper.

Stan made some beautiful pictures there. They were always Indian pictures, of dancers and hunters and falsefaces and pipes and things like that. I loved them, even though all I wanted to draw was super heroes, from the pages of tattered comic books my mom bought me once at a rummage sale.

One day, in the summer, when I was about ten, The Bug and I were listening to his old portable radio. It was getting to be about six, after supper, and I thought I might be able to cadge one of those molasses cookies. After the six o'clock news, The Bug shut his radio off and headed into the other room. I thought maybe he had to take a leak or something.

"Gotchee!" he said and I obeyed, following him into the spare room. "Here, hang on to this," he said, handing me one of Stan's charcoal pencils as he hobbled past me, back into his kitchen. He lugged back one of his mismatched chairs and pushed it up against the wall. "Here. That's your place, now. When you're done, you can put that pencil back in my top dresser drawer. That one's yours. I bought it from Stan."

"Thanks, Bug, but what's the chair for?"

"So your pictures will be just as tall as Stanny's. Now, go on. Quit asking so many questions. You only got a few hours of daylight left."

By the end of that day, the falsefaces were joined by Captain America, but when I was done, it didn't at all compare to Stan's work. The Bug said he liked it, and he always pretended that he did. Even when I had outgrown comic books and really wished the drawing would just disappear, he claimed to like it.

He used to show the drawings to the people who came to drink at his house. He'd drag them in and most of them were smart enough to go along with it. And if we happened to come in, he'd tell his company that we were the ones who had done the drawings. This was fine for Stan because his drawings were great, but The Bug always insisted on showing mine, too.

So one time when I wandered over to The Bug's, this guy who lived just down the road was sitting there. He was my friend Nathan's dad. I grabbed a beer and we all started talking, and, at one point, The Bug got up and headed for his bedroom. He kept a pot to piss in by his bedside so he wouldn't have to strap on his leg in the middle of the night.

"Hey, boy. Have you ever captured the real Bug?" Nathan's dad asked me quietly, once we heard The Bug pissing.

"The real bug?"

"Yeah, you got all these fancydancers and whatnot, old fashioned Indians, and that's fine," he said, waving hands in the general direction of the spare room. "But somebody should be drawing the real Indians. Take

Guggins, and Beaner, and Inchie, for instance. Man, they're gone, and all we got left is some old fuzzy black and whites. You think about it." As he mentioned them, I couldn't remember what those guys looked like. And some of them had only been dead a couple of years then.

But I was only drawing "barbarians" at the time and didn't want to be bothered with his idea. And besides, I'd never forget what The Bug looked like.

As the years went on, my drawing career ended. Life seemed to get in the way of picking up a pencil. But I always wanted to do something for The Bug.

I had this trophy of a lacrosse player that had fallen off the shelf in my trailer. The figure survived, but cracked at the upper right thigh, the same place The Bug's leg had been cut off at. And now the leg was slightly off in the wrong direction. I always thought he deserved a trophy. Both for his leg and for the guitar playing. It isn't everyone who could survive being run over and laugh about it. He didn't talk too much about the incident, though. When he did, he mostly laughed about my mom, at how funny she looked standing in the middle of the road wearing a torn skirt and a bra.

She had wrapped her blouse and the strip of skirt around his crushed leg after he had been run over in front of her house. She had stopped the bleeding long enough for the ambulance to get there. She had saved his life. He had been passed out in the middle of the road. No one knew it until they heard first the tires squealing and then The Bug yelling at the top of his lungs. My mom had never approved of his drinking and in fact had even taken a baseball bat to him once when he tried to fight with her one night when he'd had too much. He never tried that one again. But he was still her brother, and we loved him.

The Bug always had time for us when no one else did. He sang us the blues before we knew we'd need them. He laughed when I gave him the trophy, and set it on his shelf. I had glued a small plastic guitar to the lacrosse player. Sometimes he told us that he had played the six-string with Hank Williams when they were both in the army, but he didn't tell me the story that day.

"Pick up that six-string, will you?" he asked, and I brought it to him. "Did I say to hand it to me?"

"No, but . . ."

"Put it on. Play it."

"I don't know how to play," I said, but he motioned for me to slip the strap on, anyway.

"Now, gotchee. Pull your chair up closer." He wrapped my fingers around the neck and helped me play a few chords.

"Okay, now you play 'em on your own." I played them through a few times until he seemed to be satisfied I had them down. He took it back and played me some songs that day, but when the room began soaking up the new darkness of sunset, he didn't get out the lanterns. He played in the near dark for a while and just before he shagged me out, he put the guitar away and walked me to the door. "Now, you listen to me. If you learn to play that old six-string from me, I'll just hand it right over." As he shut the door, he said: "Somebody's got to play for the kids."

That was about two years ago. This summer, after we left him in the ground over on Upper Mountain Road, I went back to my trailer and sat there for a while, listening to some old Hank Williams records. We'd just had this really stupid send-off for The Bug, with the minister and all that bullshit. As far back as I could remember, I had never seen The Bug in a church. He needed a better goodbye than that.

It was nearing sunset when I stepped outside. I stood on my cinderblock front steps and watched the sun creep into the trees. "You going to go play kickball?" my mom asked from behind her screen door. I wasn't the only one who thought the formal service was just a bunch of oot-gweh-rheh. All my cousins' and friends' cars were pulling into The Bug's driveway. They were carrying cases of beer from their cars.

I grabbed the case I had in the fridge. It was almost full. I headed down the path to The Bug's house. My mom didn't follow, and that was as it should be. I pushed the old back door open and walked into the living room, or the pool room, as it had become in recent years. Some of the others had already started in.

Innis was racking up the balls for a game. He passed the cue to me, like I could take it. I made a motion to the case in my hands, and as I did, my sister Kay, who I guess had walked in right after me, lifted the case from my hands without stopping. I relieved Innis of the cue and broke for stripes or solids.

After I quickly lost the game, I passed the cue to someone else and Innis racked the balls again. He had always spent the most time at the table, anyway. I knew I had just been his first victim. With all the practice he got at The Bug's, he almost always won at the city bars.

"Hey! Where's that case I brought in?" I shouted, heading through the velvet curtains to the next room. I hoped they had put it in the fridge to keep it at least a little cold. The Clorox jugs all sat on the floor in the corner next to me. I picked one up and found it to be empty.

Stan's wife, Mel, was leaning over one of five coolers lined up in a row across the kitchen floor. She was loading the last of the beers into place among the crushed ice in the cooler. She handed me one as I stepped in the room.

"Nyah-wheh. Stain didn't come out, huh?" I asked needlessly, as I helped her up.

Whoever lined the coolers up tried to cover the dark rust blood stains that had soaked into the wood floor. The Bug had been laying in a big puddle when Stan walked in one morning. Stan searched him frantically for some wound. The blood seemed to be everywhere. The Bug woke up long enough to tell Stan that he was throwing it up. By the time someone had tried to clean the puddle up, it was permanent.

"Doesn't matter, anyway," Mel said. "You wanna go back over to the graveyard? I wanted to pick a rose out of one of the arrangements. You know, press it into a bible, and I don't wanna go alone."

"Sure. I'll drive," I said, pulling out my keys. I thought The Bug would probably find that bible thing pretty funny.

Stan and The Bug had always stayed close. More recently, I had made it over to The Bug's maybe once or twice a week, aside from the jug carrying visits. But Stan spent at least an hour a day with him for as long as I can remember. So Mel did, too. She seemed to miss him almost as much as we did. It was just her way of saying goodbye. She never was much of a beer drinker.

"So, what'd you mean, 'it doesn't matter?'" I asked as we walked the back path to my driveway.

"Hank's gonna move into the house," she said. The Bug's son, Hank, who was named after Hank Williams, we mostly never saw anymore, because he lived in the city.

"He's already put in key locks on the doors. He just let us use the place for tonight," she said, as we climbed into my car.

"Hey where is he, anyway?"

"Dunno. I saw him when he first let us in, but after that, I don't know. Wasn't he in the pool room?" I shook my head.

"Anyway, you know he's planning on gutting the house and starting over, electricity, wall to wall carpeting, the works. Probaly even a new heating system. "He told Stan that if he wants the drawings, he could come in and cut the plasterboard pieces out before they sledged the walls. He's going to do that in a couple of days. You want him to cut your drawing down for you?"

"Funny," I said, as we walked to the grave.

The arrangements looked kind of nice waving in the July breeze, against the dim sky. We stood by them for a couple of minutes. As Mel was picking out the rose she wanted, I opened my pocket knife and cut off one of the ribbons that had "The Bug" in gold letters glued on it. I handed it to her. It seemed to be what she needed.

"So, what's gonna happen to The Bug's stuff, you know?" I asked her, on the way back to the house. Not that he had too much, but it would have been nice if we each had something to keep him around with.

"Hank's keeping it all," she said, smoothing the ribbon on her lap.

By the time we pulled back into the driveway, they had gotten out the kerosene lanterns. The old orange glow was coming from the hinged pane as we walked up the old steps. As I reached for the door, I could hear some music coming from inside the house. In the time Mel and I were gone, one of my younger cousins had gone next door and brought back a boom box. They were playing some compact discs. The one playing was some rap star.

I picked up the stack of discs on the table and held it close to the lantern so I could read the titles. No Hank Williams there. In fact, most of the discs were rap music. I headed into the pool room. Everyone who agreed with me about the music had already moved in there. Someone let the heavy velvet curtain down that divided the two rooms. This muffled the sound a little, but not enough for most of us.

The party had divided into two groups. This room was just full of night-time kickball players. The other room was the younger people. They were always listening to machines. The cue ball cracked into the freshly racked balls and I watched them spread about the table. Innis was not one of the players. He was sitting on the arm of a chair in the far end of the room. I looked at him with one eyebrow raised, like Spock.

"This night just ain't right for winning. Something's off," he said from his perch.

Just then, Stan reached into his jacket pocket and pulled out a bottle of Mohawk Ginger Flavored Brandy—The Bug's Special Occasion drink. He cracked the seal, and, after taking a slug, passed it to the next person, my sister Kay. The bottle began making the rounds. Ace took it and exclaimed after his slug, in his best imitation of The Bug, that the brandy was "pretty dood."

Stan stepped around the pool players and sat in The Bug's chair. No one else had done so yet. He reached into his other pocket and that was when he pulled out the cassette. He slammed it into The Bug's old radio/tape player. The player had been around forever. The antenna had been duct taped on, and there were other pieces of duct tape holding the back to the front.

"Hey! Shut that shit off!" he yelled through the curtain, and eventually they did. He pressed the "PLAY" button. A guitar sounded some familiar chords from the tiny speaker. A minute later, The Bug's voice came through, loud and clear.

"I recorded this at the nursing home, during one of his rec room per-formances," he said, leaning back in the chair.

Three songs played through. "Your Cheatin' Heart" and two of those others we never knew the names of. The younger kids reopened the cur-tain, and leaned in the entryway. After the third song, while the Senior Citizens were clapping, Stan reached up and shut the tape off. We all stared at him.

"He didn't play it. There wasn't enough of us there that day," was Stan's answer as he popped the cassette and slid it back into his pocket. The younger kids let the curtain down and put their discs back on. I had noticed the six-string while the tape was playing. It rested in the corner I had set it in when we brought it back from the nursing home. I was still pissed off about Hank saying that he was going to keep everything. The Bug had said that he would give me the six-string.

I almost reached out and picked it up. But I couldn't. I never did learn the guitar from him. In fact, I couldn't even remember the three fucking chords he taught me that day. No one picked up the six-string. None of us knew how to play it. I left a little while later, but I snagged the trophy just as I was about to head for the door. Hank didn't need that.

I thought, after the funeral, about drawing a picture of The Bug, and I even sat down to do it one day. But when I closed my eyes to see him, the picture that filled my head was him in the nursing home, skinny and dazed, with one eye looking off one way and the other eye not quite looking in the same direction. And I knew that wasn't the real Bug.

So I drew a picture of Captain America.

Son of a bitch, we never got rich.

Chapter Seven

∿
∿

THE BALLAD OF PLASTIC FRED

FLOYD PAGE

AUGUST 1, 1992

We were going down to the corner store on the day I learned about death. My sister had just recently gotten her license. Or maybe she hadn't yet. I really can't remember. You didn't need a license to drive on the reservation, and its only store was the one we were going to. We could've walked, since it was at the end of our road. But Kay was just beginning to drive, and that made everything exciting. I was only four, and excitement was pretty cheap in those days.

It was summer. I knew that I'd be heading off to school for the first time very shortly. Innis had already been there for a while. New kids had been playing with him since he started school. They'd come over and visit, and he'd be gone for long periods of time, presumably visiting them. He lived next door. We had played together all the time, but not so much anymore.

I was left hanging around with his brother Ace, whose real name is Horace. But nobody calls him Horace, except for his mom when she's mad. Everyone else calls him Ace. Ace was prone to random bursts of violence, and though he was younger than me, he was much larger. I didn't hang around with him without some big person to protect me. Cowardly, but safe.

That morning Innis had actually been home. We had been playing in the mountain. The mountain was this mound of dirt which had been dug out for Auntie Olive's patio, which had never actually gotten built beyond the cinderblock foundation.

The mountain was on the patch of land between our two houses. It was small, I guess, but to us it seemed like another whole world. We had dug a hole into one of the interior folds of the mountain for later use as a cave for the six-inch plastic Indian figures we all played with. We could never quite figure out who those Indians were. They were all peach colored and they didn't really look like anyone from our reservation.

There was some speculation from my older cousins, those in the fourth or fifth grade, that one of those figures might be of Gary Lou's older brother, who had gone to Hollywood to be a star. We had seen him in some movies on tv, but I could never recognize him. He was killed by the Cavalry before he ever got any close-ups. I don't really think anyone else recognized him either, but they all wanted him to be a star so bad that they made themselves see him in "that wild horde of savages."

So one of the figure's names was always Fred, as that was our star's name. It was always the one who was in a running position, crouched with one leg up. His mouth was open wide, in either a war cry or a really big yawn. In the hand that was in front of him, he carried a hatchet, a tomahawk, and he had two feathers sticking out of his hair in the back. All he wore was a loin cloth, but when we looked underneath, to the area that wasn't covered, there was nothing there. He was a warrior without any balls. It didn't make sense to us, because we knew Fred had balls. After all, he went to Hollywood to become a star.

But it wasn't really him up there, anyway. Even at the ending credits, we couldn't find his name in the "Indian savages" list. We found out from his mother that he had changed his name. She had married a white man, who had a distinctly white last name. For Hollywood, Fred Howkowski had become Frederick Eagle Cry. Frederick Eagle Cry died daily on some tv somewhere, but Fred Howkowski lived on in California, occasionally sending his mother picture postcards of palm trees and big houses which described to her his most recent death so she could tell us and we'd all go to the movies so we could play "Spot the Savage," on bargain night.

Plastic Fred was getting a little beat. This was the figure everyone always wanted, and he usually died the most dramatic deaths of all the figures we had. He had to be rejuvenated every so often, and the old Fred would be retired to our version of the ancient burial ground. We would give the

70

Freds to one of Innis's older brothers, Ely, who either used them for target practice, or tied them to fire crackers, or put lighter fluid to them, or in some other way creatively mutilated them.

When he was done with them, he would give us back the twisted and blackened plastic, which hardly resembled a figure anymore, and we would give them to Ace. It was his job to set them strategically around the mountain for their best dramatic potential. He had quite a knack with that sort of arrangement.

This Fred's days with us were numbered. He was covered with pock marks from our discovery that we could throw darts at him and that if we were lucky, the darts would stick as he toppled from his ledge and remain stuck as he landed, which was a really cool looking death.

This Fred also had a large hardened glob of Testors Model Glue on the back of his head with a little sharp spine poking out. We had found a feather, which had fallen off of this sparrow that one of our cats had killed, and we decided to put it on Fred. Innis stole one of his dad's saws and we hacked the plastic feathers off of the back of Fred's head, and glued on the real one with the model glue. The feather lasted about four or five days and then it finally broke off and all we were left with was the mound of glue and the feather's spine. How do birds keep them so long, anyhow?

So it was still pretty early in the morning, probably around eight-thirty or nine, though I hadn't been able to tell time all that well yet. The sun was hot, but not unpleasantly so. We had shoved all the finely sifted dirt we had dug out for the cave. We had shoved it all together to create a small, very soft hill in the inner valley of the mountain, and now that the sun had reached over the mountain's edge, the hill was warm.

I took my sandals off and patted my toes in the dirt, leaving small circular prints. Innis did the same, but he hadn't had to take his shoes off. He never wore any in the summer. We wrestled toes with each other in the heated earth, stirring up small clouds of dust, which swirled in the sunlight.

We did this for a while. I asked him if Ace were up yet. Just as I asked it, I heard their screen door slam. I waited and listened for the splash that meant it had just been Auntie Olive throwing out some dirty wash water, but the sound never came. Ace was coming. He jumped down next to me and stuck his feet in with ours, sneakers and all. Ace had no aversion to shoes in the summertime.

Ace asked me where the Indians were. I told him that they were in the house. He was a little irate over this; he wanted to play right then. Innis said that he'd pee on him if he didn't behave, and this calmed the younger brother down instantly.

I guessed that Innis had made good on this threat at some time in the past, though I had nothing to substantiate this. I also told him that we didn't want the dogs to get them and chew them up, which is what would happen if we left them unattended. To pass time, we planned for our impending departure from the mountain.

We were waiting for my sister to get up. She had said the night before that if Mom would give her the keys she would drive us down to Jugg's store to get a new Plastic Fred. Maybe we'd get a bottle of pop, too. There was always pop in the fridge, but it wasn't the same as drinking pop while sitting on one of Jugg's high stools which surrounded his lunch counter. People in high school seem to really love sleeping in late.

Kay finally came out of the door. We were pretending not to notice but had been watching the door all morning. She leaned against the porch railing for a minute, adjusting her sandals to conform against her heels. She went to the car and hopped in. I grabbed my sandals as the others ran to line up at the edge of the driveway.

After some moments of adjusting the various settings of the car, Kay started it and jerkily drove to the place my cousins were standing, just as I joined them. We all piled in, Innis getting to sit in the front seat since he was older. He turned on the radio and began spinning the dial to find a good song. He found "Daydream Believer" by The Monkees and we were all happy with that, so that was what we listened to as we pulled out of the driveway.

Ace and I couldn't see too much as we were small and the seat backs were high. We entertained ourselves by pretending we were members of The Monkees. The song ended, and we all listened to find out what the next song was going to be.

The announcer said that it was going to be something new from The Jefferson Airplane. This was some new group and one of Kay's favorites. I knew that we would be listening to the new song through speakers that vibrated because the volume was turned up so high.

We never did get to hear the new song that day. In her excitement, Kay was more interested in the volume control than the steering wheel. We promptly crashed into Ardra's mailbox just down the road. We hadn't been going very fast, but we did enough damage that we had to stop. We all got out of the car and looked at the uprooted mailbox and the dent in the front end of the car.

Ardra came out of her house, wiping her hands on a dish towel. She watched as Kay picked up the mailbox and tried to stick its post back into the hole we had rammed it out of. It went back in, and actually wasn't damaged. But the hole had been widened by our hit and the mailbox sat lazily at an angle.

Ardra looked closely at it, and seeing that neither the box nor its post were any worse for the wear, told us to go along, that Enoch, her husband would put some rocks in the hole to steady it when he got home. We went.

When we got to the store, Kay told us to stay in the car, while she ran in. We started to whine, but not for long. Her mood had changed substantially since our encounter with the mailbox. She was back out in a few seconds. She threw the bag in the back seat, just barely missing me. She slammed the car into reverse and we stirred up a dust cloud in the small gravel parking lot.

We flew down to the picnic grove, just below the hill upon which the store sat. We pulled in, bouncing around in the back seat as she drove over the pitted and rutted path into the grove. She got out and left the door open as she sat down hard on the concrete bandstand. The three of us got out and walked over to where she was sitting. I opened the bag to see what she had bought.

I reached in and pulled out some bottles of Pepsi and passed them around. I pulled the plastic Indian from the bag. It wasn't Fred. It was a chief with a headdress and a bow and arrow. How could she mistake this guy for Fred? I mentioned this to my sister; she told me to shut up and snatched the bag away from me. She pulled a pack of cigarettes from the bag and ripped them open. She lighted one. I didn't even know she smoked.

We left the grove a couple of minutes later. We were all looking out the windows, studying hard the road and the ditches which bordered the road. We were looking for a dead cat, any dead cat would do. We just needed one. There was a high mortality rate for reservation cats and there were usually some dead ones laying around the sides of one road or another.

Innis had gotten the idea. We had to find some way to explain the new dent in the car. It wasn't as if the car were new or anything, or that it didn't already have some dents in it. This dent, however, would not go unnoticed. It wasn't just the fender that was dented. The mailbox had impacted with the hood and had left its own noticeable mark.

We knew that we could get away with this if we had some really good reason for the dent. We also knew that if we said it happened because of the radio, we'd be walking to the store for quite some time to come. We were in this together.

My mom loved cats. We had eight of them. When our cat had kittens, my mom just couldn't bear to give them up. The survivors from the second litter were already grown up, and the mother was pregnant again. It appeared we were going to have more. Virtually the entire population of the res knew of my mom's love for cats. Innis thought if we told my mom that we had hit the mailbox while trying to avoid running over a cat, that would be a good enough excuse. We agreed.

He thought he had seen a dead cat along the side of the road as we had headed to the store, but he couldn't remember exactly where. He did say that it was after Ardra's house. He was quite sure of that. He thought if we brought the dead cat home with us, it would be even more convincing. Kay thought this was really gross, but she was a desperate woman. We had to hurry, too. We were only supposed to have gone down the road.

Kay warmed to the idea the closer we got to the house, and the closer she got to not being able to drive for a while. She even told us that she hoped it was a fresh one, and not stiff and loaded with maggots. It was, after all, the middle of summer. A rotting cat would not be too convincing.

My mother would probably insist on a burial, and she would most certainly notice the odor of a high-summer dead cat. We hoped along with Kay. None of us really wanted to handle the cat. The anonymous plastic Indian sat casually on the back seat.

I spotted the cat. Innis was right. It was beyond the spot of our collision, but not much. It was in front of the field next to Spicy's house. On the other side of the field was Ardra and Enoch's. As we got out of the car, we could see the lounging mailbox. Enoch apparently hadn't gotten home yet. We walked over to the cat. It was an orange one, the color of Creamsicles, my mom's favorite cat color. It was still alive.

Someone had hit it not long before Innis had seen it the first time. It was lying in the gravel and dirt which edged the road. There was a trail of streaky blood from the place on the road where it must have been hit to the place it now rested. It must have dragged itself. The blood had come from its rear end. Its back legs were bent at impossible angles. It was breathing heavily, panting. Its eyes stared up at us as we surrounded it.

I squatted down to pet it. I didn't know what else to do. Kay yelled at me and pushed me aside before I could reach it. She said that the cat might try to bite. She said that she couldn't do it.

"Sure you can, just do this," Ace said, moving closer to the cat. He was out of reach for any of us. I was still sitting in the weeds. Kay and Innis had already turned and started moving toward the car.

Ace stomped hard once on the cat's neck. The cat made a small squeaking noise and then did not make another. The cat expired under the hot summer sun. We had all seen it go. I wondered who would be putting food out for it tonight, how long those scraps would sit before they knew the cat wasn't coming home.

We started walking back to the car.

"Hey, aren't we takin' this?" Ace was holding the cat by the tail, lifting it out to his right, like a fisherman showing off his prize catch of the day. Innis told him to put it down and to wipe his hands on the weeds. He dropped the cat back to the ground and did as he was told. The cat stirred up a little dust, which blew away in a couple of seconds.

My mom didn't ask about the dent. She had been on the phone when we walked into the house. As soon as she finished talking to someone she would dial someone else's number and begin with her one greeting which always meant some serious bad news.

"Did you hear?"

Auntie Olive, who was sitting at our dining room table, told us what had happened. Fred Howkowski had shot himself in Hollywood. The Cavalry must have finally come.

My mother glanced at the old clock hanging on the wall near our phone, got off the phone and rushed out the door. She still had curlers in her hair. She was going to drive Fred's mom and dad to the airport. They were bringing him home to be buried on the reservation. The plastic Indian Chief rode in the back seat with Fred's dad.

I wondered why Fred went and did that. Maybe he just couldn't find someone to stomp on his throat.

I asked Kay if we could walk back and bury the cat. She said sure. We buried it in the mountain. We wrapped it up in an old flannel shirt which didn't fit her anymore. We put it in an old cardboard canning-jar box. We did this so the dogs wouldn't find it.

We told Mom about the dent when she got home. The plastic Indian Chief joined the tribe. We continued to play in the mountain, being careful not to dig where we had buried the cat. Whenever we went to the store the rest of the summer, we walked. We drank a lot of Pepsi. We occasionally bought a Mountain Dew.

We never bought another Plastic Fred.

Chapter Eight

∿∿
∿∿

KEYS

I

Floyd Page and Janice Freen stood on the roof of the Nursing building. It was sometime past midnight on a Saturday night. Jan had worked as assistant on a project for one of her professors in the Spring semester and had a key to the building; Floyd had a key to the roof access. It was one of his responsibilities when they got to the site every morning.

"I've never been up here. It's really beautiful. You get so much better a sense of the campus," Jan said, strolling in a large circle around the roof's perimeter.

"Better than what?"

"Better than from in a classroom, silly. Where else?" She started to laugh, but when he didn't, she stopped.

"Oh," Floyd replied, quietly. As Jan looked out over the rest of the university—relatively quiet this late—out of her view, Floyd practiced the most basic steps of a Social Round Dance, but he still couldn't get it. He tried listening to the rhythms in his head, but his feet just would not move with them.

They had just driven back to Buffalo from a social at the Cattaraugus Longhouse. He had told her about his memory problem a couple weeks before, right after they had first met. On the slim chance they might get involved, he didn't want her wandering into a bad situation. Though he felt as though he were getting a bit better, and that his notebooks were

77

really helping him along, he had no way of knowing what would happen next.

"None of us do. That's part of the fun," Jan had replied over burgers one day at lunch. Later in the conversation, when he had informed her that there was no Longhouse at Tuscarora, she invited him to theirs, and now he had been to his first social. He had watched her glide across the floor in graceful fluid movements; all of them moved that way—the way of people who'd been dancing all of their lives.

Floyd had not joined the group and danced, even at several adamant invitations. He couldn't. He hadn't danced since he'd been a kid, and that had been a good number of years ago. His feet felt like wooden blocks. Maybe he had just lost the memories of those dances as well, but he didn't really believe that. It had just been too long.

Jan turned around quickly and caught him in mid-move. She'd obviously heard him trying to shuffle rhythmically in the cinders. "You know, if you'd try that in the Longhouse, you'd be surprised."

"No, you'd be surprised . . . at how bad I can be," Floyd replied, stopping, embarrassed.

"Okay. Don't they do any dancing on your res?" she asked.

"Sometimes. Not too often, though."

"When are you going to take me out there, anyway?"

"I dunno. There's not much to see, really. Some houses, people. I suppose I could take you to the dike, or on top the school. I hung out on that roof, too. Like I told you, there's no Longhouse."

"No. I mean to your family. I couldn't show you mine. I don't have one, any longer. The closest thing I have are those people in that Longhouse you met tonight."

"Well, you know, they're not too traditional. I mean, they have their own traditions, but they're not like the ones where you come from. It's just . . . different." Silence.

"Yeah, sometime." Floyd said finally when Jan didn't respond to his excuses. He walked over to the roof's edge and looked out over the campus. He agreed with her that it was a sight. She brought a different subject back around.

"Look, dancing is easy. It's just like this," she said, her body instantly moving in the same magical ways it had been under the big caged lights of the Longhouse an hour or so before. She grabbed his hand and held it, pushing her body in his direction, forcing him to move with her. Floyd moved, turning his body so they met head on instead of side by side. They stopped for a few seconds. "Some dances are even more natural," he mumbled, pressing closer. Her breath hitched and she ceased moving, then met his pressure.

"Here? On the roof?" she whispered, nuzzling her chin against his neck. He kissed her gently behind her right ear.

"I told you, I'm kind of partial to roofs. There's a sense of freedom here, only the stars can see your missteps, this way." He slid his fingers into the waistband of her jeans, feeling the warm, firm flesh of her bottom, gently lifting her closer with one hand and eventually moving the other to meet the brass button at the fly. She reached down and helped him, gently guiding his rough and coarse fingertips.

They folded into one another, beginning a different sort of dance in the cinders. Their bodies glowed in the moonlight.

II

Earlier that evening, before the daylight had vanished, Hank Jimison walked through his evolving house. They had all started work on it recently. While the house was nowhere near livable, he had taken to stopping off there, after work. Today, though, he and the others had been laboring at it all day. Floyd had cleared out early, not saying where he was going. Innis didn't like him heading out alone like that, but Floyd was a big boy.

Hank wandered through the partial, tentative rooms. Supplies and tools were piled in the old bedroom which housed the drawings. He kept telling himself that he came out here every day to see the progress, map out his furniture, that sort of thing. But he knew the real reason. He always checked the locks as he strolled around, and this time, like all others, as he looked at the tools, he could not help but take an inventory of everything there. As usual, he found nothing missing.

He stepped into what would be his living room. Out the window, he could see his Uncle Frank, just finishing replacing some lattice work on the gazebo behind their house. He noticed that the gazebo was meticulously finished, but that the house sorely needed some new siding. He wondered vaguely if hiring his cousins was not the smartest thing to do.

Hank stepped outside on his way back to the city and as he was about to lock the door, he watched his uncle walking with his tool box. He slid it into the small shed attached to the back of Olive and Frank's house. It did not appear that the shed had any door, and Hank shook his head. He slid his key into the ignition of his Firebird, but sat there for a minute.

He unlocked and re-entered the house a few minutes later. He unlocked the heavy brass deadbolt he had installed on the side door. He tried to slide the big wood block into place that The Bug has used to keep the door from opening, but the deadbolt blocked it from sliding.

A few minutes later he was knocking on Frank and Olive's back door. He could hear the tv going in the living room.

"Who's knocking?" Frank shouted from the couch.

"Hank."

"What the hell you knocking for? Come on in." Hank stood in the kitchen entryway and shouted over the tv.

"Maybe I shouldn't come in. I'm all grubby."

"Me, too. It didn't stop me. Pull up a chair. There's glasses over on the counter and some iced tea in the fridge."

"Actually, I just stopped by for a minute. You got a Phillips head I can borrow for a minute?" Hank had gone through all of his tools and had no Phillips head screwdriver. He was at first suspicious, and having second thoughts and then remembered he had used it recently at his mother's house in the city.

"Yeah, yeah. You need some help with something? It'll only take me a minute to slip my boots back on. They're right here," his uncle said, standing up and coming into the kitchen, holding a pair of grimy boots in the air. Up to this point, the two had just been shouting to one another through the rooms and over the squawking voices on the television sit-com Frank had been watching.

"No, it's a small job. I'll be done in a minute."

"Sure?" Hank nodded a reply and his uncle continued. "There's a couple of 'em in my tool box in the back shed. Just take one. If I need it, I'll just come and pick it up sometime. If you need anything else too, the door's always open."

Hank thanked him and headed for the shed while his Uncle Frank went back to his tv show. The shed did have a door; it was just, as Frank had said, always open.

The job did indeed only take a minute or so. When he was done, Hank noticed the new hole in each of the doors, like a cavity, or an area where something bad had been removed, something cancerous. There'd be no way of filling those holes without it showing, but he had made up his mind. It would just have to remain that way for a while. Anyone could slip a finger in the hole and slide the wood block away, opening the door; the back door didn't even have that.

He turned the key that had sat in his ignition the whole time. His key ring jangled a little less; it was lighter by two keys. Those two keys were in a little brown paper bag in the back seat, along with the entire deadbolt mechanisms he had removed from the doors. He was taking them back to the city, where he would undoubtedly find a use for them.

Chapter Nine

ᗰ

GAZEBOS

FLOYD PAGE

AUGUST 18, 1992

Jan wants me to bring her out to our reservation, but I just don't know, particularly already having to deal with Hank and all his shit. Hank being out here reminds of the time I brought someone back with me to the reservation last summer. I got a lot more at stake here this time, in both of these cases. I'm going out with Jan and, as much as I hate to admit it, Hank is blood. The other one was, I guess you could call him a buddy, but he was a white guy. He saw the gazebo, but just didn't understand it. He almost got it, but I felt it fly in the night air, with the gray wood bonfire smoke.

It was mid-July. I had been working on the roofs down at the University then, too—the new section. They were in pretty bad shape. The buildings had been designed in a stupid way with flat roofs. With our winters, practicality should have taken the lead. They wanted interesting looking buildings to impress or something. But flat roofs are practical only for roofers around here. All those stress repairs keep us off unemployment lines. We keep saying we're snow dancing overtime winters to secure work in the spring.

We mostly liked our work. The pay was good, and it was as close as most of us were going to get to college. We laughed when we put those University parking stickers on our bumpers, wondering who we were going to fool on the reservation, but not really. We knew we weren't fooling anybody. But they did offer us pretty steady work. We'd work on one set of buildings one year, and at the end of that winter, a set we had worked on a number of years ago would end up needing repair. It was a big school, so there were enough repairs needed to keep us busy all the time.

I think this was our fourth or fifth summer. We were working on the Social Science/Humanities building, and we always had our lunch on these benches that were sitting in the shade of these trees by the building's main entrance. We saw some of the professors go in and out, and lots of kids, too. Funny though, it was supposed to be the professors who were the smart ones. But even though it was July, they were still wearing suit jackets. The kids wore T-shirts and shorts. Seemed to us that they were more aware of their surroundings.

The kids didn't usually talk to us, but we didn't care too much. Actually, it seemed like most of them didn't even see us, but again, we didn't really care. At least they knew when it was too damn hot to wear a jacket. Most of the professors didn't talk to us that much, either. Most looked at us and nodded. They usually also included that fake smile that the recipient always knows is a fake smile, because it looks more like a wince than a smile. I guess sometimes pain and pleasure go together, but I just don't know when any of those times are.

Occasionally one of those professors would stop and say something stupid about the building. We'd all laugh with him. The women professors didn't ever stop. It was always the men. I guess the women just weren't interested in architecture. Although they could stop. Having no knowledge in architecture did not seem to stop the men professors from making comments. And besides, what the hell did we know about architecture ourselves, except that they shouldn't have built these pretty buildings in this area of the country?

So one day, one of them stopped while we were on lunch. He looked as tweedy as any of the others, but a little bit younger than most, maybe closer to my age, which was twenty-eight at the time. He didn't have dress pants on, though. They were like jeans, but they seemed to be purple, kinda weird. He had one of those bad professor haircuts; you know the one. Trimmed around the edges of the salad bowl, it made him look a little like Moe from the Three Stooges.

But he didn't talk to us about architecture in general, or the building in particular. He edged a little closer, waiting for us to offer up a part of one of our benches. We didn't move. So he sat in the grass. He folded his legs in front of him, Indian style. He didn't say too much. He seemed to be more listening to us. That wasn't fair, so we shut up, and went about eating.

Nathan Buck, who still lived down the road from me and took turns with me driving to work, said that this stupid white guy was going to drive him crazy. Now of course he didn't say this so the white guy could understand. He said it in our language: "Dee(t)-quah Cree-rhu-rhit Jeh-oos-eh Ah-kree-aw(t)-nes." We all laughed. None of us could speak the language all that well, even though they had taught it to us in elementary school. Our families didn't speak it very much, and we mostly lost what we had learned.

But there were certain words and phrases we all knew, because they had frequent use, and were useful, for occasions such as this. The words were particularly handy when you wanted to say something funny about a white person, and they happened to be standing there. Not only could you say it and they wouldn't know what you said, but they also usually knew you were talking about them, and they would leave you alone soon after. You could also tell them you said something entirely different, and they might believe you. This way, you got more mileage out of the joke.

But this guy just smiled. He didn't leave or anything. So I'm drinking down this Pepsi I got from the machine inside the building when he finally says something to us. It was something stupid, but something we're used to hearing, anyway. Some funky misconception.

"I did my fieldwork with some Indians out West a few years back, Lakotas," he said to no one in particular. He smiled some more.

"Oh yeah, I did some work in the fields out West, too. With some white guys. Californians, I think . . . you know 'em?" It was Nathan. We all started laughing. That had been a pretty good one. Even that professor laughed. He stood up and brushed off his pants. He looked at the bunch on the bench closest to him, expecting the guys to move. No one did. He thought that laugh had been his admission price; he didn't know there wasn't one. He said see ya later and we nodded. After he walked away, Nathan repeated his joke and we laughed again.

He showed up again on Friday, but not at lunch time. He must have been waiting in the air-conditioned building for us to come down, because he appeared right as we were walking the ladders down. He watched without actually talking to anyone. He looked like I guess people do at art museums, studying. He went over to Mike Bronson and asked him if we were maybe going out for a couple of beers when we finished.

"Nope," Mike said. "More'n a couple, I figure," he finished and laughed. He continued tearing down, not really looking at the professor. The professor asked Mike if he would mind one extra person. "It's not my bar," he replied. He was being ornery that day; he was working on a hangover from the night before. The professor was looking bewildered, but persistent.

"Hey, c'mere." I decided to give the guy a break. I started to tell him where the bar was, and then I changed my mind and yelled to Nathan that after we punched out, I would ride down to The Den with the professor and I'd meet them there. We loaded up the trucks and made sure we had everything secured. I was getting ready to climb up when The Hack told me he'd punch me out on the clock. If I was riding with the professor, it was the least he could do. I took him up on it. Whenever we left our cars at the main office because we needed the big trucks, I always got stuck sitting next to the door in the tight cab and the window knob constantly jabbed into my side. Sometimes I think Mike hit the pot holes on purpose. He had kind of a mean streak in him, so I was just as happy.

So me and the professor headed out to the Faculty Parking Lot, and when we got there, he pointed to this really nice car. It was a Bonneville, or something like that, really classy.

"I was wondering," he said, as he unlocked the car's trunk, "if you would mind sitting on these." He pulled out some neatly folded newspapers, from one of the corners. I didn't mind. I had sat on worse things in Nathan's car. I looked down at the floor. No pennies, no weeds, no old and cold french fries from Burger King—Hell, the newspapers themselves were almost a luxury.

As we pulled out, he pushed some button on the stereo and it just swallowed up this tape; he hadn't touched the tape at all. It was something really fierce and unfriendly sounding.

"So," I asked, "you got any of them Hank Williams tapes? Senior, not Junior, or any of that new shit." He got the hint and pressed that same button and the tape went dead and came sliding out, like somebody's tongue who doesn't like you, or who likes you an awful lot.

"Well, no I don't, but I might have something in which you'd be interested," he said, pulling it out and setting another one in its place and then pressing that first button again.

The music this time was these flutes and drums. It was all kind of dainty sounding. The professor was smiling away, almost like he had just put on the best blues record on earth. I asked him what the hell this was supposed to be. He handed me the little case that the tape came in. I was surprised to see that someone actually put the right tapes back into the right cases.

There was some Indian on the cover. He was wearing feathers and leather and what looked like one of those fluffy neck things girls used to wear in their High School Senior Yearbook Picture. I opened up the case and unfolded the little cardboard sheet inside that told you all about the singer, or performer, or whatever. This guy was supposed to be Chief something or other, but it didn't say what he was chief of. He looked kind of Indian under all the feathers and such, but it was hard to tell. It was what they call a "New Age Recording." I had to give it that. It was New to me. I continued my search and eventually found what I was looking for. It didn't really take all that long. This was, after all, a small piece of cardboard, about as tall as a cigarette pack. The line I was looking for told me that this tape was recorded entirely in Tokyo. Boy, those Japanese have everything over there. So by the time I found this, we had reached the last section of the perimeter road for the University and were about to go on the regular roads.

"Which way?"

"Go right," I answered.

"I feel this music is very peaceful. It has such a sense of balance, a sense of harmony," he said, still wearing his light and airy smile.

"Yeah, I could see myself falling asleep to it," I agreed. He thought this was a compliment.

As we got closer to our destination, I told him that we were gonna be way too early. The others wouldn't be arriving for at least another half an hour. He asked if there was usually anything I'd do in the meantime. I said that yeah there was, that I'd be showering back at the main building with the others, trying to get rid of the day's grime. I didn't have one at home, so I'd have to end up taking one of those stupid step-by-step baths with a wash pan. But I didn't tell him that much. I suggested that we could go and hang out at Bond's Lake.

"Is that something you all do?" he asked.

"Sometimes, but it's mostly something I do." We didn't do *everything* together.

I asked him if he knew the way and he said that he did.

"I went to high school at Lew-Port," he explained, "and we used to hold our Class Day down there every June." Class Day was the end of the year drinking free-for-all that all the area high schools seemed to do. The schools themselves didn't, but all the kids did. Bond's Lake was usually where the party ended up, so schools all set up different days as their Class Day; kids from different schools only seemed to rumble whenever they got in rumbling distance of each other.

"I went to Wheatfield," I laughed. "We probably rumbled with each other at some time."

"What's 'rumbling'?" he asked.

"You know, 'rumbling'!' Brawling. Gang fighting. You know."

"I have never rumbled," he said very seriously. "However, something very funny did happen to me at Bond's on one of those Class Days, my Senior one, in fact." I asked him what, and he said he'd tell me when we got there.

So we got there. He pulled slowly into the pathway that served as an entrance to the park. He drove a little way in and pulled into the clearing. There were several other cars around. They were pretty beat up cars, with big rust holes in the quarter panels and such. Mostly Welfare mothers from the res and their kids. They had nothing better to do, so they sat at the picnic tables and smoked while their kids played. The tables were closer to the road than we were, so I just waved. I knew them all.

We got out of the car and he pressed some button and the door locked. I looked to him for an explanation. He said that it was just a force of habit, but he didn't press the button again to unlock the door. He just shut it. We walked to the edge of the lake. He was leading me to a particular spot. It was an area where the ground just sort of dropped off. It wasn't that deep of a drop, only about three feet or so, but it was different. There was no gradual incline to the water's edge here, like there was around most of the rest of the lake. We stood, looking out over the lake, which wasn't very big, but a pleasant sight all the same. I didn't know what it was we were supposed to be looking at, but I like to look anyway.

"Right here was where it happened," he said. "My father had just purchased a brand new Trans Am as my graduation gift. My mother had paid for the registration, and also said she would pay for the insurance while I was in college, and probably throw in gas money every now and then. After all, what fun is a sports car if it's sitting at home with an empty tank? They had suggested that I give my old car to my younger brother. I hadn't wanted to do that. I thought it would be great to have a winter car, so I could put this baby up. I, of course, relented when they reminded me that they had bought the original car also, and were still taking care of all of the expenses. It was a bummer, you know?" I didn't say anything. Couldn't relate.

"I had this fine young woman with me—natural blond—and I decided to impress her by doing backwards doughnuts right here in the clearing. I threw the car in reverse, turned the wheel as sharp to the left as I could and kept it there, and then stepped on the gas. People had cleared out of there; they of course knew what I was planning. We laughed as we spun around in tight circles on the clearing, stirring up dust. I knew that she'd be mine that night. We laughed right up to the point where we went over that embankment!"

I knew that was coming. But he had said that this was a funny story. He continued. Maybe the humor came later. He started laughing, saying how the car was hopeless. They couldn't get it out of the water. It was ruined. He couldn't get out too many long sentences, because he would keep breaking them apart with laughter. He said that his parents were really mad, and that they made him get rides from his little brother for the whole summer, until they got the insurance thing squared away and he could get his new replacement. He said he could have had it sooner, if he would have taken a different color, but he could deal with the humiliation of riding with his brother so that he could have his car just perfect when he got it.

I told him it was time to go. He looked at his watch and noticed that not a whole lot of time had passed since we'd gotten there. I thought for a minute. I told him I wanted to stop at my house and at least change my clothes and wash my face. He seemed kind of excited about this. I guess it was that Indian thing. We had people driving through the reservation all the time, with the little kids staring out the windows in the back seat. Could never figure out what it was they expected to find.

One time when I was a little kid, this car pulled up to me as me and my cousin Cynthia, Innis and Ace's only younger sister, were playing in the cherry tree that sat alone on the edge of our property right near the road. We had planned to run, because both of our mothers, and I later found out, most mothers of the reservation, had told the children to beware of "The Pecker Man." He was called this because he had cut the peckers off several little boys. As things turned out, this guy had lived in Baltimore or some damn place, and had been caught years before we ever heard of him. All the same, it was a pretty effective way of making sure we didn't talk to too many strangers.

But this car that pulled up was a family, so they seemed considerably less suspicious. It didn't seem likely that "The Pecker Man" would have a family in tow on one of his outings. They asked us to come down and we did, but I told Cynthia to stay behind me so she could run for help if there was any trouble. So I got up closer and thought "wow". This family looked just like the people in our Jack and Janet, Tip and Mitten book at school, although I didn't see any dog or cat with them. But the people looked the same.

They asked us if there was any place they could visit on the reservation. So I asked them if they knew anyone. I named off some people I went to school with to see if those names rang a bell for Jack and Janet's father. He meant something else, he said. Like a gathering place. I told him he could go to the picnic grove, but there probably wasn't anyone there. He asked when there might be someone there. I told him during the National Picnic. When he asked when that was, I told him it was when they play fireball. He said thanks and Jack and Janet waved in the back seat as they pulled away. Me and Cynthia went back up into the cherry tree.

I didn't know that he was looking for a tourist place, because we didn't have one on our reservation. So I had never heard of them. We still don't. There's one in the city now, so people go to that. But they don't see any of us. They see jewelry and beadwork and arrowheads and pictures. We're just as happy. We don't really have anything to say to them. And that's about the way I was feeling toward the professor. I didn't really know why he wanted to hang around with us.

So we pulled into my driveway. Well, actually, it was my mom's driveway we pulled into. My trailer is just behind her house, so I just use her driveway. He came in and had a beer while I filled the big tea kettle to heat some water so I could wash up. I went back into my bedroom and got out some clean clothes. The water was heated so I went into the bathroom and plugged up the sink and poured the warm water in. I did a quick wipe with the washcloth over the sweatiest parts of me and put on the clean clothes.

As I came out of the bathroom and threw my dirty clothes in the bedroom, I noticed the professor looking out the kitchen window to behind my aunt's house next door. I looked too. Nothing unusual there. Auntie Olive and a couple of her grown-up kids, the girls, were sitting in the gazebo, and my Uncle Frank was making some weight adjustments with big rocks on the car tires which held up the volleyball net. The little kids must have been playing in it, again.

We left and began pulling out when Ace came running over. I told the professor to stop for a second. I pressed the window button and the window hummed down.

"Hey, check this out," Ace said, wedging a new record in the window. "Mind if I use your stereo? Innis is already using ours, and he ain't gonna be done for a while." It was some Billie Holiday that I myself had contemplated buying. I told him to take one of my blank tapes and record it for me. He took off down the driveway and we pulled out.

"How is he going to get into your trailer?" the professor asked as I hummed the window back up.

"Through the front door, how else?" I answered.

"I can't believe you don't lock your door. You've got a really great stereo. Don't you mind that some other person will be fussing with it?" He was just using it, I told him.

"But it's so expensive," he repeated, like I didn't know this. I said that was why Ace wanted to use it. He shook his head and so did I. To change the subject, I asked him what he had been looking out the window at.

He was quiet for a minute. He asked me what the deal was with the gazebo. I said my Uncle Frank built it; he was a retired carpenter. The

91

professor hadn't wanted to know where it had come from, but why it was there. I didn't know what he meant. I thought it was pretty obvious why people put up gazebos, to sit in them and enjoy themselves. But what about all that shit around, he wanted to know. I didn't remember seeing any shit, so I asked him what shit he was talking about. He mentioned all the heaps of torn down wood, and a couple of old kerosene barrels and the stove and all that junk aound in back of my aunt and uncle's.

I told him that they didn't want to sit on those wood heaps; who would, anyway? That was just the old tool shed we had torn down last year. Uncle Frank even used some of the wood in the gazebo, but not too much. Most of it was too rotten or weak to be trusted. The professor said that was what he meant about it. Why keep this junk around? He was pretty stupid for a professor. So we went to the bar in silence. We could both see that this conversation was going nowhere, but we didn't really know why.

Everyone was there before us. We walked in and I could see the Hack waving way up in the air to get our attention. The Hack is a white guy, with a big bushy white guy beard, but he acts like a regular guy, doesn't treat us like archaeology, and we don't treat him like an exploring alien. His waving worked, and we wormed a path through the packed room to where the rest of our group was waiting. It wasn't that hard, actually. The crowd all kinda wanted to get a look at the guy with the suit jacket on. I guess they all wondered, as we did, what he was doing there. We got to the table and someone poured the professor a half a beer, draining the pitcher. Mike suggested that the professor might want to buy the next round.

When he said sure, they lifted the other two empty pitchers to him that had been sitting on the table. He walked to the bar. The Hack made the observation that the professor sure did an awful lot of smiling for no damn reason. We had to agree there. Everyone knew how shitty it was getting stuck with the "half a glass beer run." The trick was to figure out how to get out of it once you were tagged for the run, but the professor didn't even try. He just smiled some more and took out his wallet. No fun.

We stayed until about ten, or so. It would have probably been longer, but someone complained about Mike pissing in the men's room sink, like anyone actually used it to wash their hands after taking a leak. Anyway, he got thrown out for a week, which was serious for him. He kept claiming that the guy was lying, but who could say? He'd be lost at night for that week. One of us would probably have to keep him company at some different bar. Anyway, once the group breaks up, even a little, that's usually about it for the night. Nathan asked me if I wanted a ride. I told him the professor was gonna give me a ride.

This was news to the professor, but he just smiled some more. So we drove away from The Den and back towards the res and my home. I hummed my window down again; that thing was like magic. He offered the air conditioner. I told him this was better. As we went past the dike, I could smell the summery water inside. A ton of dike-bugs appeared in the headlights and began smashing into the windshield, blurring it up. He tried the squirters, but that only made it worse. I told him we had Windex at home and we could clean it off when we got there.

As we pulled into the driveway, I could see the fire burning as I had hoped it would be. Now he'd understand about the gazebo. He stopped the car and I got out, telling him I'd be right back with the Windex. I went into my mom's house and looked around. There were some lights on, and the tv was on, but that didn't mean anything. She always left things on. I glanced at the tv. Boy, she had a nice clear picture. I called to her but I didn't get any answer. I grabbed the blue spray bottle and some paper towels and headed back out.

I squirted the windshield and the whole front end of the car suddenly smelled like Sanborn Field Day french fries. The professor frowned, so I said that she must have been out of Windex. When she is, sometimes, she just pours vinegar into the bottle. It has the same effect, just smells a little funny is all. The windshield cleaned up just fine, the dike-bugs disappearing into the paper towels.

The professor started to say that he was gonna get going now, but he was interrupted by a big explosion of laughter from the gazebo. I told him to come on. He didn't have anything better to do, and he'd get a chance to meet some more Indians. I knew that would get him, just like those Jack and Janets. He reached into the car for a six pack he had bought on our trip here, but I shook my head and he left it.

Some of my cousins were laying on blankets near the fire. A couple of them had pillows, but most of them didn't. They were talking about different things, mostly the stars, in the sky and on tv. They were all the people I grew up with and we'd had the same conversations many times. They were always good and always a little different. Auntie Olive and Uncle Frank, my mom, and some little kids were either in or hanging around the gazebo.

I could hear Billie Holiday. Someone had brought out a boom box and it was sitting on one of those fifty-five gallon drums. It was decorated with some feathers that were attached with a roach clip. Auntie Olive stopped humming along with Billie long enough to tell me that was my new tape. I agreed that it sounded good and asked where Ace and Innis were.

She said Innis went out, but that Ace took the car to get the kids some marshmallows down at Nyah-Wheh's. That was what we called this little store named Mr. Thank You's, which was just off the reservation. Our name was Tuscarora for the same thing. Ace was going to be right back. Auntie Olive asked the professor if he would like some coffee. He introduced himself. His name was Tim. I guess I didn't know that.

He had been warming his hands at the fire. Reservation nights were cool even in the summertime. He said that he didn't want to put her to any trouble. She said that it was no trouble. She pointed to the drum that the tape player was on. The electric coffee pot was also there. They were both plugged into this extension cord that ran from her house and snaked down the path here to the gazebo. She told him the cups were in the house.

There was another cord running from the extension cord outlets. It ran up to the gazebo. There was a Bearcat Police Scanner sitting on the gazebo's railing. The red light scanning all the channels casually blinked through its pathway, on the lookout for gossip. The professor followed the thick orange extension cord to the house.

My mom asked who that was, and I told her it was some professor from the University. Auntie Olive was taken aback some at this. She thought he was from the reservation, since she really couldn't see him. But she had thought it was weird that he introduced himself. She laughed when she thought about him walking into her house, because she knew it was too late to call him back.

Since I had brought him here, it was my job to get him. I ran over, but he was already inside. He was just standing there, looking at the kitchen.

You couldn't really see the table. It was covered with stuff. There was real limited storage space at my aunt's house, so the table had just been used as more storage space. No one ate in there, anyway, and it was very easy to reach whatever you needed. It was all in plain sight. I scanned the table and reached for the stack of styrofoam cups.

I looked at the professor, but he seemed to be occupied. He could see into the living room. There was a large floor model tv, and on the shelves above this, a lot of records and a stereo system like mine. He peeked around the corner to see the rest of the living room. There were a bunch of magazines stacked up in the corner by the couch. Above the couch, there were more shelves that were filled with plastic model cars, and lacrosse and basketball trophies. He held out his hands, palms open to the two rooms. He seemed like he was going to ask me something, but just then Ace flew into the driveway. We could see him through the bay window my uncle had put in a couple of years before.

Ace came running into the house to get a sharp knife so he could cut some roasting sticks for the kids' marshmallows. He said hi, and told us to come outside. He seemed really excited, so I grabbed a few cups from the package and we all headed out. As we headed down the path, Ace said that there was a car on fire down by the dike. I said that I didn't see it, and I had just been by there. The professor shook his head to confirm what I had just said. I told them to hang on a second and passed the cups to Ace, so he could put them in the bag. He saw what I was doing and gave the bag to the professor to hold. We grabbed some of the bigger pieces of wood from one of the heaps. We were careful to watch for nails, and though there were some, we didn't get poked.

As we got closer to the bonfire, we could tell that the others had heard about that other fire from the scanner. The tape had been shut off and the scanner's volume was turned up. Everyone was huddled near it. We set the wood down near the fire and joined everyone else at the gazebo. We could hear the cops and firemen talking to each other. They all talked about how it figured that a call about a car burning was on the reservation. They always were.

We turned the scanner down and put Billie Holiday back on. Ace and I laid some of the boards we had brought on the fire in an old fashion tepee style. They would burn better that way. Once we were sure the boards wouldn't cave in on themselves, Ace and I went looking for sticks to cut to make the kids' marshmallow poles. Everyone settled back into their old places, listening to my aunt hum away with the tape. But the kids quickly stood at the fire, waiting anxiously for us to bring their sticks back. The oldest of the kids held the bag, so that they wouldn't get dropped and spill all over the ground. The professor joined us as we headed to the bushline.

I asked Ace if he saw anyone at the car. He said he had seen a car pulling away, but it wasn't any car he had ever seen before. That didn't surprise me. The professor asked us why nobody seemed too concerned. Didn't we think we might have known the people involved? I explained to him that someone from the reservation probably wouldn't steal a car and then bring it back to the reservation. And they wouldn't be burning it, either.

It was true that some people from out here did steal cars, but only for the car's main use; they took them for rides. They usually rode around in the city, or went to Buffalo, or sometimes went as far as Rochester. They could be on reservation roads any time they wanted to. If they were going to the trouble of stealing a car, they certainly wouldn't use it to do something as boring as driving past their own homes. Think about it.

As I was telling the professor this, he seemed to be getting more and more frustrated. Ace and I both figured that he was going to go into some big speech, and neither one of us really wanted to hear it. But since I had brought him out here, I figured it was again my job. I handed the sticks I had broken off to Ace and he added them to his own collection and headed back to the fire.

I continued to walk along the bushline. I got up to this stack of old tires we had lined up at one point and told the professor to pull up a tire. He brushed one off and sat down.

"How could this happen?" he began. "Why don't the police know that it isn't reservation people? Why haven't you ever said anything? What could be done? Why was the reservation suspected? Have you ever thought of getting a coalition together? To make a presentation to the local law enforcement agencies? It's the way you live. I'm sorry to say so, but it's true," he surmised. "It's all the junk laying around, making everything look cluttered. That's a sign of no self-respect. You need some priorities. All it would take is a little bit, everyday. And more focus.

"Instead of buying colored televisions and VCRs and stereos, you could put in plumbing. There aren't supposed to be outhouses in twentieth century America. And that bay window, the house could have been sided for the cost of that. And that fuckin' gazebo, why did he build that fucking gazebo when the house needs so much work?"

I asked him if he were through, and then I told him that the house didn't leak anywhere, and that it was warm in the winter. It didn't need a lot more than that. I thought he understood about the gazebo. He had been there. But he hadn't really sat in it, I guess. We walked back and I poured some coffee and handed him one. We both sat in the gazebo with the others. My mom had just begun telling a story about the time she and Auntie Olive had first moved off the reservation and into the city. She said they kept burning or freezing themselves in the shower, because they just couldn't get the hang of those faucets. They both told us more stories. The professor asked her how she finally resolved her shower situation. She told him that she began to take baths.

The tape had shut off and all we could hear were some summer bugs, katydids or Jeh-ees geh-geks, as we called them. There was an occasional squawk on the scanner and we could see faint lights flashing in the sky way beyond the trees, so we knew the police were still at that car.

The professor didn't stay much longer. He didn't seem to like the gazebo too much. As he pulled out, I could hear his tape deck. He had thrown in his Japaneses-Indian flutes and drums music.

I walked over and flipped the tape that was in the boom box. The Jeh-ees geh-geks were joined by Billie Holiday and my aunt humming. Later, we watched the sun rise through the gazebo's lattice work. It was nice.

Chapter Ten

∿
∿

AMONG THE SHADOWS

I

Jan Freen rode in the darkened back of the ambulance with Johnny Flatleaf. No lights flashed and no sirens sang as they left the reservation for the city. Beginning the semester on an ambulance bench was an unwanted addition to the already overloaded clinical schedule. She was only two weeks in and it looked as if taking care of Johnny were going to be as big a priority as keeping up with her day to day school work. She had finally convinced him that an amputation might give him a little longer. He had been concerned about being disabled in the after life, with only one leg, and it had taken quite a bit of convincing on her part for him to finally agree.

He'd lain in his darkened house, refusing to move as the cancer diligently converted him into a dead man. He waited patiently for the Eel to walk in his door, and the only light he kept on was one over the front door, so he could see the Eel in the entrance and know he could safely make the passage. But of course the Eel hadn't shown, and the only person entering his doorway was Jan on her routine trips to check on the old man.

Jan hated her entrance, more every day. She'd see, when she stepped into the light, that expectant look, not totally obscured by shadows, fall to resignation. She'd taken to singing as she walked up the drive these last few days, hoping he would be prepared for her. He had never greeted her in this pained fashion, even on those days in her childhood, and there had probably been many, when he might not have wanted to see her.

He had always smiled then, and welcomed her in and sat her down at the table, ready to pour her a cup of tea. He seemed to know when she would arrive; the water would be at a perfect boil. Now, when she walked in, the first thing she did was put the water on. This gave him a moment to regain the face he liked to wear for others. It was getting increasingly harder each day for her to commute back to the reservation to care for him though, now that the semester had started.

She'd made a number of pleading requests to have her rotation changed, and now was able to tell him she'd be working at the hospital in which he'd be staying. He finally agreed. The ambulance brought him in on Labor Day. The surgeons were all out at the country club, no doubt, but at least this way, she wouldn't have to be making daily trips back out to the reservation. He was calling to the Creator, to hold off on taking him back to the sky, when they arrived at the hospital. By late Tuesday, however, Johnny was in recovery, and Jan had been able to sneak in and check on him. She had just strolled assertively onto his ward and found him. Her temporary student hospital ID probably helped.

Johnny came out of the anesthesia briefly while she stood there and he spoke, with great difficulty, through a brittle throat. "Brian said that an Eel was coming to help me. You the Eel?"

Jan shook her head softly. He probably didn't recognize her, as she had initially surmised. He had known for years that she was a member of the Snipe clan. He had been with her when she'd buried her mother, had stood with her, even when the other Snipes wouldn't. It was not that they had any dislike for her or her immediate family, but they knew they should have, as clan members, taken her in. None among them could really afford to feed another child, though, not even one who could work her board off around the house. Johnny, an Eel, had stood with her and had held her when the others left her mother's death feast with averted eyes. He'd stood with her for years, as she'd gone on to college, a career, and now back to college.

"If that Eel shows back home, they won't find me. Make sure they find me, okay?" he asked, struggling to stay awake long enough to hear her response. She nodded and whispered to him that she would.

Jan left the hospital a while later, and on her way home, she swung by the campus, to see if Floyd were putting in overtime. He wasn't—none of the roofers were. The only people around were other students, already involved in intense research, even though the semester had just begun the week before. She'd be seeing Floyd tomorrow. She drove back to her apartment and tried to do some reading, but the potential of the next day kept forcing the words on the pages of her nursing texts to shift gracefully into meaningless symbols as she read, a secret language.

II

Floyd Page sprawled in his day off. He would have liked to have been with Jan, but he knew she was spending time with someone who wasn't doing too well down on Cattaraugus. It was just as well. He wasn't sure if he were ready to introduce her out here, yet.

Even in their own maturity and identities, the family members still reaffirmed their connections for holidays. Sometimes a holiday was just a day off, and Labor Day certainly qualified as that. In the afternoon shadows, the tables and their empty platters spoke of a satisfying meal. Still, some folks picked at the few remaining fragments of Nora Page's fry bread. She only made it on special occasions, as a compliment to her corn soup, and though the soup had been finished over an hour ago, discerning fingers still snatched at anything large enough to put butter on.

Innis leaned back against the large picnic table, talking with Kay and Peter about past parties. Peter excused himself and went over to talk with someone else; there had been some parties in the past that he'd just as soon forget. Floyd sat at the shaded area of the table, spread across the opposite bench, listening in, but not really contributing too much. He seemed intent on absorbing the words of the others.

Ely walked up to the two and said that he was collecting. They each reached into their jeans pockets and pulled out a few rumpled dollars. Innis glanced over at the coolers, as if he could somehow sense the number of beers still floating within. He called Ely back for a minute. He suggested they get Hank to make the run. Their city cousin agreed amiably enough. After he took the money and asked about any brand preference, he jangled his keys and walked toward his car, only to be called back one more time.

"Hey, Hank! Whyn't you take Floyd along? Help with those cases." Innis expected a dirty look from one or the other, but Floyd just stood up and Hank unlocked the passenger door as well as his own.

They silently listened to the tape playing in Hank's deck—Hank Williams. The recordings were foggy; the tape masters they'd been taken from were limited, filtered through primitive instruments.

After loading the car and cruising back to the party, Floyd finally spoke. "Smell that," he said, closing his eyes and leaning out the car window, slightly.

"Smell what? All I smell is the reservoir water," Hank replied, punching the car lighter in.

"Dike."

"What?" Hank lighted his cigarette and tapped the lighter into the ashtray before replacing it.

"We call it the dike," Floyd explained slowly, in a voice not entirely clean of annoyance.

"Whatever."

"Pull over. Let's go up. You ever been up?"

"No way. What the hell do I want to go up there for? I been up before. There ain't nothing to see but dirty water."

"Well, let me out, then. I haven't been up in a while." Hank pulled over at the path and Floyd got out. As he climbed the steep side wall, he watched his cousin's car, reflected darkly along the inside of his sunglass lenses, as it wavered and twisted on its way back to the remains of their family's plot. He reached the top and stared out across the empty expanse, noticing the distinct lack of swimmers, fishers, drinkers, and sunbathers. They were still gone. He tried to will some of them to appear, thinking of the past and, briefly, he could see people with whom he had spent many hours. They sat casually on the rocks, laughing and smiling. A sound behind him distracted Floyd and the people around him dissipated into the late haze. He turned and looked back to the direction from which the sound had originated, watching Hank as he appeared over the reservation horizon. "Thought you were goin' back to the party," he said, matter-of-factly. He did not seem to care one bit that Hank had come up the reservoir. Secretly and silently, though, he celebrated.

"Changed my mind," Hank wheezed.

"Over there's where our land used to be. Innis showed me before," Floyd said with the authority of a tour guide, pointing out an area of the vaguely shifting water.

"There, too," Hank replied, pointing out another area. "I used to have a tire swing in this big old maple on our property over there. I watched them bulldoze the whole area."

The dike had played an important role in Floyd's life. It had been there since before he had been born and, to him, it was a strong part of reservation life. Occasionally, stray thoughts would occur to him concerning their predicament. That it was Labor Day made him recall another holiday, and the odd fact that they celebrated it: the fourth of July—Independence Day. It wasn't their Independence Day; it was more like Dependence Day.

He also sometimes realized that he and the people he hung around with associated the dike with the reservation. It was almost as if they had forgotten the land it rested on had been forcibly purchased from their families by the state. These thoughts never lasted long, though. Floyd never had an answer for the questions they raised in him, so he let them slide away to wherever it was they resided.

Up to this point, it had never occurred to Floyd that Hank even had a history out here on the dike like them, or anywhere on the reservation, for that matter.

"Dad played his guitar, sittin' in the tire swing sometimes," Hank said, pulling two Molsons from his pocket and handing one to Floyd. They were sweating and slippery. He had grabbed them from the cold case they had slid into the back seat.

"The Bug fit into a tire swing? Man, that must have been a long time ago," Floyd laughed, cracking the beer.

"Yeah," Hank growled after a deep pull from the bottle.

"Yeah," Floyd echoed.

"So, what else was there?" he continued after a moment.

"Lots of stuff." Hank sighed and frowned, trying to remember. It had been a long time since he had thought about the few years he had spent on the reservation.

The two climbed down the inner wall, sliding on the unsteady smaller rocks, and sat down on a couple of large, stable boulders. Hank started talking, telling him pieces of family history that had not even occurred to him. Like Innis, Floyd had a very abstract idea of the family connections under the water.

"Well, Umma, you probably don't really remember her, do you?" Floyd shook his head. Their grandmother had died when he was less than a year old. "Shoot, she used to ride you around in her wheelchair all the time. Almost like you were attached to her.

"Anyway, she used to always come through the woods, when she could still walk, to our place. It wasn't that far, and she always had a saucepan with her. Used to pick all kinds of stuff, different medicines and berries, stuff like that.

"She always wanted me to walk through the woods with her, learn to pick out the medicines. I guess her legs were already beginning to bother her, just like Selina. But I was only a little kid, and I was afraid of the woods. She dragged me out there, one time, told me the little people would protect me, you know, that's what they're supposed to do, protect kids lost in the woods.

"She pointed them out to me when we were out there, but all's I saw was our own shadows on the undergrowth. She kept pointing, but she coulda pointed all day, and it wouldn'ta meant nothing to me. Anyway, I moved into the city with my ma not too long after, when the state started bulldozing all this." The two walked closer to the water's edge.

"Never did see those little people. Probably drowned when they flooded this. But the woods were all gone then, too. Maybe they were just bulldozed out to some other part of the reservation."

"Well, you know, sometimes the little people are supposed to appear only as shadows. Maybe you did see them," Floyd said, watching his own shadow swaying on the waves which splashed near his feet.

"Nah. They were only our shadows, one little, one big."

"Could use some little people about now," Floyd said, removing his wet sneakers and socks. He slapped the socks against a boulder, leaving impermanent Rorschach blots, to be absorbed by the dry porous surface.

"I think I'm just a little too old for the little people. They only help lost kids," Hank said. "Besides, I'm not lost."

"I was talking about me."

"You're grown up, too, man. We're on our own, here." Hank stood and stepped up a few boulders, clearly trying to get his cousin to follow. Of the two, however, Floyd felt even stronger that he needed to take the lead, here, even though he didn't really know where he was headed, either, like swimming in the dike. There were drop offs among the boulders. You could have a sure footing one second, and in the next, slip into water ten feet over your head—always a footstep away from disappearing, viewing the world through the murky green light.

"Jeez," Floyd said, retaining his position. "Even after hearing it, I still have a hard time picturing anything but the water here. We been coming up here, forever. It's one of those landmarks. Everyone brings their kids here to go swimming. Cheaper than going down to those public pools at the State Parks."

Hank looked around. They were the only people there.

"When you get old enough to climb the dike wall, you know you're growing up."

"Shit, man! I must be barely grown up, then. I just made it up that fuckin' wall," Hank said, and they both laughed. Floyd continued.

"And once you make it up that side, you're allowed to go down this side. Come on, let's go swimming." Floyd tossed his wet sneakers and socks onto a higher boulder.

"Neither one of us are wearing shorts," Hank observed.

"You got your reservation swimsuit on. Come on," Floyd said, undressing and tossing the rest of his clothes up to join his sneakers. He dived in, his brown body cutting the water smoothly. When he surfaced, Hank shouted again the thing he had said to himself as Floyd had slid beneath the water's surface.

"I'm not going into that fuckin' water naked! What are you, crazy?"

"Nobody here cares, Hank. This is just the way it is out here."

"Nobody cares? There's nobody else here!"

"So what's your point, man? Come on, the water's great."

"What about the party?" Hank said softly, kicking off one of his sneakers.

"They'll still be there when we get back. Besides, I've got an idea," Floyd said, swimming out farther.

≈

After a while, they climbed out and sat, letting the sun dry them like a couple of lizards. Hank had put his briefs and jeans back on immediately, but Floyd just sat on the rocks.

"Whyn't you put your jeans on, man, or at least your shorts?" Hank said, looking self-consciously up at the perimeter road. "What if somebody comes by?"

"I wouldn't care if they did. Neither would they, but they won't anyway, so don't get so bent," Floyd replied, rubbing his hands along his legs to dry them faster. He supposed it was about time they were getting back. He grabbed his shorts and put them on.

"What makes you so sure?"

"Oh, this is about it for the summer. It's been a bad one. That body they found here in July? Some girl from Town of Niagara. That just about ended swimming up here. Cops started watching the place all the time. No one wanted to bring their families down here, anymore. No more kids riding down here on the roofs of cars. No more parties. Just a few of us. Maybe next summer it'll be back to normal. That'd be nice."

"Know who did it?" Hank asked in a low conspiratorial voice.

"How the fuck should I know?" Floyd grabbed the rest of his clothes and began putting them on.

"I don't know. Just thought you might've heard. The gossip train seems to work pretty well out here."

"Next I suppose you're gonna ask who keeps stealing cars and bringing them out here to burn. If you killed someone, let's just say, you think you'd bring the body to your home to get rid of it?"

"I'm not a killer. How would I know?"

"We better get back," Floyd said, climbing the rocks and boulders. Hank followed him, trying to grab the same secure boulders on his way up, but often missed, sliding a bit back toward the water.

"Maybe you should reconsider moving out here. Who knows what you'll be bringing home?" Floyd huffed, reaching one of the highest boulders and sitting on it. "Here, sit down.

"You know, last summer, there was this car fire down here?"

106

"Last summer! There was one last week!"

"So, last summer, there was this car fire down here," Floyd continued, ignoring his cousin's editorial. "And it just so happened that I was getting a ride home from the Den that night, from one of the professors down at the University . . ."

By the time they headed down to Hank's Firebird, their shadows had grown long and had surrounded them, slowly dissolving into the weeds in the late, cooling sun, which dipped gradually behind the dike's far, off-reservation border. They did not leave until they were both sure they were heading home.

Chapter Eleven

∿
∿

INDEPENDENCE DAY

FLOYD PAGE

SEPTEMBER 7, 1992

Though we really have no reason to celebrate the Fourth of July, we're fairly adaptable and usually use this day to celebrate our survival. I wondered, after the Fourth on the year I was thirteen, if some others looked at it that way, too.

Early on the morning of the Fourth, the phone began ringing. Kay was on the other end. Normally, I'd have yacked with her a bit before handing the phone over to my mom, but Kay didn't sound too happy. Her in-laws were supposed to be leaving for the small patch of tribal land they lived on. She liked them, but she and Peter had a small trailer in a cramped trailer court. There just wasn't room for guests. Her in-laws never noticed, having lived in a two-room house their entire married life.

Kay was twenty-six. She had round Janis Joplin glasses, and her hair was long. When she wasn't working, she wore Levi cut-off shorts and baggy T-shirts, and if she wore anything on her feet, it was those foam rubber flip-flops. She worked as a cashier down at the grocery store in Lewiston. The job, with its drab blue smock requirement which hid her true nature, was turning her old, fast. By the time they'd have enough saved for their goal, getting a bigger trailer, they'd be too old to enjoy it.

My mother took the phone, and, as I crossed through the screen door, she turned her attention to Kay's sad voice coming over the lines. "Well, just bring them along," I heard her say as I headed next door to see if my

109

cousin Stan was around. Stan had been doing carpentry for a few years, and sometimes he came home with some pretty interesting stuff.

$$\sim\!\!\sim$$

He pulled up in the company truck one day in early June. Innis, Ace and I ran up to greet Stan as he climbed from the truck's passenger side door. He reached back in and pulled out this big misshapen cage made of chicken wire and some boards. It was kind of rough looking and you could tell that whoever made it wasn't very handy. He asked Innis to help him and the two of them brought it over to the front porch. I still couldn't tell what was in the cage, but it wasn't moving around too much.

When they set it on the front porch, I could finally see it was a crow. Stan told Innis and me to carefully take it over to The Bug's house and set it on the back porch. Just before he climbed back into the truck's cab, he said the one thing we hoped he wouldn't. He told us not to open the cage.

It seemed like hours before he got back, but it was really only about forty-five minutes. By this time, at least eight of us had gathered around the cage, taking turns squeezing in to get the best view. Throughout this commotion, the crow strutted back and forth inside the rickety cage, scoping us out with its shiny black eyes, occasionally letting out a loud, sort of cheerful squawk. It almost seemed to like being in the cage.

Stan finally pulled up and ran over to the porch, telling us not to crowd the bird. Some of us stepped back, but others just moved in. Stan didn't want it to be too scared in its new home. Auntie Olive could see that he was getting a little worried, so she commented that the bird didn't seem to mind, at all.

Stan started to work on a sturdier cage while we watched the bird's every move. He told us the bird had lived with this old couple whose house he had been working on. It had crashed into their front picture window when it was small. They had taken it into their house and the old man had quickly put together the old cage from gardening supplies he had in the basement. His wife had kept the bird wrapped up in a towel until he was done. She kept petting it, stroking the feathers on its head. They put the cage in the garage and so that's where the bird lived.

They had the bird since January, and by the time Stan saw it, the novelty had worn off for them. They were bored and had been planning on leaving for vacation but they didn't know what to do with the bird. They had tried setting it free, but it liked the cage, liked being fed, and didn't feel like flying away. The couple even tried locking it out of the garage, but it retaliated.

They had taught the bird to be comfortable around people and it had taken to standing on either of their shoulders, or even on their heads, sometimes. When they tried locking it out, the bird sat on top of their house and swooped down to ride around on them any time they tried to leave, or whenever they came home. They gave up and let it go back to its cage in the garage. Having the bird around had quickly become a pain in the ass.

"Here, watch this," Stan said, as we brought the newly completed cage over to the old one. He reached into the cage, and the bird hopped up on his arm as if it had done this thousands of times before. He gently pulled his arm out of the cage and the bird flapped a little. He transported it to the new cage, where it excitedly jumped around, apparently relieved to be caged again.

"That's exactly how it was when I met the crow," Stan continued. "He just hopped on up, as if I'd known him for the longest time. And man, as soon as that old man saw us, he offered up the crow, just like that."

So now we had The Crow, as he'd come to be known. Not very original, but he didn't seem to mind. After I checked with Stan on the morning of the Fourth, I opened the cage door and The Crow hopped out and on to my shoulder. I liked to walk around with it up there, and see my reflection in The Bug's window, but not for too long. I was always afraid that The Crow might shit on me.

Sometimes, though, The Crow didn't want to get off, and I had the hardest time making it go back into the cage. I'd try to reach up and get it, and it would take off, flying a few yards above my head, and re-landing on me when I put my arms down.

On these occasions, I waved it off and went inside The Bug's house to watch The Crow from the screen door. It would sit on the porch for a little while and yell, but when I wouldn't come out the door, it would give up and climb back into its cage. Then I had to sneak around to the side door, running up on the cage from the other side. The Crow was always too startled to think about jumping out, having been watching the screen door the whole time.

We had to go through this routine on the Fourth of July, twice, actually. The Crow seemed to finally figure out that The Bug's house had two doors. When I came running from the side, The Crow was watching for me and flew out to land on my head. It bit my ear, but not too hard, just to let me know that it had won. So I finally got it in the cage and wandered back to my mom's house.

She was off the phone, but still cooking up a storm, when I came in. "Here, stir this." She handed me a spoon and a bowl.

"So, what's up with Kay?" I asked, swirling the egg whites.

"She'll be here, but Peter's folks are coming with them. They never bring anything but their appetites. What's wrong with them?" she sighed her mad sigh. "I guess we taught them that, though." My mother was wrong. They did always bring something. Peter's dad had a pistol that he kept in a holster at his belt. I had never seen the whole thing, just the handle sticking out. It was dark and shiny. I imagined him saving the day under all kinds of circumstances. Since it was the Fourth of July, maybe he'd shoot a couple rounds when we let off some firecrackers.

It wasn't that I had never seen a gun, before. We had lots of rifles around, particularly Stan, but a pistol was something else. It was like what the cowboys and police had on tv. I even told Ace and Innis about it, when I first saw the handle.

Though everyone else arrived around one-thirty, carrying their dishes-to-pass, Kay didn't get there until quarter to two. They had come up in Peter's folks' van. As Peter's dad stepped down from the van, we could see the gun's butt sticking out of the holster on his belt. Kay carried this huge clear serving bowl filled up with salad, and Peter's mom and dad carried nothing.

"Jeez, they must think we're the government or something," Auntie Olive, observing, mumbled to The Bug. "Next thing, they'll complain 'cause we didn't make their favorite foods. Did you bring the commodity cheese?" The Bug laughed quietly.

Later on, after we'd eaten and had blown off some small firecrackers, I asked Peter if he would get his dad to shoot the gun, but he said I'd have to ask, myself. I finally got up enough courage, as I didn't really know him, but he said no, anyway.

A bunch of us kids drifted down to The Bug's house to check out The Crow. It squawked and began pacing around. Though we weren't supposed to, we let it out. It walked around the porch and its cage and hopped up on some shoulders, but it was a little jumpy. There normally weren't this many people around, and it seemed to want to try every single shoulder.

But someone, I don't even know who—no one would admit it later—lit off a few firecrackers all strung together. The Crow flew up and landed on The Bug's house, at the peak. Innis and Ace ran for a ladder, hoping no one would see us from my mom's house.

But before we could get the ladder over to catch it, The Crow spotted the party. A bunch of us were out in front of The Bug's house, watching the peak, and the two brothers were about halfway down the path with their ladder, when The Crow took off.

We all chased it down the path, but it got to the party before us, not having to follow a path. We wanted to tell The Crow which heads not to land on, but we didn't make it.

∿∿

Peter's dad had been drinking a beer in the shade of the big lilac bush, when he'd heard this rustling through the bush's top and had looked up in time to see The Crow land on his forehead. That's what he said later, anyway. We heard the shot fired from down the path, and we froze for a second, but then we took off, running even faster, through the burdocks and the prickers, forgetting about the path.

By the time we got there, the pistol rested back in the holster, but the shot was still echoing off in the distance, from one field to the next, and the next. The Crow was over on the front end of our lawn, perched on top of the power lines and squawking. Nothing we did convinced The Crow that it was safe to come down. It left a while later, flying out over the fields.

This put a damper on the rest of the party; most folks left a little while later. Melisa's mom offered to take Ace and me with them to the fireworks off the reservation, down in Lewiston, and then have us stay overnight. Most Indian communities didn't officially recognize this holiday, but who

113

doesn't like fireworks? When I went and asked my mom if it was all right, she seemed relieved. "I was gonna take you, but I'm too tired. Too much Independence for one day," she said, taking her shoes off and putting her feet up on the couch. "I just wanna watch some tv and then go to bed."

Before we left, we propped The Crow's cage door open, thinking it might miss its cage, and we left some scraps for it, but it didn't come home. After a few days, we finally shut the door. But that night, when we still had hope, we headed out, forgetting him, and finished our Independence Day celebration.

The grown-ups drank through the fireworks, staying in the car while we sat on the roof, and by the time the big finale came, they had decided the party had just begun. They dumped us off at Mel's and told us to go to bed. They'd see us in the morning. We watched the car pull out of the driveway and then we were out on the road, ourselves, down to the elementary school at the corner. We never wanted to be there when we had to, complaining about Tuscarora language classes, culture classes and the like, but now that those things were in our past, behind locked doors, we kept returning—at least to the roof, the closest we could get.

First, though, we headed for Nathan's house, almost across from the school, to see if he and his sisters were home. We could see this bright glow coming from their front lawn when we were about halfway there. Nathan and Violet and Dory, his sisters, were standing around this really bright firework. All three were close in age and looked alike, tall and skinny, very wiry kids who could climb better than any of us.

"Hey, guys, what's up? What the hell is that?" I asked.

"Car wreck flare," Nathan said. "My dad got drunk all day and passed out before he could take us to the fireworks."

"Jeez, you could've come with us," Mel said, staring at the flare. "We had room, didn't we?" she asked Ace and me.

"Anyway, I got this idea on how we could make our own. I lifted my dad's car keys and dug these flares out of the trunk. I knew they were in there, wrapped up under the jack. Cool, huh?" Nathan said, stepping on the butt end to make the flare stand up.

As the flare sputtered, we heard their door slam, and a second later, Nathan's dad was yelling for him. We kicked dirt onto the flare to put it out.

Nathan ran up to see what his dad wanted and we hid in the bushes, listening as he was being yelled at for something. When his dad was drunk, sometimes even Nathan didn't know what he was being yelled at for, going along with it until his dad forgot he was mad, and then things would be fine.

From the bushes, we heard someone coming. Boots clicked in a steady beat from up the road. They sounded like cowboy boots, like Quinn Trost, who wore cowboy boots, no matter what. We flagged to Quinn and he joined us in waiting to see what would happen to Nathan. Nothing did, and we headed to the school in a few minutes. At first we contemplated staying at Nathan's, but he didn't know if his dad might wake up again and give him some more shit. He still had three more flares, but he said we could only shoot off two. He was going to put the third back in the car's trunk before morning. If all the flares were gone, his dad would know we had taken them, and Nathan would have been hided for sure, but if we left one, he might not ever figure it out.

We got to the school and headed straight for the roof tree, which grew branches a couple feet above the big concrete stairway.

"Wait a minute, you guys." Quinn walked over to the flagpole and began unwrapping the drawstrings, or whatever they're called, those ropes that the flag goes up on.

"C'mon, forget the flagpole," Ace said, itching to get at those flares. Most of us didn't feel like flagpole swinging, but Quinn had a way of pulling us in, and we held off on the roof for a while. After his first swing, each of us wanted a turn on the flagpole. The rope ended in a small loop, just enough for an arm or a foot to get in. You had to be pretty coordinated to get your foot up into the loop. Quinn thought he was.

He took a few runs around the pole to get up enough speed and finally started his swing. It was slight at first, but every time he came around to the area of highest ground, he'd spur it to give himself some more speed. When he got his swing going pretty fast, he scrambled up the rope a little bit and eventually got his foot in the loop. He swung like crazy, and we helped him along to keep his speed up, since he couldn't touch the ground, anymore.

Right in the middle of his swing, we heard this car come flying down Snakeline, slam on its brakes, and then a little while later, peel out again, heading in our direction. We ran to the bushes growing against the entryway. Quinn still swung and he whisper-yelled at us to come and stop the swing so he could get off. "You guys! You guys!" we heard over and over when Quinn's arc brought him around closer to the bushes.

We wouldn't come out. It could be pretty serious business if you got caught by the wrong people, and none of us wanted a permanent scar to remember this Fourth of July with. Quinn tried to jump from the loop, but he didn't make it. His cowboy boot heel had gotten tangled up with the rope, so he crashed head first to the ground and got his head dragged in the grass until it finally slowed him down.

All that was for nothing, really. The car didn't even slow down, and we got a pretty good look at it, except for Quinn. It didn't belong to anyone on the reservation, too new. We climbed out of the bushes and helped Quinn down from the loop.

We were on the awning a minute or so, later. Quinn's boots slowed him down again, and he finally took them off and threw them up to us, so he could climb the tree in his bare feet.

On the awning, we were out in the open, even in the spotlight, actually, but just above the awning, there were about four more feet of brick front before the actual roof started. Mounted on the bricks here were big concrete letters that spelled out TUSCARORA INDIAN SCHOOL. Small spotlights built into the awning shone on these letters, twenty-four hours a day.

We didn't like being in the spotlight, but the letters were perfect as steps to the roof, particularly the A. I wanted to get to the roof that night as quick as possible, and only partly because I wanted to light up those flares. Since it was the Fourth of July, there were bound to be more cars flying by the corner. I didn't want to get caught.

So I started right away. We couldn't hear any cars, but not every one of the letters would be useful and we had to share the good ones. The longer we stayed on the awning, the more likely it was that we'd be seen. Dory and I were on top before any of the others. I had used the A, and she used the H.

Mel was a little impatient. Ace and Nathan were climbing the good letters, so she decided to use one of the O's in SCHOOL. None of us had ever done that before. In a couple seconds, we knew we never would again, either.

"You guys, my foot's stuck. I can't get it out," Mel whispered, twisting her leg in all kinds of directions, trying to break free. "This is serious, guys, c'mon. Help me," she said, her whisper getting louder. Nathan cracked one of the flares open and we laughed as she danced on the O—Quinn, most of all.

It took us a while to free her, and we were lucky that no cars had come. We laughed the whole time we were trying to get her out. That, and probably the flare, was what drew the girl to us. Quinn had just gotten Mel's foot through the letter and shoved her over the edge to the roof top. He pulled his boots on and had one foot into the H when the girl called to us.

"Hey! Can you tell me how to get to Lockport?" In the night when we were trying to be so quiet, here was this shout across the school's tiny front lawn. We grabbed Quinn and dragged him across the letters to get him on the roof. Once we had him over, we ducked behind the low wall that surrounded the entire roof. Nathan jammed the flare into the bricks, trying to put it out, but it just lighted him more. He was a brilliant, glowing red. Finally, he just swore and threw it as hard as he could toward the back of the building, where it fell onto one of the other levels.

"Hey! I see you up there. I need some help gettin' to Lockport. Where is it from here?" Quinn peeked over the edge. He figured that he had already been seen, anyway. He ducked back down after just a few seconds.

"It's some black girl," he whispered. "Never seen her before," he added, like he really had to. Not too many people other than Indians ever came out to the res, and they sure wouldn't be walking. The few strangers we did get were mostly white, too, so this girl was really sticking out. We didn't know what to do, caught as we were by this stranger in no position to do us harm, but Mel made the decision for all of us, jumping over the wall and back onto the awning. We followed.

The black girl was kind of tall. She wore this hot-pink outfit made out of towel material, a tank top and a matching pair of shorts. She had flip-flops on and was carrying a pair of white roller skates slung across her shoulder, tied together by their laces. From where we stood, her skates looked kind of muddy, but it hadn't rained in over three weeks.

"Meet us there," Mel whispered, but the girl couldn't hear.

"What!" she yelled back. Mel pointed to the bushes where the school-climbing tree was. We started down the tree and when the girl saw where we were headed, she followed, taking her skates off her shoulder.

117

"How do I get to Lockport from here?" she asked again, waiting at the bottom as we jumped from the tree.

"What are you doing out here? Do you know where you are?" Nathan asked, brushing some tree bark from his hands.

"Not really. Sanborn?" she asked, raising her eyebrows.

"This is the reservation. How did you get here?" Nathan continued, staring at her. She didn't seem to realize what serious trouble she could be in. If you weren't from the reservation, and you were caught on the roads at night, you had to pay a pretty heavy fine. Territory is a serious issue with us.

"I was down at Carousel. They were having a big Independence Skate tonight, but when it was over, I lost my friends and didn't have a ride home. Some old white guy asked me where I was going. I told him Lockport. He looked like he worked at Carousel or something. Had on a tie and a jacket, and some nice shoes, so when he asked me if I need a ride home, I said 'sure.'"

We listened to her story, but also listened for cars. If any came, we would have to duck deeper into the bushes, with her on the inside. That outfit would be spotted for miles.

She said they were driving out here, and she didn't really think anything of it. She didn't know how to drive. Even though she looked older, she was only fourteen, about our age. So she didn't know for sure that this wasn't a way to Lockport. All of a sudden, the guy pulled off into this small path not too far from here. We looked at each other; we knew the path. It led to some of the field car paths that ran throughout the reservation woods. Most Indians learn how to drive on these paths. Though I wouldn't be getting a license for at least three years, I was looking forward to driving in about six months. You didn't need a license to drive on the reservation; you just needed long enough legs.

"So he pulls his nasty thing out and tells me he'll give me a ride home and ten bucks if I suck on it. I said no way and tried to get out, but he grabbed me by my hair and shoved my face down on it, and yelled at me to suck it.

"He grabbed me so hard that he ripped the pick right out of my hair. I had this pick that matched my outfit. Anyway, that's when I hit him in the head with my skates." She held up her skates and we could see it was blood, not mud, on them.

"Oh man, you shoulda' hit him in the nuts," Mel said.

"So I ran out his car and hid in some brush until he pulled out. I didn't know where to go, since it's already after midnight, and I didn't want to wake anybody up. That was when I heard you all laughing." We didn't think we had been that loud. That increased the chances of someone going over there and checking out what was up.

"So how do I get to Lockport from here?" the girl repeated.

"Getting to Lockport is the least of your worries," Violet, who had been quiet up to this point, said softly.

She was right. We had to get this girl off the reservation first. But none of us knew how. We didn't want to walk the several miles it would take to do that. We definitely had to be back to Mel's house before the sun came up. "I got a plan." It was Nathan. He could be counted on to have a plan. Some of us went with him while the others kept the girl hidden in the bushes.

A few minutes later, we were back with his dad's car, silently pushing it up the small hill the school rested on. We got to the top and the girls came out. "What are we gonna do with Dad's car?" Dory asked accusingly, sliding up next to Nathan.

"If you'd get the hell off me, I'd show you," he replied, pushing her away. He dug into the front pocket of his jeans and pulled out the keys, jingling them in front of her. "Dad's passed out, we gotta move before he wakes up. Let's roll." We climbed in. He slid the key in the ignition, and started the car. Before we left, Nathan told Dory to get out. She had to sneak into their upstairs window to make a phone call in about five minutes. She complained but got out and we pulled onto the road.

"Do you really know how to drive?" I asked, when we turned the corner a little sharp, heading onto Snakeline.

"Sure. My dad lets me drive all the time, when he gets too drunk to drive home." Nathan was my age, thirteen. He was just tall enough to reach the pedals, and we were making it, barreling our way to the reservation border. The girl sat quiet, apparently not too sure we were legit. Her hands hung on tight to her roller skates, in case she might need to use them on us.

119

We reached the border a few minutes later. As we got close to it, marked off with the signs announcing the reservation, almost unreadable through the buckshot scars, Nathan cut the headlights and pulled over into the field car path we knew bordered Snakeline. Quinn got out and ran silently—his boots left in the car—to the reservation's edge, where Snakeline met Clarksville Pass. He waved us forward—no cars. We walked the girl to the border and watched as she crossed.

"Here, take this. Celebrate, when you get home," Nathan told her, sliding one of the last two flares into her bloody skate.

We were going to walk her further, but Violet pointed to the bushes at a nearby house, noting that we couldn't hide there. They were clipped too rigid, no natural hiding places. Ace looked behind us, back to the reservation side and found some better bushes there as car headlights appeared on the horizon. Dory had gotten through in her call to 911. A patrol car pulled up as we crawled in deep. Dory was supposed to try to sound grown-up and report she had seen a young woman wandering aimless near Snakeline and Clarksville. There must have been a patrol car near by. The cops never respond that fast to a reservation call.

We watched the girl tell the cop the same story she had told us, only changing the location of the white guy's car. "He was probably an Indian, this close to the reservation. They do things like that. And some of them look as white as . . . well, as white as me," he informed her. Things played out and the cop offered to take her home. Nathan's plan worked. She climbed into the patrol car. As soon as they were out of sight, Quinn ran up to Clarksville again and waved in the same way.

Nathan pulled back onto the road and a few seconds later, we were passing the buckshot sign. Reentering the safety of the reservation, Nathan stepped on the gas and floored it. We guessed it was somewhere around two o'clock. The roof was calling us and we still had one last flare.

Chapter Twelve

ᨑᨑ
ᨑᨑ

PLAYING CHICKEN

FLOYD PAGE

SEPTEMBER 8, 1992

Innis stopped by this morning before work with the paper. I usually read it after work, but he wanted me to see something. He had it folded open to the second page. There, a small story told how Sherman Koslik had died. He had been hit by one of the trains some time during Labor Day. That didn't really surprise me. Every once in a while, when the wind is right, I can hear, right from my bedroom window, the train whistles over in Belden Center, and I always think of Sherman.

Sherman went to school with us, junior high and high school. There were a lot of low-income kids in our school system. The reservation was certainly the lowest, but there were other kids in our system who also shopped down at the Salvation Army stores, or "Dig-digs," as we called it.

These were the kids in the school most of us knew. We never hung around with them, mind you. We used to fight with them. Everyone had territory. In some cases, it was all they had. The kids from over in Belden Center were some of the roughest. They lived on the edge of the city, but before the suburbs. Their houses and apartment buildings were mixed in with junk yards and industrial suppliers.

They always looked tired in school, even in early junior high, when they were probably too young to be smoking up. They were also a little too young to know much about territory, then. Sherman was one of those kids.

He was a big guy, even for being eleven years old. He naturally got the name "Sherman Tank" when he arrived in junior high. He might have even been called that in elementary school, but I didn't know him then. In fact, I didn't know anyone who wasn't Indian, but I was soon to.

When we left the reservation elementary school in June, we figured we'd be together again in classes at the town junior high. We all saw each other through the summer and didn't think things would change. On the reservation bus that first day, we talked about the Border Crossing, the National Picnic and other stuff like that. But when we got off the bus that first school morning in September, I ran to the room that I had been assigned to. My shirt still smelled like starch, or whatever that new shirt smell is. I always wore my new school shirt on the first day, so people could see that I had gotten one.

As I reached my classroom and looked in, all I saw was a group of three white kids, sitting at desks, and taking up one whole corner of the room. I didn't really want to walk in there alone, but I wanted a back corner and one was already gone. So I put my book bag, with four fresh new folders in it, down on the desk in the back right corner.

When the bell rang a few minutes later, I realized that I was the only person from the reservation in the whole room. All the other kids seemed to know someone. They all sat in little groups of three or four, talking about their summers, just like we had on the reservation bus. But none of them talked about the Border Crossing, and I knew they hadn't been at the National Picnic. I would have seen them.

One other person sat alone in the room. In fact, he sat right in front of me. As I stood at my desk, he asked me if I wanted to trade. I said no and sat down quickly. I wondered why he was sitting alone, and then I realized. He was the "fat kid." None of them wanted to talk to him. He didn't even wear a new shirt. He had on some T-shirt with a bar's logo on it. It looked like it was an adult size T-shirt, but he still had it stretched pretty tight against him. It was so distorted, I could barely tell what bar was being advertised across it.

I asked him what he did over the summer. He said that he didn't do anything. I tried again, asking him if he knew anyone in here. He squinted and pointed to a couple of people at the front of the room, and informed me that he knew "that bunch of assholes up there."

122

He swore, right in class on the first day of school. I was going to watch out for this guy. Even with his name for them, though, I couldn't figure out why he didn't want to sit with them. He finally said that they didn't want to sit with him.

The teacher came in. He was this older guy with silver hair and he wore a soft looking maroon colored felt jacket. As he passed by, I noticed he smelled like cinnamon or some other spice. The big kid noticed it too, and looked at me, crinkling up his nose. I crinkled mine in agreement.

As we filled out those stupid three-by-five cards, I peeked over the big kid's shoulder to see what his name was. It was Sherman Koslik. I passed my card up to him when the cinnamon teacher told us the cards all had to go to the front of the room. Sherman didn't even glance at my card. He just put his on top of it, as instructed, and passed them to the kid in front of him.

When we got to the next classroom, I stepped in the door to find that Sherman had beat me to the corner seat in this room. He smiled as I sat down just in front of him.

Throughout the day, we tried to beat each other to the next classroom to score the far corner seat. By the end of the morning, the split was even, and that was okay. At lunch, I was getting ready to join all the reservation kids, but the lunchroom monitors wouldn't let us do that. We even had to eat at the same assigned lunch tables with the kids in our sections. I was in section 6-2 for the long haul.

So Sherman and I sat next to each other, even at lunch. At the end of the day, we headed out to the buses, fast at first, but then slowing down as we reached the outside. It still seemed like we should be in summer laziness, and we also had to look around among the buses to find the correct one.

"Hey!" Sherman said as I headed off toward my bus. I turned and he smiled that same desk beating smile. "What the heck is your name, any-way?" he asked. After I told him, he nodded and said "See you tomorrow," and walked off in another direction.

Innis saw me and stopped by the building's front steps, to wait for me. He had seen me talking to Sherman. "What's that kid's name?" he asked when I got up close. I told him and he continued. "Yeah, I thought so. He looks like one of those Kosliks." He nodded to himself. "You should stay away from that kid. He's only gonna bring you trouble," he answered, when I asked him what he meant.

Sherman and I hung around through junior high, and in that time, I got to find out why all the Belden Center kids always looked tired.

"We all live right near the train tracks," he explained once. "The train whistles scream by our bedrooms every fuckin' night. They ain't supposed to use their whistles that late at night, but some of the older kids are always playing chicken with the trains up and down the tracks, daring the trains to pick them off, and jumping out the way at the last second. Fuckin' crazy bastards."

One day, at the end of junior high, out of nowhere, Sherman said to me: "I tried it, man," and I knew what he was talking about. "And it's a fuckin' rush like you never had before," he whispered in the back of Regents Earth Science. He never asked me to try it with him, and I was just as happy.

That summer, fresh out of junior high, I was old enough to get a job with the summer work program. I worked at our school system's bus garage with a lot of the other Indian kids. But that didn't happen until my second summer of work. The first year, I worked on the school paint crew. The program was for low-income kids to have these summer jobs. It was intense at first, but things eventually worked out.

That first summer, when I got the paint crew job, I was happy to find that Sherman was on the crew, too. He had been a natural for the job. His older brother worked on it, and had put in a good word with his immediate boss, who had at least some say in the matter. With that kind of influence, the crew was mostly Belden Center kids, and an occasional Sanborn kid thrown in for good measure.

It was unusual that I had gotten the job. There were so many low-income kids interested in the jobs that you usually had to go through a year waiting period from when you first got put on the "qualified" list before you got the job. But I got called on the morning the summer jobs were starting. It was the day after the fourth of July.

The reservation kids usually worked at the garage and that was where I was hoping to get. But when I got into the library, where they were assigning positions, there weren't any more Indians there. There weren't too many people there at all. The job assignments had already been given out and everyone was going to their posts.

"You're late," a man in plaid pants who was standing at the front desk said, putting papers into a briefcase. He was the job coordinator. "You're on paint crew," he continued, snapping the case shut. I asked him where they were and he sighed, as if it were a great effort for him to tell me.

"They've already gone down to the Military Road School, but you, young man, are fortunate that the school is on my way and I won't be too terribly inconvenienced in taking you there," he said as we walked out the front door. The coordinator let me off in front of the school and told me to walk around in the building. I'd find either the crew or a janitor who could tell me where they were. As soon as I stepped in, I could hear people laughing and I just followed the laughs. They were in the gym. Some were standing around and others were already working.

The boss stood at the center of the gym. He had taken off his pale blue work shirt and his T-shirt. He had just wanted to get rid of the T-shirt. It was too damned hot in the gym. He put the work shirt back on and undid his dark blue chinos, letting them droop a little below the waistband of his undershorts, so he could tuck his shirt back in.

The pale skin on his belly was almost as white as his briefs, only the blue waistband stripe and a few sprigs of belly hair distinguishing them. But above the pasty white belly, his chest changed colors in the shape of an upsidedown triangle, the tell-tale signs of a v-neck T-shirt tan, a farmer's tan. His coloring there, and on his face and arms, was nearly as dark as my own.

He tucked his shirt in, did up his pants, and buttoned the shirt buttons. The white belly disappeared. I walked across the gym and up to him. An ally whose skin was burnt red was better than none at all. And then I spotted Sherman. He was already on the floor, painting dotted lines of demarcation for basketball. I waved to him as he glanced up, but he quickly ducked his head and went back to his painting.

"You're late," the boss said. "Here, take this," he continued, handing me a brush. "Just join up with someone, and they'll explain what you're supposed to be doing."

So I joined Sherman. He didn't say too much to me all morning. We just painted dotted lines and solid lines, being careful not to go over the borders.

At noon, the boss yelled for us and we all piled into the paint crew van, actually a retired mini-bus, the kind they used for taking the handicapped kids to school. We rode around to the back of the high school and pulled up to a couple of picnic tables that were under this nice shade tree.

The boss opened the boarding door to let us out. I climbed out first and Sherman was right behind me. The other four guys stayed in the van, and as the boss shut the door and pulled away, he told us they'd be back in about an hour. We sat down at the tables and I asked Sherman what his problem was.

"You can't tell anyone on the crew where you're from, man," he said, ripping into his lunch. "And if they figure it out," he muffled, through half a sandwich, "you're gonna be hurtin' for certain." I didn't know what he meant. I thought it was kind of obvious where I was from. "Most definitely not, man, or you wouldn't even be able to eat that lunch of yours. Those guys must think you're Italian or something like that. And if you're smart, you'll keep it that way." He wedged the other half a sandwich in his mouth and continued.

In that hour, I quickly learned that Belden Center and the reservation were not places that mixed too well. In the two weeks we had been out of junior high, Sherman had been taught the ins and outs of what it was going to be like in high school. The most obvious of these things, he told me, was that we were not going to be able to hang around in school together, in the fall.

Once you got into high school, things were a lot different. Territory became a real important issue there. You had a little more freedom in the classes you took and in who you hung around with. You didn't have to eat lunch with a section, because you weren't even assigned a section anymore. You had to seek out your own kind of section. Belden Center and the reservation were clearly two different sections.

"The fights between the two sides been going on for more than fifteen years," Sherman claimed. "Shit, man, even the schools know it. Why do you think, if you're in the summer job program, you usually gotta wait a year to get the school jobs?" I shook my head. "Don't you see, stupid? They try to work out the jobs so that the Indians worked only with other Indians and the Belden Center kids worked together. Simple as that."

I asked him to explain my job, then. Why wasn't I working over at the garage with the other Indians?

"A Belden Center kid had your job up until last night, but at about two this morning, that asshole lost the game of chicken to the train. So they had to replace him. You gonna eat that?" he asked, reaching for a half a sandwich I had left sitting on its wax paper for a few minutes.

"You see," he said confidently, "the way they tried to keep things fair was by, you know, alternating the hiring. Since I was the last one hired, the next opening was supposed to go to an Indian. Turned out to be you. You know, I can't hang out with you on this job. Man, if those other guys found out . . ." he whistled. "I figure my brother would just as soon beat the shit out of me for hanging out with you. I mean, he'd beat your ass, too, but I might be first, and no thank you."

We still had some time on lunch, and I wondered where the boss and the older kids had gone. Sherman said that since they were older, they got to go eat with the boss. If we were around for another year, we'd be able to. I had no plans of being around that job long enough to chow down with the boss, but I did want to survive long enough to make it over to the garage.

The rest of the summer, I spent most of the days dodging questions and remembering the lies I had already made up to answer those I hadn't been able to dodge. And when the screw-up came, it really had been Sherman and not me. I hadn't said a single word.

Late in August, we had to paint the new parking lot lines before school started, and it didn't look like it was going to cool down any. The boss didn't want to make us do it, but the school district superintendent had told him it was one of the priority jobs for that summer. There was no avoiding it.

The boss tried to help us out by bringing a cooler with ice in it, if we wanted to load up on pop at the machine in the building. But hot is hot, and by nine-thirty, we had all taken off our shirts, even though it was against the rules. The boss had left us at around quarter to nine, saying he had to run some errands and that he'd be back by noon.

Since it was August, we had been working together for about a month and a half and were all getting along pretty well, playing jokes on each other and all that. I had pretty much gotten my story down, by that point. I even almost believed I had that other life, where we had a car and a shower and a flush toilet. Sherman and I still ate lunch by ourselves, and we could still talk and be friends for an hour a day.

But that morning in the parking lot, we had drank ourselves out of pop by about ten-thirty. Our shirts were all piled at one end of the parking lot, with an unopened can of paint on top of them, so they wouldn't blow away. Even though the crew believed I was Italian or something, I still felt conspicuous parading around in my dark skin, while their shoulders and bellies were frying in the August sun.

At around eleven-thirty, we stood around the cooler, taking turns reaching into it, to splash cold water on each other's backs. It didn't matter that our pants were getting wet. The waist bands of our jeans were already soaked with sweat, anyway.

Sherman's brother had just finished splashing my back and I stretched, feeling a little bit cooler. I reached into the cold water to do the same for him when Sherman killed the summer.

"So I bet you'll be glad to get home today, huh? Go swimming in the reservoir?" I stared at him. His brother turned around and stared at me. The water I had just splashed connected with his face, spotting his mirrored sunglasses.

Everyone knew that only Indians swam in the reservoir. Sherman's brother and a couple of the others chased me around the parking lot. It didn't take them long to catch me. They were a lot bigger and a lot faster. His brother tackled me and we crashed almost softly into the grass. That was all I was hoping for.

But it didn't matter. The others crowded around and dragged me on to the hot asphalt. It burned against my back. One of the guys sat on my belly, while Sherman's brother covered my mouth and nose. The other two each grabbed one of my arms and began grinding them and my shoulders into the scorching parking lot surface.

The boss pulled up a couple of minutes later and the guys quickly jumped off of me. One of them grabbed my T-shirt from the pile and told me to put it on. The boss asked what was going on and when no one said anything, he told us all it was lunch time.

I wasn't hungry, so when they dropped Sherman and me under the old tree, I just sat on the table's edge. I didn't know what I was going to do for the remaining week we all had to work together and from the panicked look on Sherman's face, I guessed he didn't know what he was going to do, either. But he still finished his lunch and mine.

He said his brother was going to beat the shit out of him. As we had gotten out of the van, his brother had whispered "traitor," in his ear. I asked him if there was anything I could do, out of friendship more than anything else. My ass was going to be in worse shape than his, I guessed, before this was over.

The boss stayed around for the rest of the day, so nothing more happened. We all punched out and left at the usual time. One of the mothers came and picked up all the Belden Center boys. I waited until they left before I started walking home. I had almost gotten to the edge of the reservation when I heard a car slow down behind me. I looked to the woods for my easiest possible escape.

I didn't need it, though. It was the boss. He asked me if I wanted a ride. When I got in the car, he wanted to know what really happened and I told him. He nodded and pulled over to the side of the road and told me how it was.

"You know," he started. "Next summer, you'll surely be moving onto the garage with the rest of the Indians and you won't be on my crew, anymore." I nodded and we sat there a minute before he spoke again. "Those other boys are good workers and I need them. I trained them long and hard, and I don't want to have to start off with a totally inexperienced crew next summer. You know they'll all be fired if you report this." I just sat with my scorching back leaning against the cool air-conditioned vinyl. "Tell you what," he said. "If you don't report this, I'll give you a fine recommendation for rehire and for transfer to the garage. If, on the other hand, you want to file a report, I'll file one, too, against you. You won't ever be able to work for the district under the program again, I assure you." I chose his recommendation; we shook hands on it. "Well, see ya," he finished.

We looked at each other for a minute, and then I got it. He wasn't actually giving me a ride home. I got out and he turned around in a nearby driveway. We left in opposite directions.

For the remaining week of work, he kept me separated from the Belden Center guys, doing some line painting all on my own. I didn't even get picked back up for lunch. I ate by myself wherever he had set me up.

I didn't see Sherman again until we started high school two weeks later. We were all groping our way through a new school, new teachers, and new rules. We didn't all have to stay together in groups, anymore. Many times, we were hardly with the same people from one class to the next.

I passed Sherman in the hallway between classes sometime in the middle of the day. He was wearing a T-shirt with a bar's logo on it, same old Sherman. He also had a pair of mirrored sunglasses on, just like his brother's, but I could see the black eye behind the reflective lens. It went along with his right arm, which rested against his body in a heavy plaster cast.

I asked him what happened, even though I already had guessed. All he said was: "Fuckin' Indian. Get away from me before someone sees me talking to you and the other one gets broke. Too much risk, man." He walked on without altering his pace.

That was the last time we ever talked, but it didn't really surprise me when, almost two years later, Innis was suspended for fighting some Belden Center kid and it turned out to be Sherman. Sherman had developed an instant hatred of us when his brother broke his arm for being friends with me. From what I hear, he sucker punched Innis right in the lunchroom.

Whenever I hear the train whistle, I wonder what the chicken players love more, the friends who help them to believe it's cool to flirt with an oncoming train, or the train, itself.

Chapter Thirteen

~~~
~~~

TERRITORIES

I

Floyd Page hung up the telephone. He had tried calling Jan to let her know that he couldn't make the date they had planned for that night. He had gotten her answering machine and left a lengthy, rambling message about feeling some kind of need to go to Sherman Koslik's wake. It didn't seem to matter to him that Jan would have no idea who Sherman Koslik was. Innis sat on the couch, uncomfortable in his dress shirt.

He had walked in a few minutes earlier and, as usual, Floyd had been sitting at the table with one of his notebooks. After Floyd hung up the phone, he went into the bedroom to grab a tie. He, like Innis, did not have a dress jacket or sport jacket. He picked up his leather jacket but thought it would look unusual and set it back down; it was warm out anyway—the summer had not passed yet. From his closet, he grabbed the one tie he owned. It hung from a nail, still tied from the last time he had worn it, at The Bug's funeral.

"This go?" He pulled the tie over his head and it rested down the front of his dress shirt.

"How the hell should I know? Who's gonna care anyway . . . not Sherman." They both smiled, and Floyd yanked his collar through the tie and cinched the knot.

They were on the road and leaving the reservation a little while later. The funeral home was in the Town of Niagara proper, neutral ground, but as they had grown older, territory had gradually become an abstract and meaningless idea. The two cousins had both, in the last few years, worked on jobs in the heart of Belden Center.

At the corner of Lockport and Military, where Floyd should have gone left, he took a right. Innis sat quietly as they rode under the viaduct and headed into Belden Center. Floyd was watching the roadside intently and, seeming to recognize something, pulled over.

He got out and started walking down the cindered edges of the train tracks they had just driven over. Innis followed him after locking the Nova's doors. They only walked a short distance when they spotted a group of men standing around a point where several track lines converged into the main line which headed to the station a few miles down the way.

"Maybe this ain't such a good idea, Floyd. It's been years, but hey, some people can remember for a long time," Innis whispered as they got closer. He squinted, apparently scanning the others' faces as they got closer, to see if he recognized any old brawlers.

"Hey, what are you doin' out here?" one guy asked, when Floyd and Innis reached the group. "D'you know Sherman?"

"A long time ago," Innis replied. The man asking the question was George Spinner, one of the other carpenters in Innis's union.

"Well, here then. You gotta have a drink in old Tank's honor," George said, passing an open bottle of Jack Daniel's to Innis. "But I guess that's what you're here for, anyway, ain't it," George continued as Innis took a pull.

"Actually, we didn't . . . " Innis started.

"Yep, that's why," Floyd said, pulling a bottle of Mohawk Brand Ginger Flavored Brandy from his pants pocket. He cracked the seal, took a drink, and passed it to George. "It's pretty dood," he said.

George looked at the bottle, took a swig and grimaced at the sweet liquor. He quickly passed it back to Floyd, hoping to save the rest of the group from Floyd's bottle. Innis signaled to Floyd, who passed it.

II

Sherman had told Floyd of this place, this crossroads. He used to go there to get away. There were usually a few people partying there, and Floyd, even now, could see the remains of a recent bonfire; apparently the crossroads was still an active party place. While the others drank, Sherman had said, he dreamt of catching one of those trains, riding it away from there, but the one thing that always prevented him from doing this was the belief that he'd just be riding into someone else's territory, anyway. This was the first time Floyd had actually been to the place, but he'd seen the suggestion of it, glimpsed fleetingly through the trees many times as he drove along the thruway on his way to other places.

"It's getting to be about time," one of them said, and the bottles disappeared into a bag. None of them had dress jackets, either. They all turned and meandered down the tracks. When they reached the road, Floyd and Innis walked to their car and the others headed for cars in nearby driveways. They all drove to the funeral parlor in one, unbroken line.

As they got out of their cars, George Spinner called out to Innis. The cousins walked over to where George and some of the others were leaning up against a car, smoking a joint. "So, listen. We're going out after this shit is over. You know, send Tank off the right way. Thought you might like to join us."

"Sure," the cousins said simultaneously. The group nodded an affirmation and walked into the building. They sat through the standard polite wake lies: that Sherman had been an exemplary Sunday School student; had tried to be a role model; had worked with Senior Citizens. Floyd wondered to himself if any of those things were true. He supposed any of them were possible, but that most were unlikely.

After the service, the minister made an announcement that refreshments would be available in the church hall, about a block away, but none of that group planned on going anywhere near the church. As they walked out, Floyd noticed a familiar orange Datsun parked right next to his Nova.

"Hey, In," he said, grabbing his cousin by the shoulder. "Why'nt you catch a ride with your buddy, there? I just remembered something else I was supposed to take care of tonight. Maybe I'll catch up with you later, but if I don't—don't worry, okay?" he continued, watching alternately the people who were coming out of the building, and the orange Datsun.

"You sure?"

"Absolutely."

Innis yelled to George Spinner, and Floyd watched them leave. There were very few people coming from the building and he went in to look.

When he came back out, he spotted her, leaning against a light post across the street, waiting for him to notice her. He waved and they began walking toward one another.

"I wanted to have a cigarette and let the smoke float up toward the lights just like in those old movies, but then I remembered that I don't smoke," Jan said, waving her hand nonchalantly.

"Funny. How'd you find me here, anyway?"

"I can read the papers as well as you. I looked up where the service was being held. You're not getting out of a date that easy. Who's Sherman Kolsik, anyway?"

"Koslik, " Floyd corrected. "He was just someone I knew a long time ago. When territory was important. Hard to believe it ever was that big a deal. I don't even know why I came here."

"Territory's always important, and that's why you're going to show me yours, tonight. Come on, we'll take my car, and you can tell me all about Sherman Koslik on the way to your res."

III

"Well, this is it," Floyd grunted as he heaved himself over the letters and landed on the roof. Mounted on the front of a half-wall which bordered the roof over the main entrance was a series of concrete relief letters which proclaimed TUSCARORA INDIAN SCHOOL. Jan slipped her foot into the bridge in the letter A and lifted herself up, as he had instructed. They had been on top of the dike earlier in the evening, sharing the rest of the bottle of Mohawk, and waiting for it to get late enough. At first, he was just going to show her the dike, but as they got to talking about it, Floyd had remembered the incident with the Rawleigh Man, and the effigy site, and Jan said she wanted to see it.

Floyd told her they'd have to wait. Now it was past midnight, and he was sure there'd be nobody around, or at least it wouldn't be likely that anybody would see them. That was a funny thing about the site, he had told her, nobody wanted to go near it—like it was bad luck or something. They had climbed down the dike wall in the late dark, and headed down Dog Street toward Snakeline, toward the center of the reservation. They passed by his family's land, and he pointed to his outside light, informing her that was where his trailer was. As they had reached the corner, Floyd told her to pull in behind the school; the site could wait. He had instructed her to park her car behind an entrance to the kindergarten. No one could see it from the road that way. They walked until they reached a side entrance, and Floyd began climbing a tree growing next to the steps. She followed.

"I guess I was a born roofer. Been spending a lot of years on top of them. I haven't been up here in a long time, seems too much like work now, but when I was a kid, we used to sneak up here all the God damn time in the middle of the night. The same way we came up. One time, one of us got caught in the letter O. It was Melisa, my cousin Stan's wife."

"Stan the one who was with you tonight?" Jan looked out over the expanse of the roof.

"No, that was Innis. He wasn't with us that night."

"What night?" Jan asked. They heard a car coming down Snakeline and Floyd grabbed her, and pulled her down behind the half-wall they'd been leaning on. She frowned at him.

"We're not supposed to be up here," Floyd reminded her. "The night Mel got her foot caught in the O, that same night, we met this black girl. We were only about fourteen. In fact, we even stole, borrowed, my friend Nathan's dad's car to help her out."

"Out of the letter?" Jan was lost.

"No, no. The black girl. That's what I mean about the site. The clearing. It seems like only bad things happen there. When we were helping Mel out, the girl, I think her name was Yolanda, heard us laughing and came to ask us for help."

"What was she doing out here? Strangers on our reservation are a pretty rare thing."

"Here, too. She was only about our age, I guess, but she'd been skating at this rink in the city and she said some white guy in a suit and tie offered her a ride home. I guess she had somehow gotten left behind. But anyway, he brought her out here, you know, and pulled into that same clearing. He, um, he was looking for . . . he wanted her to suck him off. She didn't know where the hell she was, but she got away from him and, oh jeez, she whacked him in the head with her roller skates. They had blood all over them."

135

"She should have whacked him in the nuts."

"Hah! That's just what Mel said. I gotta get up." They had still been crouched behind the wall, but now stood up and walked around the roof. Floyd jumped up to another level and pulled Jan up. He pointed to an area down Snakeline Road. "That's where they were at. You see that big tree there, that's the tree. You ready?" Jan nodded and as they climbed back down the tree they had come up, Floyd told her of how they secretly borrowed a car, lifting the car keys from the pocket of his friend's drunk father, and getting the girl at least off the reservation. That was their responsibility, they felt, to see her through their territory. She could find her own way to Lockport.

IV

"Cut the lights and slow down. Here it is. Pull in." Jan's Datsun softly rolled over the sparse grass. After the burning of the effigies, the grass had just never grown back. They got out of the car. The clearing was not that far from the school, and they could still see the parking lot lights from where they stood.

"Seems like I keep saying this, but . . . this is it. Not much to look at, huh?" The clearing was under several older maples, one of which was the enormous tree Floyd had pointed out from the rooftop. The trunks still held scars from the flames of over twenty years before. The bark was twisted and charred and the new growth had gone on in spite of the damage.

"I think these trees feel it. They've just been kind of left here, you know. Something good should come from the place. This is like that McDonald's in California where that guy shot all those folks. I mean, McDonald's tore the place down and put up a plaque—what the fuck is that?" Floyd said, trying to pick some of the blackened outer layers off the trees.

"Something good could come from this place," Jan said, reaching up and taking his hand away from the tree. She held it in hers, brushing away the old soot crumbs. He touched her cheek, leaving a small streak on her face, moving his finger to absently create the symbols he and his cousins had made up for the milkweed wars, years before. He licked his thumb and tried softly rubbing the brand away.

"We could make our own good thing come from out of here," he said, caressing her neck, leaving a faint trail of smudges along her nape. He slid his hand around and gently cupped one of her breasts. She softly moved into his hand.

They had done this just once before, and only recently, and it had been more of a physical thing, rolling around in the cinders on top of the Nursing building. It had been crass and they hadn't even undressed. When it had been over, they'd awkwardly stood, picking small cinder fragments from their skin before readjusting their clothing.

This time, he unbuttoned her shirt—she wore the Navajo print again—and slipped it off her, setting it on the hood of her car. She undid his blue tie. They smiled when, even after it was off, the tie held the creases it had kept for so long. He unsnapped her bra and lay it next to her shirt. As he unbuckled his belt, she tried pulling off one of his boots, but they both lost their balance and fell on the ground. They lay comfortably in one another's arms, each getting to know the other's body on the soft dusty earth.

They stood momentarily after a while and fully undressed. Floyd admired her in the moonlight. She was not traditionally beautiful, but her presence, her mixture of moonlight and shadow, he believed, forced any bad image he'd had of this place into that area in his mind where he forgot things. As they joined, he feeling the softness of her body really for the first time, a Jeh-ees` geh-geks began calling. It was answered by a cricket. Amid the accompaniment of the insects, the two made love.

Afterward, they lay together listening to the night songs, she lightly pressed against him. He slid his hand gently, tracing the swoop of her collar bone, the orb of her breast, her gradually sloping belly, her down-feathery pubic hair, over her raised thigh to the smaller orb of her knee, eventually gliding his hand down her shin and feet, stopping at the thickly callused soles of her feet. His fingernails across them sounded like the Jehees` geh-geks. They looked at each other and as he kissed her, she mumbled, "Too many years of moccasins." She pulled her foot away and turned toward him. As they continued to kiss, Floyd slid slowly into her and they began once more.

As they dressed, later, Floyd asked her what she meant about too many years of moccasins.

"Moccasins are only a layer of skin between your skin and the earth. Here, don't put that boot back on, yet," she said, walking over to him. She took his hand and ran it along the sole of his own foot. The sole was mostly soft, with only a few calluses, where the heel supports pressed against them. "Too many years of boots. You don't know the earth, anymore."

A train whistle sounded far off. The moment passed and Floyd slipped his boot back on. "You know, if Sherman lived out here, he probably would never have discovered the trains."

"Well, how well do you think he would have fit in out here?"

"Pretty well, I'd have to say. Really. There wasn't much difference between us, I don't think. Except our territories. And you know, we don't have any trains out here. Maybe that's why we're still here." He slipped on his other boot and stood.

"What's the matter?" Jan could see that Floyd was listening for something. "What'd you hear?"

"Nothing, yet. But folks you know always die in threes. My uncle was first, and now Sherman. I was just listening for the Ski-daw-dee."

"What's that?"

"A skeleton. It lets us know when and where someone is going to die. I wonder who it's going to be," he answered, opening the car door. "We better get back to my car, before that funeral parlor owner decides to have it towed."

"We have one of those callers, too. We call him 'Boney-Ass,' same thing, it sounds like. You're going to hear him from that direction," Jan said, pointing to the south. "I know who it's going to be, but you should know him better before he passes. We'll go sometime, soon."

They passed out of the reservation and into neutral territory.

Chapter Fourteen

≈

THE RAWLEIGH MAN

FLOYD PAGE

SEPTEMBER 9, 1992

The Rawleigh Man used to come on Saturdays. They must have been Saturdays. Everybody was around and it was the middle of the day. He must have come by all year round, but I only remember him in the summers. We'd all be playing in the mountain when we'd hear his weird horn.

His car horn wasn't like the usual kind. It didn't just honk. Instead, it played this little song. Years later, I heard these sorts of horns all over the place, mostly on customized vans and trucks with the monster tires. But back then, The Rawleigh Man was the only one who had a horn like that.

As soon as we heard it, we just left our plastic Indian tribe in the mountain and ran to the big open space between my mom's house and my aunt's. That was where he used to pull into.

Until Jan and I were talking about the dike, I hadn't thought about The Rawleigh Man in years. After last night, I figured I'd be able to forget about the last time I saw The Rawleigh Man, but there it was, still in my head when I woke up this morning. So, before I went to work this morning, I stopped into my mom's house for a second. She was sitting on the couch, sipping from a cup of coffee and doing some sewing.

"Hey, what did The Rawleigh Man sell, anyway?" I asked. I couldn't really remember what his main goal in visiting us was.

"Oh jeez, lemme think," she said, setting her material down after poking the needle through it. "It seems like it was mostly cleaning stuff. Sponges,

139

cleaners, brushes, and funny things, too. Medicines, healing balms, salves. Spices. I remember this one time I was right in the middle of cooking some spaghetti, and I needed some oregano. Just then The Rawleigh Man came pulling up like clockwork, and I sent Kay out to buy some from him.

"But I didn't have enough money for it, and when Kay came back and told me that, I was just gonna skip it. But then The Rawleigh Man showed up at the door and said I could have it as long as he got to eat some of that spaghetti. I think that was the first time a white person was ever even in here. He even poured himself a drink from the water pail. He didn't seem to mind that we didn't have running water. What made you think of him?" she asked, smiling.

"Just thinking," I said and walked out the door. I was kind of baffled by that answer. I didn't remember any of that. I must not have cared too much about that kind of stuff. What I remember most about The Rawleigh Man was the little red radio-controlled car and the cat masks. He kept these, with all of his other stuff, in the trunk of his car.

As he pulled up into the clearing, all of us kids crowded around his trunk. Even now, the smell of exhaust fumes weirdly excites me. The Rawleigh Man got slowly out of his car. He was a pretty old man to have this as his job. His skin was really pale, and his silvery hair was almost all gone on top. The few strands there floated around in the breeze whenever he moved his head.

He wore a suit. I'm not sure, but it seemed like it was always the same suit. Either that or he had a whole closet full of dark gray suits with pale yellow shirts. The suit was kind of crumpled looking. He brushed at it with his thin, blue veined hands as he got out of his car and walked slowly toward us. It never did any good, but he brushed away as if his hands were irons, magically straightening the material.

The Rawleigh Man was something else. It wasn't that we never saw white people. We saw them at the store and places like that, and they sort of looked like The Rawleigh Man, but we never talked to them. And the white people we did know didn't look anything like The Rawleigh Man at all.

They all lived in trailers. Most of them wore dirty white T-shirts that were stretched across huge beer bellies and work pants that didn't fit too well. They were always hiking their pants up, even if they were wearing belts. Their faces were gray with stubble because they didn't shave too often. They also usually had these really nasty dogs tied up right near their trailers.

They had been living on the reservation since the days when the state built the dike. They had come in to work on its construction and after it was done, some of them must have liked living with us, because they stayed. But not everybody was too happy with this. The state had taken a big part of our living area, and now because of them, we had to share what we had left with those who had helped take the rest away. When we asked the state to get rid of their old workers, they told us they didn't have any jurisdiction out here.

We tried to discourage the old workers from living with us, asking them if they wouldn't like running water better. But a lot of them, when you asked them this, would simply crack another beer and say that pissing on the ground was just as easy as pissing in a bowl. So some people tried heckling them, I guess. They did things like driving cars in circles on the lawns where these men had settled, making big doughnuts in the grass.

With one particularly sickening guy, they shot out the transformer that kept his electricity connected. That seemed to work, and the guy left within the week. But this was not all that practical. When they shot out the transformers, about eight other houses lost their power, too. But people had gotten the right idea. We had to scare them off. Giving them hints wasn't working.

Someone got the idea to burn some dummies dressed up like the trailer guys. A lot of people went down to the "Dig-digs" to see if they could find some clothes that looked like the trailer guys' clothes. They found some old work pants and T-shirts, and Mel's mother, Vonnie, even donated one of her only good white sheets, for the dummies' faces and hands, so no one would miss the point. They stuffed the bellies extra full and painted big red mouths on the faces.

They selected a clearing down on Snakeline for the burnings. That way they wouldn't have to worry about catching someone's field on fire. My mom wasn't planning on going. She was worried that the trailer guys might do something back and she didn't want us kids there. Then Kay offered to watch me if my mom really wanted to go down. She said okay, maybe for just a little while.

"It might be too dangerous the first time, and besides, there's going to be plenty more," she replied to my whines about wanting to go, as she fixed her hair in the mirror. "You'll have your chance after I check it out. And besides, you're only six, and I could decide that you can't go to any burnings until you're grown up and then you can make the decision all on your own."

With the threat, I went outside and sat on the porch. As she came out the door, she reminded me: "It's Saturday."

"So," I replied, frowning at the ground.

"So, it's Rawleigh Man Day," she smiled, trying to force me to return it. I finally did. "I'll be home later," she called back into Kay as she drove out and headed toward Snakeline. Innis saw me and walked on over, to see if I wanted to go and play in the mountain. I shook my head, not interested. He said that he had some new ideas and this would be a good one, but I didn't take him up on it. He went to the mountain and brought the plastic tribe to our porch. We started playing and eventually we did move over to the mountain.

The hours disappeared as we gave our plastic Indians a whole new war to fight. Innis was right. We hadn't thought up this one before. He had boosted some Barbie doll Country Camper from the dumpster at school. It had been in the girls' toy box, but the girls in his class had totalled it and the teacher threw it away, deciding that it would be no good to anybody.

Innis hid from the bus when we were leaving to go home. He squatted in the group of kids after their teacher had counted heads and had then rolled into the shrubbery. He had to wait a half an hour as his teacher got the room ready for Monday. But she finally left and he ran over to the dumpster and crawled in. He found the Country Camper and walked home.

Innis brought the Country Camper home for his sister, Cynthia, but she didn't have a Barbie to go with it. The Camper became a fort for some of the Indians, and others attacked to try and get control of it. After one was counted dead, we set it aside, but only for a little while. Then it came back as someone else. There weren't too many Indians so we had to bring the dead ones back to have enough people to fight.

When The Rawleigh Man finally did show up, I almost didn't want to leave the battle, but Innis reminded me about the cat masks and the radio-controlled car. Maybe he'd drive the car.

He pulled up to his spot, and I ran into the house to tell Kay that The Rawleigh Man was finally here. Peter was in there with her. They weren't married, yet. They had just started seeing each other, so they were making out whenever they had the chance. I still have no idea how they met, since Peter was from another reservation a long ways away.

Wherever he did live, he came out to our res pretty often these days. They seemed like they were going to get married, already. I could especially tell when Kay said she didn't want to go see The Rawleigh Man because she and Peter were busy. Her loss.

I ran back out and the trunk was already open. My Auntie Olive was even there before me. Cynthia stayed in the house; she didn't like the cat masks. At first I thought that I must have taken longer than I thought, but then I noticed that she had her poncho folded over her arm. She picked out a few things, paid with a couple of crumpled up dollar bills that matched The Rawleigh Man's suit, and sent Ace back to the house, carrying these things.

Innis and I were trying on our cat masks. They came in different colors, but most of them were either blue or red. They looked just like a cat's face, right up to the muzzle. There was no chin on the mask. But it had whiskers, on the top and bottom, and big cat ears, and eye holes shaped like cat eyes.

The masks were made of plastic and were shaped to fit kids' faces perfectly. They fit Innis and me, but not Ace. He had a really round face, and the masks just sort of sat on his eyebrows for a few minutes before the cheap elastic that held the mask on broke. Ours always broke in a few days, too. The Rawleigh Man kept a stack of them in his trunk. He knew that when he showed up the next week, these would be broken and lost, too.

So for Ace, he always kept something else. Once it was a balsa glider, and another time it was a parachute man. Ace always tried the mask on, anyway, in hopes that this week, it wouldn't break. This week, of course, the mask broke as usual. But before Ace could even receive what The Rawleigh Man had especially for him, Auntie Olive had sent him into the house with her supplies.

Innis and I were looking at the radio-controlled car in the trunk with our cat eyes when Auntie Olive spoke to The Rawleigh Man. "It probably isn't such a good thing for you to be on the reservation today. Maybe you shouldn't make your usual stops today, and just keep going. Next week, things'll be better, okay?"

She sounded pretty serious. "Looks like we ain't gonna see that radio car this week," Innis whispered to me, and Auntie Olive whipped one of her "bad kid" frowns at him. Occasionally, The Rawleigh Man hooked the car up and drove it around in the clearing, hoping one day someone would buy it for us kids. No one ever did, but we still liked to see him drive it every once in a while. He hadn't done it at all that summer, so it seemed like the time was right, until Auntie Olive spoke.

She quickly walked away and The Rawleigh Man seemed to have gotten her message. He closed the trunk up and got in his car. He pulled out even before Ace could come back out of the house.

We went back to war in the mountain, but that didn't last long. Kay leaned out the front screen door and yelled for me to come and get some shoes on. We were going somewhere. Peter was driving. Innis came running, too, but Kay said he couldn't come this time. We were going down to the dummy burning, and she didn't want to be responsible for him.

Just before we left, I promised Innis that I would remember everything and tell him all the details. He said he'd try to make a little cloth dummy, so we could act it out with our Indians once I got the scoop. I hopped in the car and as we drove away, I watched Innis and Ace out the window. They were looking grim.

Peter was usually a really nice guy. As we pulled out of the driveway, he said he was taking us to get ice cream before we went to the burning. We drove by the site and a lot of people were milling about. Some were in the trees, stringing up the dummies, and others were on the ground, admiring the stuffed figures, and the handiwork skill in some of the stitching.

We didn't see any white people on the road, but we got kind of a strange look as we cruised by. As we were almost past, a solid, hard noise came from the back end, then another, and another. We were being bombed with dwarf green apples. I knew what they sounded like hitting cars. I had hit some before.

144

Peter slammed on the brakes and, throwing it into reverse, plowed his car into the clearing. A big group immediately surrounded us. Some people held onto boards with nails in them and others had baseball bats. Peter jumped out of the car, swearing at whoever was closest, asking them if they were nuts.

They all looked at each other and then shifted, moving a little closer. Kay figured out what was going on and opened her door. Peter stuck his head in the window and told her to stay inside. She didn't listen. In fact, she grabbed me and dragged me out her door. She began shouting even before we were halfway out.

By the time we got out, a few inches were all that remained between Peter and some of the other men. Finally, it happened. "Hey! It's all right! It's just Kay Page," someone shouted. They backed right off and Kay started yelling at some of them. They hadn't recognized Peter's car as belonging to any Indian they knew, so they bombed it.

Before Kay could get too far into her rant, we heard the sound of more apple bombs going off. The kids in the bushes had been instructed to bomb any car they didn't recognize, especially any new looking car. The only people who had new cars on the reservation were the chiefs and they were already at the protest.

The car being bombed went off the road and almost landed in the ditch. It came to a stop and the bombing started again. Some of the men headed toward the road to see what the driver was going to do. I could see through the bushes that the car was maroon, the same color as The Rawleigh Man's car.

I moved to another opening and could see the car's window. It was The Rawleigh Man. I could see his old blue eyes, bugging out behind his old glasses, his forehead looking furrowed like a plowed field. They had to stop. Why were they going after The Rawleigh Man? He never refused to leave, or anything.

I started shouting for them to stop. I figured that it worked for Kay, and I felt like I had to do something for him. But before I had gotten more than a couple of words out, my mom had magically appeared next to me and covered my mouth with her hand. She squatted down and whispered in my ear. "We can't help him right now. He has to get out of this himself."

145

The Rawleigh Man eventually recovered enough to get his car moving again, but by then, it was dented all over the place. It was getting a little darker, and I couldn't see his blue eyes, anymore. I had closed mine, anyway, and twitched every time another apple smashed into his car.

As the shadows grew thick, and more people arrived, the men went to the trunks of their cars. I heard the latch and almost felt that Rawleigh Man excitement, but I knew they didn't have any cat masks or radio-controlled cars. They pulled out some five-gallon gasoline cans and set them down near the ghostly dummies.

A few guys scrambled back up the trees and when they were steady, someone handed them the cans. They poured the gasoline on the dummies and after they climbed down, everyone gathered around for the lighting. The dummies danced in the igniting flames, and then twirled like ballerinas as they burned.

Most everyone seemed to be having a good time, but no one mentioned the trailer guys. They only talked about what good times they used to have, before the state changed everything. I thought about the good times I wouldn't be having anymore. Though it's usually the state's fault, this time it really wasn't. With a few more burnings, we finally got rid of the trailer guys, but I didn't even care anymore.

When we got home, Innis asked me to tell him everything, but I wouldn't say anything. Someone else must have told him, though. He didn't seem too surprised when The Rawleigh Man didn't come by the next week, or the next, or the next. But I never spoke of it. I didn't want anybody to look back on that day with fondness.

Chapter Fifteen

∿∿ REBOUNDS

I

Jan Freen sat in the uncomfortable visitor chair, waiting for Johnny to wake. She had always felt that the chairs were purposefully designed to be uncomfortable, so family members would be easier to get rid of when visiting hours were over. A good number of people in her profession found that family just got in the way, and would just as soon they not visit at all.

This had always been her big difficulty with the world of science. She had gotten through nursing school with almost a perfect 4.0 average, all "A's," but the nursing world was a harsh one, and she was encouraged to not get involved with her patients. She had worked at one of the largest hospitals in Buffalo for several years, and, though the pay was good, the forced isolation from people had driven her to want a change.

Within reservation society, the family was seen as one of the most important aspects of the healing process. They worked as much as any western medicine could at bringing someone back. She, herself, was at a distinct disadvantage in this respect. When she was seventeen, Jan lost her mother to a car accident and she hadn't seen her father since she'd been three. She wanted to work in a setting where families were respected for their inherent value.

With her Bachelor's degree, she could not really go back and work at the reservation clinic. They already had a glut of nurses from the reservation working there, and a waiting list for others who wanted to get in.

What the reservation needed was a doctor. The doctors they got were serving out student loan obligations and couldn't wait to get out of that atmosphere and into private practice in offices with reception areas that had prints of sailboats on the walls instead of posters that listed the signs of Fetal Alcohol Syndrome. Jan certainly couldn't afford medical school, and had felt stuck.

But one day a co-worker of hers, another part-time reservation clinic nurse, had passed on a notice for a University scholarship program in the Family Nurse Practitioner Program, specifically for Indians. She had made the call that day and was registered for classes within a month. The Master's program would give her that opportunity she had been looking for. Though she wouldn't be the physician the reservation needed, she would be considerably closer to being one than her Registered Nurse degree allowed for. FNPs, as they were called, had many rights physicians had, including that of writing prescriptions and making diagnoses.

However, she was still almost six months from that point, and her attachment to Johnny might force her to lose it all. They were very much alike; both were alone in this world. Jan had lost her parents and Johnny had been an only child who never married. He had outlived the rest of his family and now stood to leave this world alone.

Jan had convinced him to enter the hospital to give a little more time for the Eel to arrive, the thing he felt was most important. She did not know where this person was going to come from, but she wanted to give him whatever she could. It hadn't occurred to her that, if his condition worsened, the administration would not let him go home without some family to watch over him. Johnny had made it clear that he wanted to die at home. She looked at his chart a little earlier, and he seemed to be improving. Maybe the amputation had slowed down the cancer's progression and they'd let him go on an outpatient chemotherapy schedule. She hoped.

She knew that, whatever it took, she would see that Johnny made it home.

II

None of Innis's brothers, or even his sisters, for that matter, believed in the reservation medicine man. They all went to regular doctors, and, truth be told, Innis did, too, whenever he needed one. But none of them had come up with a situation like Floyd's, either. And none of them had seen the milkweed that had been picked over a month ago and still looked fresh, as it spun in Floyd's ghost machine.

Innis had tried to keep a look out for Floyd, ever since that day on top of the dike. He still didn't know how Floyd had gotten his Nova up there, but he assumed it was the way they had eventually gotten it down. They drove to the top of The Dike Road, where it still existed.

When they had reached the bottom, where the road ended in mounds of ruined earth, they'd driven straight off The Dike Road's edge, careening down the steep incline of the dike's outer wall. Crashing into the ditch, they'd crushed the radiator and lost a tire, but they had made it down. That had been almost three months ago.

He had gone over to Floyd's trailer on Monday, after work. Floyd was sitting at the dining room table. Innis wasn't surprised. Aside from Fridays, lately, this was where Floyd could be found when he wasn't at work.

"So what's up, man? Anything interesting happen at work today?" Innis had taken to casually interviewing Floyd about his days, to judge how much Floyd was remembering. Initially, when asked, Floyd sometimes described the same events several days in a row.

After Floyd had visited Brian Waterson, though, and had gotten the milkweed, things changed. He gave a lot of details about things that had happened during the day, but by the time Innis was ready to leave, their topics had always switched to events that had happened years ago. That didn't concern him, though. Floyd seemed to recognize that he was talking about the past.

However, Monday was different. It seemed the same at first. Floyd sat at the dining room table, writing in a spiral notebook. A stack of them were leaned up against the wall on the other end of the table. Their bindings were bent, where they had been folded back, and in some of them, extra sheets of paper stuck out of the tops where they had been added.

Innis was curious about the contents of the notebooks, but he never asked. Floyd never offered, either. They went about the routine they had established a few weeks before. However, this time, when Innis had asked if anything had happened at work, he got a different response.

"I asked this girl to come over here. Really, I first met her a while ago. You know, down at the University, when she was in summer school." As he spoke, Floyd put his pen down and folded the cover shut on the spiral notebook. Innis silently noted the continuity in Floyd's story. This one actually had a history of over a month.

"She's Indian, from down on Cattaraugus. She goes to school at the University. Her name is Jan. Janice, actually, but she lets me call her Jan," Floyd continued, liking the sound of her name. "We're going out Saturday night, and then she's coming over. Maybe you'll meet her Sunday morning.

"She's a little pale, for a Dee(t)-quah." He rattled off a few more mundane facts or speculations, which Innis observed were very detailed, to the point of being uninteresting.

"Lots of times, she wears these brown shoes, but today she was wearing a pair of sneakers."

"So, what is this thing, man?" Innis was excited that Floyd had retained all of these details, but he really did not want to hear about this Jan's shoes. He switched to his weekly Monday night test. He had pointed to the ghost machine, as it spun casually in the breeze. So far, he had heard the story three times. Each time, though, it was consistent.

"I told you, last week. It's the ghost machine. The Hack gave it to me. Don't you remember? Jeez, maybe you're coming down with what I got. Go see Brian Waterson. I bet he's got something to fix you up." Floyd got up and spun the ghost machine slightly.

"Oh yeah, I remember. Well, I guess I'll head on home. See you tomorrow." Innis walked out the door. It was a clumsy exit, but he wanted to think, alone. He tried to remember some of the facts about Jan. He wanted to be able to test Floyd out later in the week. For all he knew, Jan might be some girl Floyd remembered whom he had really met years ago.

As Innis walked in the door that night, though, he felt pretty confident. Whatever Brian Waterson had done, it seemed to be working for Floyd, belief in the medicine or not.

"You know, I wish I could meet this Jan, just to see, you know, if she's really who Floyd thinks she is," he said to Ace on Thursday night. They had all done some work down at Hank's house and then had moved on to the picnic table in their back yard, knocking back a few sixes. Floyd, Stan and Ely had left a few minutes earlier and the two brothers sat alone.

"Ain't you ever gonna let up, man? It's some girl. What's to think?" Ace was worried about Floyd, too, but being preoccupied with a hopeless situation was not his idea of living. He hadn't changed his brother's mind any.

"Look, if you're really so interested, whyn't you just ask the guys he works with? I'm sure Nathan or the Hack has seen this chick. Particularly the Hack, that guy knows everybody's fuckin' business, he does," Ace said, standing up and stretching.

III

Hank stood in his new living room. It wasn't really finished yet, but he did have some of the other rooms blocked out. He could see the strong suggestion of his new house. He was mapping out the wiring system so he could begin installing outlet boxes soon. None of the others were around. It was a Thursday evening; Floyd would be around the next night, but he didn't know about the others.

He stepped into the kitchen and sat down at the old table, the faded oilcloth sticking to his elbows as he stared out the front window. He looked out on trees he had not grown with, trees he did not know. He had never lived in this house. It was still being built when his mother had taken him to live in the city. After the reservoir had come, the three of them were to have moved in with everyone else at the family homestead, in the house Nora Page now lived in. The house could not accommodate that many people very well, and the clutter that would be inherent in such cramped quarters had been too much for his mother. They left one day while Sy had been at work.

He laughed to himself. Even in death, his father could never be "The Bug" to him. He knew that was what everybody called him, but to Hank, it seemed so demeaning.

He heard some laughing and walked back into his new living room to look out the side window. He could see his aunts and uncle and some little kids he assumed were his cousins. They were all at the gazebo. Auntie Olive was sitting on one of its benches and Uncle Frank was running the old orange extension cord out to it. Auntie Nora had brought a big pitcher of iced tea and, after having set some cups on an old oil drum, poured for the kids. He could hear mumbles from the group and every so often, a cloud of laughter erupted from them.

He walked away from the laughter and stepped into the spare bedroom. He touched one of the drawings lightly. It left a dark smudge on his finger; the drawing wasn't sprayed. The walls in this room were intact, as he had agreed to leave them. He examined some of the drawings closely. Of particular interest to him was a drawing of a Longhouse. It, like all the other drawings, was a representation of a traditional form. The sides and roof panels of the oblong building were thatched, while the integrity of the building's rectangular shape was maintained by boughs that had been bound together at cross joints.

In addition to that drawing, there were illustrations of eagles, sun symbols that Hank thought seemed like Western symbols, an eagle dancer who was spreading his constructed eagle wings out in mid-dance, a peace pipe, even one of the Maid of the Mist, that ran from the top of the bathroom door frame to the bottom, ending in a big mist cloud at the floor. He noticed the incongruous, poorly drawn Captain America figure on the far wall and wondered about its origin.

As he studied these drawings, the cans of beige interior latex lingered in his mind. They sat just inside the room's door frame, still in the bag from Hector's Hardware. He pulled one of the cans from the bag and read the label; it claimed one coat cover, but he didn't think these drawings would disappear quite that easily. He shook the can, listening to the heavy liquid slosh around. As he did this, he went back to the Longhouse drawing.

Hank wondered if Stan had ever even been to a Longhouse. He had been to one with his mother, on the reservation where her family lived. She did not practice the religion, but a relative of hers who had practiced it had died, and the funeral was a traditional ceremony. Aside from the fact that it was a long rectangular building, the Longhouse did not at all resemble Stan's drawing. It looked more like a community center, maybe erected in the middle of the century.

The floor had been constructed of planks and at some point in the past, it had been sealed, and the light source was the sort old gymnasiums used—hanging reflective bowls with oversize bulbs in them, the bulbs protected by heavy gauge wire cages. The hard wooden benches were constructed of plywood, as were the window shutters. A Franklin wood stove sat at one end of the room and a brick fireplace covered almost the entire opposite wall.

From this room, Hank could hear the laughter at the gazebo through the open window. He stepped over some boxes of junk he still had to go through, trying to get to the window. As he shut it, he could hear music coming from the group across the way. It was Hank Williams. Traditional music, he thought. Crossing through the boxes again, he stopped and pulled a thick book with rigid pages out that had been jutting skyward from one of them. He flipped it open randomly. It was a photo album.

Among photos of all of his cousins at different parties and different ages were studio school pictures of him. His mother, and eventually Hank himself, had sent one out here every year. On the back of each was his grade and age and "To Dad, From Hank." He spotted one picture of himself as a boy in the tire swing at their old place. He sat back down at the kitchen table and flipped more carefully through the album. He found one other picture from his childhood. He was standing on the homestead's back porch and held a baby; he looked to be about four or five years old.

He carefully peeled back the cellophane from the page and lifted the old black and white from the adhesive covered page. Some of it stuck, but he could still read the faded pale blue inscription on the back of the photo: "Hank—6 Stan—2 months." He stuck the picture back in its position among the others and, closing the book, put it back in the box.

He looked a little longer at the pictures on the wall, but the sun was setting and the walls were fading into dark obscurity. On his way out of the room, he lifted the Hector's Hardware bag and carried it into the main bedroom.

A few minutes later, he meandered out onto his back porch and looked out over the fields and the bushline. The fields had corn planted in them, and he knew, from stories Sy had told, that the cousins had an annual corn roast just behind his house. Harvest time would be coming soon.

The gazebo crowd shouted to him and motioned for him to join them. He strolled over to watch the last of the sunlight fade behind the trees with his family.

IV

Innis showed up at The Den on Friday. He knew Floyd had promised to work some on Hank's roof so they could continue on the interior all day Saturday. He'd be able to quiz one of the other roofers. He started talking with the Hack and they eventually gravitated to the pool table. The Hack broke and ended up with stripes. Innis showed no preference. The game would be his regardless of what he got.

"So Floyd's been okay?" he asked again, banking a shot across the table. He stood up and chalked his cue, giving the Hack a chance to reply.

"Yeah, he's been chasing that girl around, lately, though. Foreman's gonna be pissed off if he catches him, both at Floyd and at the rest of us up there," the Hack replied, chalking his own cue with what he thought was style.

"Combination, four off the two; why would the foreman be pissed at you?" Innis asked, smoothly executing the awkward shot he had just called. The balls rolled, almost as if magnetized. He was relieved he didn't have to find some way of bringing up the Jan business, himself. If she weren't real, he didn't want Floyd's co-workers knowing about her.

"We're still supposed to be watching him, or I am, anyway. But he just doesn't need it. When this thing first started, shit, we never knew what he was gonna do, but now . . ." the Hack waved his fingers, ending with the palm open—nothing.

"Two, side pocket. So is this girl nice?" Innis let the ball falter. He wanted to continue.

"Yeah, not bad. But she's, what did he call it, 'Deetgaw,' twelve ball." Innis laughed to himself. The shot the Hack picked was the easiest one on the whole table. When the ball went in, the Hack looked as if he'd just had an orgasm.

"Dee(t)-quah," Innis corrected. "Yeah, that's what Floyd said. Young?"

"Average, maybe late twenties. Not like Glynny, anyway," the Hack said, pointing with his chin at an older woman sitting at the bar. She thought he was greeting her and waved.

"I'm leaving in a little while Hackie, if you need a ride," she yelled across the room.

"Thanks, anyway. I'm playing a game here," he yelled back. He had gotten used to being called the Hack, but clearly did not like the name "Hackie."

"Anyway, she's not bad. I've talked to her a couple times. Lunch break, you know. We get to eat anywhere we want, so she's been joining us lately, well really joining Floyd. Gonna be a nurse, I think. Maybe that's why she took such an interest in him," he laughed.

"Just shoot." Innis could recognize a stall tactic when he saw one. The Hack didn't have a good shot, so he tried to screw up any possible shot Innis might have.

"Has Floyd said or done anything weird this week? Anything at all?" Innis asked as he cleaned up the table with efficient, calculated shots. The Hack thought about it as he watched the game disappear before his eyes.

"He did say one thing," the Hack announced, just as Innis was shooting for the eight ball. Innis missed the shot, only kissing the eight and moving it out of the Hack's way.

"I hope that was just the shitty move of a desperate loser."

"No, really. He did say something," the Hack replied, trying to shoot, now that only his balls were on the table. "He said he was thinking about starting to go to the Longhouse," the Hack finished, losing his turn again, missing another easy shot.

"But I didn't think there was one on your reser . . ."

"There isn't." What the Hack didn't know, not having come from the reservation, was the Longhouse religion had not been practiced on the Tuscarora Reservation in a long time, not even in their lifetimes. Christianity had obliterated the Indian religion on Tuscarora around the beginning of the twentieth century. The Hack shrugged his shoulders, putting his cue away. He knew already he had lost the game.

"But other than that," he said, pulling out his wallet, "he's just like he's ever been. If that's any help."

155

Innis sunk the eight and began walking back to the table as the Hack strolled over to the bar. Innis stopped in his tracks and followed the Hack.

"One more thing I wanted to ask you. What's this 'ghost machine' you gave Floyd?"

"What's what? Oh, wait a minute, ghost machine. That was some ugly piece of junk my uncle brought back from, um, I think China; I'm not really sure. When he was in the war. I had forgotten about that. It spooked my old lady, and it was gathering dust, anyway. So I gave it to him. I didn't have the heart to throw it out. Family and all that shit. Why?"

Innis shook his head, seeming to dismiss the conversation, and silently thought about the Longhouse.

V

Floyd showed up right after work. He didn't even change, since he was just going up on another roof. He reached out to knock on the door, but before he could, Hank pulled it open. Floyd walked in and sat at the table Hank had been at the evening before.

"Beer?"

"Yeah, sounds good." As Hank handed him the beer, he asked about the drawings on the wall.

"Oh, Stan's drawings. I don't know. A long time. I can't even remember a time when those walls were bare," Floyd said, looking over his shoulder into the room.

"Did Stan do all of those drawings?"

"Yup."

"All of them?"

"Yeah, why? Oh, that damn Captain America, huh?" Floyd looked slightly embarrassed, as he always did whenever that picture came into his consciousness. "No, I did that one."

"Pretty amazing stuff, capturing pictures from Indians all over the country and such," Hank said, getting up.

"What are you talking about?" Floyd asked joining him in the room. He looked at the walls, trying to see what Hank saw.

"Well, like here. This stuff is from out West, ain't it? Looks Navajo or something to me."

"Oh no. Everything up here has something to do with Tuscarora, Seneca, Onondaga, Mohawk, Oneida or Cayuga—Iroquois Confederacy only. Those things there are some Mohawk pictographs. Like the kind Ray Fadden did over in Akwesasne. Navajo images are Navajo territory, and Iroquois images are Iroquois territory."

"I guess they just look alike."

"Not if you really look."

"Yeah, I guess you're right," Hank said, walking out of the room.

Floyd stayed in the room a moment longer, debating whether his cousin were earnest or not and, deciding he had been, rejoined him at The Bug's old oilcloth covered table to finish his beer before heading to the roof.

"Hey," he said, draining the bottle. "How about a little one on one? I'll even spot you ten points—city boy handicap," he laughed, standing and putting the empty back in the case.

"Shit, city boys play a hell of a lot harder than you guys. I ought to be giving you the spot," Hank replied, finishing his own beer.

They played on into the dusk, first for the best two of three, and then the best three of five, and on. Eventually, they called the game on account of darkness during a wild tie-breaker, both missing dreadfully in the new evening's relentlessness. The ball abandoned on the shadowy court, they headed back to Hank's and finished the case by kerosene lantern light as the autumn night settled on Hank's forgotten roof above them.

Chapter Sixteen

THE GRADUATION CANOE

FLOYD PAGE

SEPTEMBER 18, 1992

I tried to explain territory to my cousin Hank today, but I'm not sure he got it. It can come in all sorts of different forms. It can cause fights or cause enlightenment. It can even cause summer school. It did for Innis. He and Sherman Koslik got into a fight over territory, and actually, we ended up in one with Mr. Underwood, the art teacher, too.

Sherman and Innis fought in the high school and it had been a pretty spectacular one, too. Innis was eating his lunch and Sherman came up to the Indian table, and asked if anyone had an extra cigarette. The people at the table all just looked at each other. They couldn't believe that this Belden Center guy was asking for a cigarette at the Indian table. Innis said, to no one in particular, but obviously directed at Sherman, that if someone wanted to smoke, they should buy their own.

Sherman walked over to the middle of the table, where Innis was sitting, and asked him to repeat that. Innis gave the standard line: "Blowing make you deaf?" and took another mouthful of mashed potatoes and turkey gravy.

He took the mouthful, but he never swallowed it. Right in mid-chew, his jaw was plowed into by Sherman's huge fist. Potatoes, gravy and spit flew from Innis's mouth and splattered several people sitting across from him. He bounced off the person sitting next to him and, on the rebound, grabbed his tray and flung it up in Sherman's face. The rest of Innis's pota-toes scattered across Sherman's constant mirrored shades.

159

As Sherman stumbled, trying to wipe it off, Innis jumped out of his seat, shaking the table and rattling trays. He slipped in some of the fatty gravy now smeared all over the floor. Losing his balance, he plowed into Sherman, and they both went down. They rolled a little while, and finally Innis had the upper hand. He sat on Sherman's belly and slammed his gravy covered head into the tiled floor.

A bunch of Belden Center guys had run up by this time, but reservation folks surrounded the fighters, not allowing any interference. Mr. Kessil, one of the teachers who had lunchroom duty, broke in and the reservation group parted to let him pass. He grabbed Innis around the throat and tried using some kind of choke hold on him.

It was enough for Sherman to wiggle loose. He punched Innis in the gut, and grabbed another tray from the table. Mr. Kessil still held on to Innis's throat, but their positions had shifted. Innis moved a little and he could feel his elbow had come to rest against some softness, instead of Mr. Kessil's hard thigh muscles under polyester.

He assumed it was the guy's balls, so he shifted a little more and brought his elbow back, full force. Mr. Kessil realized what was going to happen, just a little too late to do anything to prevent it. Innis connected with his balls and the guy released his hold, crumpling down heavily with a grunt on top of my cousin.

But Innis crawled out easily. Mr. Kessil was preoccupied by that time. Innis stood up, trying to catch his breath. He saw that Sherman had gathered up a couple of trays and was getting ready to charge. Innis took the initiative.

He ran and leapt up onto the table, diving off of it and pouncing on Sherman. His momentum took them right through one of the plate glass windows that made up the cafeteria courtyard wall. I guess it was just like one of those big action adventure movies, from what people said, afterward.

But even that didn't stop them. They were still rolling around in the broken glass, cutting themselves up all over the place, when big enough teachers finally got there to break them up. Both had to be taken to the hospital, but Sherman, by far, got the worst of it. They both had to get stitched up in several places, but Sherman's nose was broken and he had to stay overnight for observation. The emergency room doctor suspected that

Sherman might have had a concussion. He was able to go home the next day. Both got to do that, actually. They were suspended for two weeks.

When they were allowed back into school, they were asked what started the fight. Innis claimed he had no idea, but Sherman said Innis started it. Innis had been heckling him. Innis didn't say anything. Sherman had come into Indian territory, and Innis knew that territory violations were not officially recognized.

They were allowed back into school after a few more minutes in the principal's office. Innis headed off to class, ready to try playing catch-up in the last few weeks of school. He had to get ready for finals like everyone else, but he also had to try making up two weeks' worth of work.

Most of the teachers were pretty agreeable. They gave him the missed assignments and a due date to have them finished. He was no genius, but he could hold his own. Besides, it was the last few weeks of his senior year in high school. A lot of the teachers weren't giving very heavy work loads. They didn't expect these kids so close to graduation to actually do the work.

But when Innis got to his art class, he got a surprise. "You can't possibly make up all the work you've missed," Mr. Kessil informed him. He knew this was bullshit. They never did a damn thing in art class. He pleaded with the guy, but he refused to listen. Innis said he needed this course to graduate. "You should have thought of that before you put that poor Koslik boy through the window," Mr. Kessil said, closing his gradebook and raising his eyebrows.

Innis told me this over a couple beers and a game of pool at The Bug's house one night after school had ended. That's why he was going to summer school. For some reason, that asshole wanted to punish him more for the fight. Innis speculated the guy's balls were maybe still a little tender. I told him to hang on a minute.

I ran home and dug out the teachers' directory I had stolen from work the summer before. I used it for revenge fantasies, but I never actually did anything with it. I brought the book back and showed Innis the proof of what I had guessed. On page thirty-four, I pointed at an address about halfway down the page. Mr. Kessil lived right in the middle of Belden Center.

We shook our heads and had another beer. "I'm still gonna get that diploma. That fucker might have screwed me out of my graduation ceremony, but I'll get the diploma before the summer's out. The only thing is, I gotta replace his art class with another art class, and you know what that means," he said, still shaking his head.

The only other art teacher was Mr. Underwood. He was a pretty calm teacher and kids took his classes because generally he was "an easy A." That was great for most. There are teachers like this all over, I hear. And that's what some people like. Innis would have liked that about then. But it wasn't to happen.

While our discovery of Mr. Kessil's dislike for Indians was recent, everyone knew of Mr. Underwood's total love for us. Not a perverty kind of love, mind you. He totally believed in us. And he believed that all Indians were incredible artists.

While he let most of the kids in his classes slide, Mr. Underwood used to keep on the Indian kids all the time. Sometimes, he even tried to recruit us to sign up for his classes. He promised to stay after school with us if we wanted some extra studio time. He promised to occasionally even let us have brief cigarette breaks in his tiny private office during class time. He even promised us some hallway passes, so we could hang out at the Indian Rail during class time, if we were mostly diligent in our art work.

What he didn't seem to know was that no other teachers cared if we had hall passes or not when we stood at the Indian Rail. There were a few groups who were untouchable in this manner. The football players got to hang around in front of the Vice Principal's office, though I don't know why they would want to, and we had the Indian Rail.

Down by the back end of the library, a fairly long rail gleamed under the hallway fluorescents. You could get about fifteen people leaning or perching on it at one time. I don't know when it got named this, but as far back as any of my friends can remember, this area has been known as the Indian Rail.

The Indian Rail was where we all went in the morning, after we got off the bus and before we had to go to homeroom to sign the attendance roster. The whole school knew that this rail was our territory. You see, the white kids had their own territories in the places where they lived. We'd had some problems in their territories, but we never had much of a chance to retaliate.

We had to go off the reservation to go to the store, or anything like that. Ace got jumped one night down at the Shop and Dine where he was buying a pack of cigarettes. Two guys hid in his car while he was in the store and they jumped him after he slid the key in, but before he could turn the ignition. He slammed his head into the one's face, breaking the guy's nose, and he bit the other one.

People from outside rarely came out to the reservation in those days, though. There was a lot of fear then. They all thought we were the worst. By taking the Indian Rail, we established a bit of territory the others had to actively avoid. They didn't have to avoid that corner, entirely. We let people pass and pretty much minded our own business. But no one else leaned up on the rail except us.

Even after the bell rang, some people stayed at the rail, skipping classes entirely. Whenever a teacher or hall monitor walked by, they sped up, pretending to be on such an urgent mission that they didn't have time to ask us for passes.

We all thought it was because they were afraid of us, but I found out a few years later that it really wasn't so. I had wandered into a beer joint, and I saw one of my old high school teachers sitting by himself at the bar. He taught Contemporary Social Problems, or something like that. I figured he'd probably be good for a beer or two, so I sat down next to him. He didn't recognize me at first. He pretended to, but I could tell he didn't really. But as we got talking, he eventually did.

As the beers went by, I asked him if the teachers were as afraid of the new Indian kids as they had been of us. He looked at me and took a drink. "That's not the reason the teachers didn't bother you guys," he laughed. "That rail had been discussed in the faculty lounge years before your group and you had ever even gotten to school. We had come to the conclusion that all of you would probably only be disruptive if you were attending classes regularly, anyway, so the other students were better off if you were out at the rail." He burped and sat there, smiling.

I thought about this for a minute, and I asked what Mr. Underwood thought of that, if he agreed with that. I was sure he didn't. "Oh, no one ever informed Mr. Underwood," Mr. Contemporary Social Problems said. "We sort of figured that he wouldn't go for the idea, too much. That's the way artists are, anyway. You know, the sensitive type. Gotta tap a kidney, empty out some of that beer. Be back in a minute," he said, standing up, and patting his belly. I left before he returned.

He was right about Mr. Underwood. The guy was a sensitive type. He really got hurt when he discovered what Innis and I were doing in art class that summer, but it was also something he needed. The Graduation Canoe helped both of them get to the other side. I took the class too, but I wasn't going to, at first.

When Innis and I concluded that he'd have to take Mr. Underwood's class, we knew he'd really have to do some art work, not like in Mr. Kessil's class. I decided I'd help him out a little, if I could.

So after the pool shoot, Innis and I went into The Bug's spare room and checked out the drawings his brother Stan had made on the walls, and tried to figure out if Innis could maybe trace some of them and pass them off as his own art projects. Since I could draw all right, I told him I could help him with the shading, if he liked.

"You know, it would be even better if you took the class with me. That way, you could help me out right in the studio classes." But I couldn't. I had to work during the time when the class was supposed to be.

I didn't mind the idea of being in the class. Maybe I could even get some free drawing paper out of the deal. But when it came down to drawing paper or paper money, I had to take the dollar bills. My drawings weren't going to keep me in cigarettes and Levi's.

But Innis was desperate. He didn't go through all those years of school to be shot down by some teacher from Belden Center, so he looked into things I hadn't even bothered to think of. He had gone and told Mr. Underwood that there was someone else from the reservation who wanted to take his summer school art class, but had to work for the school system. As soon as Mr. Underwood heard the magic word, "reservation," things got moving.

To make a long story short, he and Innis scammed some way so that for my last hour of work each day, the time his class met, I could go to the class and still get paid. Something about helping the underprivileged get more out of school, I guess.

It was in the low-income student summer work contract, but no one ever told us we could go to school and get paid. I took it. I'd go to almost any class if they were willing to pay me.

On the first day of summer school, Innis rode up to the garage a few minutes before class was about to begin. He chained his bicycle up to one of the garage's fenceposts and we walked over to the school together. The two buildings were right next to each other, so it didn't take us very long.

We walked in the front door and headed down by the Indian Rail, like we always did. It was empty. We were the only Indians in summer school. There weren't too many other kids around, so we only lingered there a couple of minutes, just long enough for the bell to ring, so we could be late for class.

We walked in right in the middle of roll call. The usual assortment of characters were there. Other people who had failed something during the year sprawled across the back of the room, while some enthusiastic geeks who just couldn't get enough of school tried to make themselves less noticeable in one of the front corners. I imagine they were hoping that they wouldn't get picked on so much if people didn't know they were there.

Mr. Underwood didn't say anything as we made our way to the back of the room, staring a couple of small toughs out of chairs we wanted. Some of the others in the back row were Belden Center guys and they stayed on their side of the row.

Mr. Underwood started us in right away on a bunch of different projects. He seemed to want to separate us pretty quickly, and sent the Belden Center crowd to another part of the room to work on drawings of a cow's skull.

I was handed a piece of soapstone and this power tool that had all kinds of drill and grinder bits. "You are going to be making a peace pipe," he said, showing me how to change the heads on the tool. I explained to Mr. Underwood that I didn't know the first thing about stone carving.

"What good would a class be if you didn't learn anything?" he asked, not really expecting an answer. Good thing, because I didn't have one. I thought about that for a couple of seconds and then started plowing into the stone. I hoped some kind of idea would come before I did some unfixable damage to it.

He brought this big white block over to Innis and set it on the lab table in front of him. He took off for a second and came back with a bunch of metal files and groovers. We both looked at the block, but could come to no conclusions as to what it was for. Innis scraped his thumbnail across its surface, and flakes built up under the thumb's ridge. We surmised it was plaster.

Mr. Underwood had taken off again. When he came back, he was carrying one of those big art books, the kind you see in the display windows down at Waldenbooks. It was called *American Indian Art*. He had strips of paper at certain pages, bookmarks. We were supposed to copy the works that were on the marked pages.

I looked at mine. It was a wolf's head peace pipe. I tried to explain to Mr. Underwood that my clan was Eel, not Wolf. "Well, Mr. Page, I don't think there is an illustration of an eel's head peace pipe in the book," he returned, not missing a beat. I really didn't think so, either, so I didn't argue. The wolf's head didn't look too hard. I'd be able to copy the carving over the course of the summer.

Innis's project was more interesting. Mr. Underwood was showing him something on the other page. "This is a woodcut from the Ojibway people," I overheard him telling Innis. I didn't think it would matter much to Mr. Underwood that we were not Ojibway, so I kept quiet.

The "woodcut" was a picture that was carved into a flat wood surface, so that it had some kind of three-dee effect to it. In it, all kinds of Indians paddled along in this big old canoe, with lots of game piled up in the middle. With the dead deer and beaver and pheasant, and all the people, there must have been seven figures in the picture, not even counting the canoe.

"Your project," he informed Innis, "is to reproduce the carving from which this woodcut was derived."

"But Mr. Underwood," Innis blurted as the teacher walked away. "I can't even draw, let alone carve. This is way too fuckin' hard!"

"But of course you can. You were all given that gift. And don't swear. It's bad for the purity of your spirit."

I knew Innis couldn't draw. He didn't even want to be able to. He was much happier playing basketball on the court we pounded the dirt into behind our houses. But you can't get grades for the art in a hook-swish shot from the back of the court.

We had to do something. Mr. Underwood had gone into his office for a cigarette. I grabbed a pencil quick and drew out a shape that sort of looked like the sky in the woodcut. I told Innis to take one of those files and slowly grind that area out, about two inches deep. That would give me some time to think up some way to get us out of this.

I was still feeling responsible for this whole thing, and those Belden Center guys didn't make matters any better. Sherman Koslik still had stitches on his face and I'm sure at least one of them saw him every day, hanging out on their street corners.

By the time our first two hour day was up, I had a plan. Innis had been able to grind the area out pretty well. He stayed accurately in the lines I had quickly drawn. I had some of the basics of the wolf's head blocked out on my project. When Mr. Underwood came around at the end of the period to see how we were doing, I asked him the big question.

I wanted to know if we could stay after an hour or so each day, to work on our projects. Before he could say anything, I told him he didn't have to stay. I knew all of the janitors and was friends with most of them, having worked around the school for over two years. We would just leave after they were done cleaning the wing. I was sure they wouldn't object.

He looked suspicious at first, but his excitement over our dedication to the projects won him over. He said that if the janitors agreed, it was fine by him. He left and I told Innis the plan. He thought it was a good idea and was confident that he could pull off his half of the work.

For the next few weeks, as soon as everyone else cleared out, I took one of the fine chisels and scraped into the plaster the outlines of the shapes that Innis was to carve the next day. Inside each piece, I put little symbols indicating how far down he was supposed to dig on that particular shape.

This was fine except Mr. Underwood wondered why my project wasn't going so smoothly with all the extra time I was putting in. I hadn't thought of everything. The only thing I could think of doing was mutilating my original carving so bad that I'd have to start over again, and make my pace seem a little slower.

So the next day, I showed Mr. Underwood where I had accidentally carved off the wolf's ear, and asked if he had some more stone. "You have to be more subtle with your tools. They are extensions of your soul. Feel the rock. Get in touch with it. Let it guide you," he lectured and I nodded, taking the new piece of stone and starting over.

By the last week of class, Innis's canoe was just about done. Mr. Underwood was very proud that he had brought out an Indian's creativity to full bloom. I was finally working on some other parts of the pipe. I had not f,nished the bowl, but he suggested I start another piece so that I'd have more prepared things to work on when the Fall semester rolled around. He was going to show Innis a carving move so that the canoe could have a scalloped frame on it, to finish it off.

When we strolled in that Monday, the thing I had expected all summer had finally come. The Belden Center boys retaliated. The whole class was standing around in a circle at the back of the room. We stepped in and saw the remains of Innis's canoe all over the floor. One of them claimed he had been admiring it when it slipped from his hands and smashed on the hard tile floor.

Mr. Underwood was shaking his head, looking at the mess. "Class dismissed," he whispered over the shattered plaster. "Would you boys stay behind?" he asked, and we knew, without even turning, that he meant us. "I am so sorry," he began, after the others left. "I should have been more careful, knowing what your relationship with those other bastards is like!" He shook and seemed almost ready to cry when Innis spoke.

"Hey man, don't be too upset. Sure, it was a shitty thing for them to do but we expected it. And, well . . . we gotta tell him," he said, turning to me, and I nodded. "Floyd did all the drawing on my thing. He's the one who should feel bad that all his work was gone. Sorry. We didn't mean to lie, but I just can't draw."

Mr. Underwood didn't quite know how to take this. He was mad at us for playing the trick on him, but he still felt bad that the work was gone. He said that we'd each get an A for effort, but an F for practices, for a final grade of C in the course. That was fine with me, so long as Innis got to graduate.

As we were walking out, he stopped us one more time. "Why aren't you boys very upset about what happened to your artwork?" he wanted to know. I told him that was easy. It wasn't really our work. We were not Ojibway. He thought about that for a minute and, finally, just as we headed out the door toward the Indian Rail, I saw him put his *American Indian Art* book back on the shelf.

168

Chapter Seventeen

$\Lambda\Lambda\Lambda$
$\Lambda\Lambda\Lambda$

FAILING LIGHT

SEPTEMBER 19, 1992

As he lay wire along the living room wall line, Hank Jimison watched Innis and Floyd's shadows fade into dark on the floor in front of him. They stood on the nearly completed roof and looked through the skylight they had just slipped smoothly into place directly above him. The roof was really supposed to be Floyd's job alone, and so far, he had laid the shingle strips alone, shrouding the exposed inner cavity of his uncle's old house. As the other cousins worked inside, they could hear him up there, and if the periods of silence bloated, one of them, usually Innis, would casually mount the ladder to see what was up. Over the past week, though, Floyd's silences were ignored as rest periods, Floyd working a nail, or some other mundane activity.

Working the skylight was the first work Innis had done on the roof. A little earlier, Floyd had seen a bank of purple, aggressive clouds cutting through the back woods, in their general direction. He had cut through the roof section as fast as he could, but eventually had given up his pride and yelled down through the hole, calling Innis up.

"Check it out," he said, as Innis reached the top of the ladder.

"Looks pretty big, man. Maybe it'll last through the weekend and you'll have yourself a day off on Monday."

"Without pay. But I doubt it'll last that long anyway. What're you working on down there?"

"Supports for Hank's outlets. I guess he wants 'em in pretty quick. Easier to work that way. No more rickety-ass generator to worry about." The generator they spoke of nearly drowned out their voices and the coming storm's thunder.

"You wanna give me a hand with this damned thing? I wanna get it in before that storm hits. I could wait, I guess, but settin' up a tarp would take me just as long as getting this window in would be, but I need a hand," Floyd said, kicking the window frame lightly with his boot.

With the two working together, the window slid in easily. Floyd's measurements and cuts had been perfect, as he knew they would be. "You, know, I almost wish I had one of these," Floyd said. Hank could hear their voices even more faintly now, muffled through the glass, but he could feel their eyes on him, burning critically into his back, where the unusual late summer heat had soaked sweat through his shirt. Knowing this, he worked continuously, only stopping once in a while to lift the front of his T-shirt to his face, wiping the sweat away.

"In your trailer? Get real. No, I think this is all Hank's. You know, it's got his name all over it, but that don't mean we can't come here and enjoy it sometimes."

"Yeah, you mean at all those parties Hank is gonna throw?" Floyd asked. Hank could hear the smirk.

"Hey, you never know, d'you ever think you'd see that?" Hank stared into their shadows across the floor, trying to will facial expressions into the blank darkness.

The storm clouds pushed their way closer, and the sunlight on the floorboards faded to nothingness, the two men's shadows grew less distinct, absorbing into the woodwork. Through the screen door, the breeze picked up and developed into a wind, and the short scuffs of their feet indicated their urgency. Floyd began caulking the window while Innis unfolded a large sheet of plastic over the incomplete roof section and tacked down some of the edges. As soon as Floyd finished with the skylight, he threw the caulking gun over the edge of the roof and helped Innis secure the plastic. The two climbed down the ladder as the first drops began tapping quietly on the tarp.

"Kinda' funny looking in here, ain't it?" Floyd said as they stepped through the threshold and glanced up toward the ceiling. Innis agreed, looking at the incandescent bulb hanging from the end of a white extension cord in the middle of the room.

Hank stood up and, brushing the dust from his knees, walked over to the others. Though he had watched their shadowy progress, he formally looked up at the skylight and nodded his approval. He also noticed the drops forming across the pane's surface and headed out the door. As the two stood in the entrance, he cut the gasoline generator's engine, and watched the light bulb grow dim behind them and finally darken entirely, leaving their obscure silhouettes.

Hank came back inside a couple minutes later and flopped down in The Bug's old chair. "I guess that's it for now; I got the plastic over the generator," he said, cracking a Molson.

"What are you talking about, man? All this storm means is that we can't work on the roof. Generator's fine running in the rain. We've done it hundreds of times," Floyd replied, getting Innis and himself a beer from the cooler.

"Yeah, well at work we use these generators all the time and we never let 'em run in the rain. How about you? You use generators at work?" Hank asked, his voice rising a little with each word.

"Well gee, no I guess we don't have much use for them. But then again, we don't use Firebirds either, but I'll bet my ass that I can run that nice little Pontiac you got out there better'n you, anyday," Floyd countered, shouting down his older cousin. "You city boys don't know Jack."

"And you do. What do you know about sports cars? The only ones I ever see out here are the ones that have been stolen and burned. Yeah, you guys sure do know how to treat a nice car," Hank said, lowering his voice, confident his words were enough.

"Is that what you think? Man, you might be as brown as me, but you sure sound like a Cree-rhu-rhit to me. Bet you don't even know what that means, do you?" Floyd returned, his voice also lowered a few degrees. Things had been going well, but he had fallen easily into the same old patterns.

"Indian words. Is that supposed to impress me? I don't impress that easy. You think some shitty little words that you picked up from some old fuck around here makes you a real Indian, some kind of movie Indian. Watch your ass for John Wayne, man. I'll tell you what it's like being an Indian now, and The Duke is the least of your worries."

171

"Yo, easy, you guys. Just drink, man. Drink your beer and shut up," Innis said, moving a chair closer, interrupting the airwaves between the cousins. His response distance was also shortened.

"No, it's all right, man. I wanna hear what old Henry has to say about being an Indian today. This should be interesting," Floyd said, leaning back in his chair to get comfortable.

"It's Hank. You can look right on my birth certificate. My name's Hank, not Henry. You see that? You don't know a fuckin' thing about me."

"I don't *care* a fuckin' thing about you either. Get on with your story, or do something useful," Floyd said, closing his eyes and listening to the storm outside pick up speed. It was getting to be a howler, and as the darkness grew in the room, lightning flashes leapt into the room through the new skylight.

Hank told them of his growing up years. He tried to think of everything that defined being an Indian in the city for him, but all that came to mind were negations. He had never considered himself to be really bad looking, but he had not dated all through high school. Some of his classmates had even speculated that he might have been gay, but it wasn't true. He didn't date for the same reason he didn't really have any friends.

He was the in-between. At the time, the white kids only associated with other white kids, and to the black kids, he was just a tan white kid. There was one half-Indian girl who went to his high school, but she knew the score. He recognized it in her from her features and her slight accent, but she never admitted it. She even did all the white girl things. She went out for the cheer-leading squad and the color guard, holding up the American flag for all to see. Among her other white girl activities, the act of not talking to him was included.

"You guys at least had each other to hang around with. I was out there all alone. All the folks around me thought Indians were extinct. This place was fifteen minutes away from most of their houses, and they didn't even know it existed. Hell, they may as well have been right. I sure didn't feel like I existed," Hank concluded.

"So why'd you leave here?" Floyd asked, undaunted.

"Jeez, Floyd," Innis sighed.

"No, it's a fair question. Would you live here?" Hank asked Floyd in return.

"We did."

"Like hell, you did. D'you watch your colored tv here? Where'd you plug it in? Or how about your stereo?" Hank smirked, knowing he had caught his younger cousin unexpectedly. He was not about to let it go, either. He had been waiting for this since they had started working on the house. Tradition was a curious thing to him. As he looked around him, he could not see anything that was particularly desirable, or anything he might want to glorify as a tradition.

"Yeah, you're about as traditionally Indian as bingo is. You go out to the Longhouse and dance to the drums, but on your way there and back, you're listening to tapes copied off of your CDs. Give me a fuckin' break."

Hank finished his beer and went to the old bedroom's back window, slid the screen over, unzipped, and pissed out the window. "And I can't wait until I don't have to do this anymore. I'm gonna flush my toilet and I hope the noise of the tank filling keeps you awake all night. Man, if you think shitting in an outhouse is a tradition, then you can have your fuckin' traditions. Me, I'll just flush mine away."

He walked back into the room, proud of himself. He had been preparing that one. He had even held off taking a leak, knowing that he could work it in at just the right moment. Neither of the other two said anything. As Hank sat back down, Stan and Mel walked in, both soaked to the skin, though their house was only a short walk away.

"I thought you guys would have these lights on and be working up a storm," Stan said, looking about the room. "I got a couple hours and a little bit of energy, so I thought I'd stop over and see what was up," he finished, going for the ice chest. Mel had brought a wine cooler with her and began walking around, checking out the progress while Stan pulled up a chair to join the others.

"So what's up?" he asked, settling in.

"Hank brought up the Longhouse," Innis said flatly, getting up to join Mel in the old bedroom. She still had a fondness for her husband's old drawings.

"That was fucked up, man," Stan said.

Shortly after the Natcha brothers and Hank had first heard that Floyd was talking about the Longhouse, they had been relieved to discover it was the Longhouse out on Cattaraugus, that it was one that actually existed. None of them were interested in joining in it; they had never really followed any particular religion and felt no driving urge to do so now. But by the same token, they were not begrudging Floyd his interest. And they all felt that he had made some tremendous improvements since he had started going.

They didn't know if the Longhouse itself were helping any, but something was, and they didn't want to take this potential help away with ridicule. There was always time for that later, when Floyd was better and things were back to normal; they always believed that would happen at some point, and had in fact stored up some smart-ass comments for when that time would roll around. They continued to make this stockpile in those hopes, Hank even coming up with some good-natured comments. He had believed this to be a part of his entrance. It was their way of praying, the only way they could see to do it—planning future jokes.

Floyd had never mentioned the Longhouse to them and, had they not gotten the word from the Hack that night in The Den, they would never have known. They decided not to discuss it with him unless he brought the topic up, and so far, he hadn't. They had, however, talked among themselves about it while working at Hank's on the occasions Floyd wasn't around, and now Hank, forgetting these conversational dances, had violated their respectful silence.

Stan got up and walked over to one of the windows to watch the storm darken their homestead. Mel came in from the other room and joined him. Stan glanced at her for a second, but went back to his study of the rain as it saturated the basketball court, the gazebo, and the paths, making them disappear in a muddy confusion.

"You could use a Longhouse," Floyd said, watching the storm himself out the side window.

"What the fuck do I need a Longhouse for? I know how to live in nasty conditions; I don't need any dancing to help me in that area," Hank said, snorting and walking into the other room for another beer.

"You could learn a lot, man. Maybe even learn to dance." Floyd felt confident that the Longhouse was at least partly responsible for his seeming recovery, though he had not learned to dance, himself, yet. However, he continued to write in his notebooks, but not as often as he had been. Most of his spare time now was being spent working on this house, and up to this moment he had not really minded it.

"I know how to dance," Hank said flatly.

Floyd had no response. Even now, though, his anger had been fleeting and was immediately replaced by a sense of sadness for his lost cousin. He planned on continuing to help with the house, but he didn't think Hank would ever really be one of them. He had been feeling hopeful, even right up to the moment the storm hit. Hank worked with them, not slacking and not taking advantage of them, as Floyd had been wary of, and could even take some harassment. But he still always went by the rules, and his alien qualities emerged at the oddest and most inconvenient times.

When this question of using the generator in the rain came up, Floyd had not been surprised. They had done it, maybe not hundreds of times, but at least dozens. Hank had apparently never felt free to experiment, to try something different, even something as simple as running a generator in the rain, and all because it was against the rules. For the first time that day, Floyd had understood a little more of Hank, had perhaps finally seen a reason, beside chickenshittedness, Hank never even tried walking the edge.

"It ain't about religion, not really," Floyd continued, getting up and walking into the kitchen. "It's about all of this. It's even about saving those pictures in the old spare room. It's about the reason we stay here. You think we like using an outhouse? Or that we wouldn't like to have a shower? Sure, I could afford an apartment in the city, so could Innis, and even Stan and Mel, here. We don't stay because we can't afford to pay rent somewhere."

"I even lived off the res for a while, but I came back," Mel added, walking away from the rattling window pane. "I don't know anything about the Longhouse, though; I've never been, myself. But this place, I don't know—I kind of need it. It's something that's just for us. Know what I mean?" she finished.

"Uh, no," Hank said with a slight irritability in his voice.

"It's all about us. This house was our house. Why do you think I wanted to save that room? Just to be sickening to you, I bet, huh?" Hank was silent.

175

When confronted with the truth, he couldn't fess up. As Floyd had suspected, Hank actually had thought it was some secret joke on him. The others stood loosely around him; he took a drink and looked out the window. Their reflections grew less distinct in the increasing dark.

"When I got sick this summer, I got to stay on. The crew worked around my problem. Why do you suppose that was, man?"

"They're a bunch of non-union fucks? How should I know?" Hank replied, his eyes remaining outside.

"Guess again, asshole. As a matter of fact, we are union men, but some times you gotta risk breaking the rules, and they did for me this summer. Know why?"

"What'd I say?" Hank shouted, angered at his cousin's seeming obtuseness.

"Hey Floyd, who's this?" Stan interrupted, pointing with his chin out the window in the general direction of Floyd's trailer. Later, Stan would tell Floyd that he had kept his mouth shut initially when he had seen the strange car pulling up the driveway, headlights bouncing with urgency. He hadn't recognized the woman who had gotten out of the car and run up to Floyd's door. It hadn't been until she had begun pounding, though, instead of knocking, that he'd figured he'd had to intervene.

Floyd, agitated, spun over to the window, irritated at the interruption in, what he believed to be, a fight he was winning. Just a few more minutes and Hank might actually make it over to their side, he thought. His arguments fled his mind entirely, though, replaced with surprise at seeing Jan on the porch of his trailer. He ran to the back door and shouted her name a few times. At the sound of it, he saw the Natcha brothers glance at each other in recognition. They all watched as she spotted Floyd waving to her from the back porch and then ran toward them down the muddy back path.

Floyd initially began shouting for her to just drive up The Bug's driveway, but it was too late; she had already stepped onto the path and didn't seem to be hearing him anyway. From that point, he observed her progress silently. He was still marveling that she was there in the first place. He didn't even think she'd be able to find his trailer. He had only brought her out to the res one time, and even then, it had been at night. They had just driven by. She had wanted to see where he lived, and as they'd passed his mother's driveway, he had pointed out the porch light on his trailer.

As she got to The Bug's porch, Floyd opened the screen door and led her in. They were both drenched and she was nearly out of breath, but she managed to get a few words out, while leaning on a stud.

"Where the hell have you been? I been trying to call you for the last two hours," she wheezed.

"I've been here. We're not supposed to get together for another five hours or so."

"Johnny Flatleaf. He's going. He wanted you to be there when he crossed over. I promised him I'd ask you, but I didn't think it was gonna happen this quick. We thought the amputation would help, but it didn't. You know, it just . . . well, will you come?"

Jan's question wasn't even finished and Floyd was reopening the door. As they ran out, Floyd turned to his cousins, who had been absorbed in the decidedly brief interaction. They would discuss their first impressions of the infamous Jan later, but Floyd ensured they'd have another topic first. The storm intensified, lightning offering quick snapshots of this family, and over the racket made by the rain smashing into the plastic tarp, Floyd shouted, stepping out the door.

"Here's your chance. The Longhouse's calling."

The thunder rumbled, following the lightning.

177

Chapter Eighteen

~~~
~~~

CALLING HOME

FLOYD PAGE

SEPTEMBER 23, 1992

I thought for sure when I lost the ghost machine, that everything was just gonna fall apart, but it didn't. But I might not have realized that until just a little while ago. It's just amazing how someone can enter your life and change it in ways you can not even imagine. And it's not like I'm in love or anything, well, maybe I am, but even if I'm not, I'm really glad she came along when she did.

I first met Jan recently, down at the University. We became friends pretty fast, intimate friends. Okay, we were getting pretty serious, but I was just as shocked as everyone else when she showed up at my trailer the day of the big storm, the same day the ghost machine stopped working, but I'll get to that, later. She was soaked and told me that I needed to come with her. She had said that she might be needing me sometime, but I didn't really know what for or think it was going to be that soon. After all, I had only been to their Longhouse twice before. I'd only known her since sometime in July, late July at that. She was in summer school at the University.

We were working on the downtown Buffalo campus. I think this is the first time we've ever been down here. We're usually over at the newer campus. These buildings were put up a long time ago, and whoever designed them knew what they were doing for this area of the country. But even old and sturdy structures need a helping hand once in a while. All roofs leak at some time or another.

179

The building we were working on was only three stories high, not too dramatic at all. I kind of like this. Being so close to the ground, we can almost see the people's faces as they walk by, going to class or leaving it. Makes them seem more real.

This was how I noticed Jan right off. She was walking into the building one day. Now I'm not saying that my memory is so good that I remember every face I looked at. But she was pretty noticeable.

I was laying a piece of tar strip and I saw this girl coming up the walk. From afar, she looked like any other person going to college. She had on some jeans and a T-shirt and was carrying this book bag thing thrown over her shoulder.

What made her most stand out was that she was looking up at us. I mean, I guess she could have been staring at the sky, the clouds, or maybe even some bird, but I could tell it was us she had her eye on. So I stared back for a few seconds, and she didn't look away. Either she was really bold or she actually was checking out the clouds.

It turned out she was bold. When she came out of the building, she looked back up at us again. That was three hours later. As the days went on, I began looking for her. She showed the next day, but at a different time. I checked around, talking to some of the kids on my lunch break. It turns out that they have different classes and different schedules for each day of the week. Also, on that next day, I had built up the nerve to wave. And you know what, she waved back. This was enough proof to me that she wasn't watching the clouds or the satellite dish up there on the school building's roof.

But we only had a little while left on that building. It looked like the next wave I was gonna make might have been a wave of goodbye. But lucky for me, we don't have a word for goodbye in Tuscarora. And to tell the truth, even if we did, I would have no plans for saying it to this girl.

I don't know what it was about her. At that point, I didn't even really know what she looked like. It's kind of hard to tell from three stories up. What could you tell from that high up? Not much, would be my guess. But I didn't have the balls to go down and talk to her, either. It was actually my old buddy the Hack who got me to go down there to really meet her after he caught me during one of our ground-to-roof waves.

180

"Hey man," the Hack said, startling me. I hadn't even heard him come up. I was busted in mid-wave when she was leaving. "Go on down and talk to her, man, or you're gonna be using that hand for more than waving tonight," he said, punching me on the shoulder. I laughed with the Hack at the stupid joke about jacking off that was always used whenever someone talked about girls, but I wasn't really thinking about that. You know, I hadn't even met her. I actually hadn't even been in close enough range to see what she really looked like. There was something else about her.

"Go on, man. I'll cover your ass up here. I been doin' it for most of the summer, anyway. What's one more day?" he said, pushing me to the service stairway we use to get to the roof.

"No. It's too late, but she'll be back," I confessed. I went down at her usual time, nervously. You know, it just might be better if she stayed being the girl I almost met.

It turned out that she was a really great person to meet, and she's one of us. Well, sort of. She's from Cattaraugus, another reservation that's not too far from Buffalo. So though she's not officially one of us, from our reservation, we still had that connection. Anyway, that's why she was waving at us in the first place. When she looked up that first day, she could tell right off that we were skins. Besides, around here, almost all the roofers come from one of the reservations or another.

It was a bit harder to tell with her. She was one of those lighter-skinned folks, and her hair was brown. She could probably pass for white among whites, but that day when I first got up the nerve to talk to her, I could tell.

When I got to the first floor, I went to the men's room. You know, I took a leak and checked my watch. I still had a couple of minutes, so I even washed my hands and tried to comb out some of my ponytail's wind snarls. I didn't want to be standing in the men's room doing nothing, and I didn't want her to catch me waiting, so I undid my belt and tucked my shirt in all smooth. By the time I walked out, I was looking pretty sharp.

But she wasn't there. I checked my watch again. I was sure she arrived at that time. Lots of other people were hanging around, doing nothing, so I stood there with them and waited. It was getting to be a while since I'd been up on the roof, so I was just going to give it up for the day.

As I turned to head back for the stairs, I saw her walking right at me with that same look she had the day of the storm. And that day had been bad enough without Jan's sudden appearance and fierce look.

∿

When the storm showed up, we had been working on Hank's house all afternoon. Me and Innis had been up on the roof, so we climbed down and went inside to wait it out. I didn't even want to be working on Hank's house in the first place, but somehow Innis rooked me into it. Anyway, when the storm arrived, I didn't think it was necessary to stop work, and neither did Innis. Naturally, that god damned Hank felt differently about the whole thing. So I started giving him some shit about it, and he jumps all over my ass. And out of nowhere, he starts giving me some number about going to the Longhouse. Now, at that point, I had only been to the Longhouse a couple of times, and I hadn't even told anyone from home about going there, so I had no idea how Hank even knew this.

I had never even thought of going to one, myself. As far as I know, there hasn't been one on our res for at least a hundred years, and probably even longer than that. It was Jan who got me to go to theirs out on Cattaraugus. She didn't invite me right off, mind you. It was after a little while after we officially met.

That first day down on the ground floor of that school building, she came right up and said she was looking for me on the roof and she tripped over one of those park benches just outside. I was ready to back off. You know, I had never even met the woman. But then I looked right at her and knew why she had come up as she had. From the third floor, as I said, I couldn't tell much about her, but from this close, I could see her slightly cat-shaped eyes and wickedly sharp cheekbones, and I knew she was a skin. In fact, she looked a lot like the Clause girls who lived down on Chew Road. She couldn't hold her fake mad-face for another second, and we both started laughing.

It actually wasn't all that long after when she took me to the Longhouse. We started having lunch together and that was when I found out she was a nursing student for sure. So over at the McDonald's one day, I asked her if she could tell me anything about memory disorders. She didn't know too

182

much without more information, and that was information I didn't have. She did know I was from Tuscarora, and asked me if I had been to Brian Waterson for help. I felt kind of stupid telling her about the milkweed and all, but I did tell her anyway. She just has this way about her that makes me talk.

Right in the middle of my story though, it occurred to me that she had mentioned Brian by name. "That milkweed sounds like a good idea," she said when I paused. "You ever thought of going to the Longhouse for help?" She didn't know we don't have a Longhouse, and when I explained this, she nodded. "No wonder Brian comes down to our Longhouse," she speculated. "Maybe you should come to ours, too. We're having a social this weekend," she prodded, and when I didn't say anything back, she took my hand in hers. "You've already taken the first steps," she whispered in my ear, as I enjoyed her warmth traveling up the veins and arteries of my arm to the rest of me.

On the way down to their res, we were listening to some Muddy Waters and she ejected the tape and threw it in the back seat. She grabbed some other tapes from the glove compartment and slid one into the machine. The glove compartment tapes were some that she had made at an earlier social. The drums and singing sounded like all the music I'd ever heard during those rare events at home. I even recognized some of the songs. When Jan eventually played them that day we flew from the hospital in Hank's car, it seemed like Hank had been listening to the songs all his life, though I would have bet money he had never heard them before.

You could have hit me in the head with a hammer when Hank showed up. In fact, if I hadn't stopped at my trailer, we would have missed him entirely. We had already gotten into Jan's car, but I told her to hang on. I figured I was soaked enough, anyway. It wasn't like I could get much wetter. I ran back up to my trailer, slid in the front door and reached up to grab the ghost machine. I thought, I don't know, maybe we could use it to keep the old man's ghost around long enough for him to make it home.

He seemed to need it more than me at this point. The old man's name was Johnny Flatleaf. I had just met him pretty recently. I had sort of met him at that first social. When we got to the Longhouse, Jan let me know that we had to split up. Women went in one door and men went in another. So I walked in the men's door and once inside, I cruised over to the other side of the room to talk to Jan. After all, I didn't know anybody else and I had no idea when the social was going to officially kick in. As I started talking away to her, she began making all of these weird faces at me. Shortly after, I realized that I was the only man on that side of the room. The old man stood on the edge of this invisible line that separated the men's side from the women's. He was looking right at me, and I could see his right hand down at his side, motioning to me with small gestures that I should get back over to my own side.

He sat me down next to him, but didn't say anything to me the whole night. At one point, during the dancing, he motioned for me to get up on the line and join the others.

I shook my head. Even though the only other people not dancing were women who had babies sleeping on them, I still felt like I would be less obvious sitting down than out on the line. He did this the second time I was at their Longhouse, too. Same thing happened. I just didn't feel like I could dance out there. It had been so long since I had done any Indian dancing and I didn't want to look like an idiot. He didn't like this too much, but even though he left me to sit on the bench and came back next to me when the dance was over, he never did say anything to me.

The next time I saw him was when I actually got introduced, and I guess because of that meeting, I ended up in Hank's car on the way to the big VA Hospital in Buffalo on the day of the storm instead of kicking back with another beer like I should have been.

"You must dance when you are approached," was the first thing he said, as I walked into his hospital room with Jan that day a while later. She told me at lunch one day that she had to go see someone in the hospital. She also said that she wanted me to know him by name. She had been doing her clinical work at the VA, but had just gotten transferred the day before. She hadn't said who it was, but when we walked in the room, I recognized him right off.

"Hi, Johnny. No, don't bother turning over. I won't be checking your dressing, today. That's what I stopped up to tell you. It will be some other nurse. I have to work somewhere else now," Jan said to him, leaning on the safety railing on his bed.

184

"How come?" he asked, forgetting me. He didn't stop lifting his gown for her. "I don't want no one else. Here, just a quick look, then I can tell them to go away later."

"It doesn't work like that, and you know it. You've been in the hospital before," she tried to tell him.

"Nope, never. Here, just one look."

"You have, too," she said, first glancing to the door and then reaching for his chart.

"Nope. Just one," he said, kind of begging her. I walked to the door and checked. There wasn't a nurse in sight. I called to Jan and nodded. I knew that she could be in serious trouble for this, and that she was going to do it anyway, so I stayed watching the hallway as she checked the bandages around the place where his leg had been cut off. She told me later that it was cancer they were trying to stop, but that she didn't think it was working.

When she was done, she told him that it looked okay, but that another nurse had to look at it anyway. I came back in and he picked up where he had left off with me, but by talking to Jan instead.

"Where's your man from, that he don't know he has to dance when someone tells him to? Who's his folks, anyway?" he asked, ignoring me entirely.

"Tuscarora," I said. "My last name's Page," I added.

"No Longhouse," was all he said, nodding. "So who's your folks?" he asked again.

"Page," I repeated.

"No. Your folks, your people," he said again, and I didn't know what the hell he wanted. Over his head and out of his line of sight, Jan looked at me and mouthed a word and I finally got it.

"Eel. We're Eels," I said. He was wanting to know what my clan was. That seemed to satisfy him as he looked up at Jan and they both nodded at each other.

I still didn't know why that was such a big deal when Jan showed up during the storm, and at first, I was more wrapped up in what had happened to the milkweed in the ghost machine. When I ran in the trailer and grabbed it, the ghost machine felt a little funny. I looked at it in the light and saw that

185

the milkweed had all dried out. The pods had shriveled so much that they looked like small silent tongues hanging off of the plant. It was only the husk of a milkweed, and the stems started to shred and crumble in my hands.

"We goin' or what?" I heard from the screen door. I looked and it was Hank standing in the doorway. I think it was the first time he had actually been to my trailer. For a minute, I was lost. I was trying to figure out why I hadn't noticed the milkweed drying out before, and I didn't really have an answer.

"I think this woman really wants you to hurry up," he said, opening the door and grabbing my arm. I left the ghost machine behind and stepped through the door with Hank. I started walking toward Jan's old orange Datsun, but Hank tugged at my arm and pointed to his Firebird. I frowned at him, but then saw that Jan was already in the back seat. "It's faster," he said, getting into the driver's seat.

He was right. We got there a lot faster than even I could imagine. It seemed like there was lightning in his engine. We flew in and headed up the stairs to Johnny's room, which was on the tenth floor. I didn't know there were stairways in the building. Well, I guess I did, but I had no idea where they were. The elevators always take forever in that building, and I figured that was why we ran up ten flights of stairs. It was not something I wanted to do again soon.

We got to the top and I leaned against the stairwell, catching my breath. Jan looked out the door and turned back to us. "Okay, this is it. Are you ready?" I nodded. Ready for what, I figured. I still didn't know what the hell we were supposed to be doing.

"Hey," Johnny said weakly as we stepped into his room. "Oh boy, my foot hurts. Can you look at it?" he asked Jan, pointing to the empty space under the sheet where his leg used to be. He reminded me of The Bug. He used to complain sometimes that his foot itched, or that his knee hurt and he knew full well that he didn't have either of those things.

"We're gonna take care of it, Johnny," Jan said to him, taking off her jacket and then her jeans. I stared at her for a second, but then I realized that she had on her nursing duds underneath her regular clothes. I still didn't know what she was up to, but as long as it didn't involve her stripping bare naked in the middle of the VA hospital, I didn't much care.

"Hey, how 'bout taking me home? I want to see my house one last time. How 'bout it? Your man here can help. Can't you, Eel?"

"That's exactly what we're doin,'" Jan said, pulling her nurse's cap from one of her jacket pockets and adjusting it in her hair.

"We are?" I asked. Hank and I looked at each other, but for only a second. He was pulling out his keys and heading out of the room.

"I'm gonna pull the car around to the front entrance, so we won't have far to take him in this downpour," Hank said, pulling the collar up on his jacket.

"No, not the main entrance. We've got to take him out the maintenance door." Jan began wrapping the sheet around Johnny and then lifting him out of the bed, and into a wheelchair that had been sitting in the corner of the room.

"What? Why?" I asked, helping her clear the sheets from the old man's body.

"Because we're not supposed to be doing this." She turned to Hank. "Maintenance is around back, on the east side. When you get up to the gate, tell the guy there, the big skin with the pony tail, that you're with me. He's expecting my car, so if you don't tell him that, he's not gonna let you in."

Hank walked out without even a pause.

Before I could say anything more, she gave me directions to a different stairway in another hall of the floor. I headed out before them and waited on the stairs. They eventually showed up and Jan lifted Johnny out of the chair and put him in my arms. He was pretty light, so I didn't have much trouble holding him while she got rid of the chair, but I thought it was going to be kind of tough carrying him down ten flights of stairs.

Jan came back in a couple of minutes and as she joined us, she supported some of Johnny's weight, so it wasn't too bad. We got down two flights and she told me to open the door and look out. I was going to ask her what I was looking for, but I just opened it and knew right away, anyhow.

We headed out into the hallway and this other skin was standing there. He was dressed in hospital clothes, so I guessed that he was a nurse or an orderly or something. He had a wheelchair and we set Johnny down in it and we followed him down that short hallway, took a left and came up to another set of elevators. One of them was standing open and, when we got in, the other skin, whose name tag read Ozzie, released the emergency stop button at the same time he pulled one of those special elevator keys from his keychain and plugged it in. We were on our way.

The elevator made its only stop and we rolled out into the boiler room. Hank was already down there, waiting for us.

Chapter Nineteen

ᨊᨊ

EEL DANCE

Innis flipped the page in the notebook, but the next page was blank. "So, where's the rest, man? Haven't gotten around to it, yet?" The big storm had only been about three weeks before, and it was certainly possible that Floyd hadn't written it yet. Innis had wondered what was going into all of those notebooks, and now he had gotten the answer, at the most unusual of times, but in perhaps not the most unusual of places.

A few hours earlier, they had been at Hank's house. The work had been completed for a couple days and Hank was now hosting a party to celebrate. He had invited everyone, and they had all come, even Nora Page and Olive Natcha, who had not been in the house since before their brother had died. They could not believe they were standing in the same house.

The plasterboard walls had been replaced and covered with a beige wallpaper print with a vague geometric pattern in it. Most of the old furniture had been taken out and replaced with a new plush overstuffed living room set that rested on wall to wall carpeting. In place of the heavy velvety curtain with which The Bug had divided the two main rooms there now stood warmly stained louvered doors. More louvered doors sealed off the two bedrooms.

"Ooh, look at all these new things," Nora Page and Olive Natcha repeated to one another as they drifted about the house together, padding softly in stockinged feet, trying to not make impressions on the plush carpeting. "Who's Patrick Nagel?" Nora wondered aloud as they examined the prints hanging on the living room walls.

"Who cares? I could do better than that," Olive responded, moving on to trace her fingers along the woodwork.

"He must be some pretty fancy artist. Look at those nice chrome frames. I bet Hank doesn't even know who Patrick Nagel is. This looks like something his mom would pick out," Nora concluded.

"She always did have that knack," Olive said. The two sisters moved through the rooms, catching bits of stories here and there and touching all of the new items in the house. Occasionally, one of them would sniff an object, to get that freshly unpacked scent new items always had, and then set it back down, careful to replace it in exactly the same position.

Quite a number of people from off the reservation were among the crowd, and they generally didn't seem too out of place. There was a keg out back, but Hank was showing off his electricity by serving cold drinks out of the refrigerator and happily plunking ice cubes from trays out of his freezer into glasses of pop and wine.

One of the people not from the reservation was Jan Freen. She had become a pretty common face since the storm, showing up fairly regularly, but she still did not know that many people. Innis, from his spot alone in the gazebo, watched her emerge alone from the back door and look around. He had come out a few minutes before, himself. Somewhere in the party, Jan must have lost Floyd. He waited until her scanning gaze crossed him and he waved to her. She nodded and walked toward him after filling her cup from the keg. She joined him, setting her beer outside the gazebo's border, on one of the old kerosene drums.

"So, how come you're not at the party?" she asked, sitting across from him.

"I'll get back there. As I was walking around, looking at all that new, I got to wondering if it's not a funeral party."

"What do you mean? Who died?"

"Oh, no one died, but it's a long story, and one I'd guess you wouldn't want to hear. You know, the past and all," Innis said. "I don't really know," he continued, regardless. "I don't think I can celebrate this. I didn't really have any trouble working on the house, and all, but now that it's fully Hank's and not The Bug's anymore, I'm just not so sure we did the right thing, after all."

190

"So, what's it like, having your family around forever?" Jan said, her voice betraying her lack of connections.

"I don't know. That's kind of like asking someone what it's like to have both legs. I don't know any different. I guess you'd have to ask that one to someone who's had it both ways. Maybe Hank could answer that for you. But if you do, make sure I'm not there when you ask him. I'm not so sure I wanna hear the answer."

"You'd be surprised."

"What are you, the voice of experience?"

"No, actually I guess I'd be the voice of inexperience," Jan replied softly.

"Why? Where's your family?"

"Don't have one," she said, stepping out and picking up her beer.

"I guess we better get over there, huh?" Innis said.

Shortly after they walked in the door, they parted. Jan, spotting Floyd, made her way through the crowd and Innis decided to rescue a lost looking Bob Hacker. As Innis and the Hack shook hands, Hank had apparently decided everyone who was going to arrive had already done so. He gathered them all in the new living room and, though the windows and skylight had amply lighted the room, he ceremoniously threw a switch, turning on the combination ceiling fan and overhead lights. They all clapped and held up their drinks in celebration; Hank smiled and then the crowd began mingling again. He walked over to a group and joined their conversation, leaving the lights on.

Even among the white people at the party, Bob Hacker had been looking as if he felt out of place. The Hack had known Floyd for a number of years, but Innis knew the way of borders—that Floyd and the Hack didn't usually hang around on the reservation. They always bullshitted at The Den, or on the job, but that was about the extent of things. He had wondered aloud to Innis what the occasion was that he had gotten invited to this party, but Innis had no answer for him. He had assumed Nathan would be here, possibly even Mike, though he doubted that, but he hadn't spotted either of them. Just as the two planned on taking a seat, Floyd caught Innis's eye and signaled for the two of them to step outside. Jan was standing with Floyd in the kitchen and they turned to leave through the side door as Innis and the Hack made their way to the back door.

191

"Let's take a ride," Floyd said abruptly, as he and Jan walked up to the back porch, their arms around one another. They turned and headed for his Nova and the others followed.

That was several hours ago and now as Innis stood up on the top ridge of the dike and dusted gravel from the seat of his pants, he understood Floyd's reason for writing down their past, but he could not figure out why Floyd wanted to share it with him, or really what any of this had to do with any of them.

He watched Jan and the Hack skipping stones down by the water's edge. It was a surprisingly warm day. They had already had a bad frost. It had come early this year, but today had been as warm as could be—Indian Summer. The sun gleamed off the water when either Jan or the Hack had gotten a successful skip. They had seemingly grown bored of his reading the spiral notebooks Floyd had pulled out of the plastic bag he had brought up with him. He also wanted to know why Floyd had stopped in the middle of the story.

"So when you gonna get to the end?"

"I'm not. Don't need 'em anymore," Floyd said, pulling several rocks from the bag and tossing them in a pile up on the ridge. Innis, out of habit, looked to the place where their land had been. "Guess where these came from?" Floyd said, making a circle out of the rocks and threw his notebooks inside of it.

"Don't know. Where?"

"Come on, you gotta know," Floyd said, removing a small container of charcoal lighter fluid from the bag and setting in on the ground.

"When did you come up here?" Innis asked, incredulous. He realized the rocks were from their homestead area, from the place he had twice tried to reach. They looked like any other rocks, as he should have known, but he'd somehow expected they'd be different, that they'd show their history.

"Labor Day," Floyd said, picking up the bottle and spraying the liquid across his notebooks. "With . . ."

"What are you doing?" Innis reached out too late to stop his cousin's actions, and then paused. "With Hank?"

192

"Yup," his cousin said, and, after lighting a cigarette, he proceeded to ignite the books.

The two men sat on some boulders and watched the books go up, Innis's gaze following a fluttering sheet of embers and ash as it floated out over the water.

"It's all up here, man," Floyd smiled, tapping his right temple.

"How do you know? What if you have, you know, what do they call it, a relapse?"

"It's not gonna happen."

"You can't know that. Those doctors still don't even know what was wrong with you. I mean, sure, they didn't find any permanent damage from the accident, and you're acting better now and you can remember all this stuff, but what happens next month or next year when you begin forgetting again?"

"You just gotta have some confidence, man, some belief. Like that old man, Johnny. You see, I guess he probably should have been dead a day or so before it actually happened. He lasted right up until we crossed the border onto Cattaraugus." Floyd closed his eyes and thought.

"We had just passed through the reservation entrance, the shot up and rusted sign announcing our arrival on Cattaraugus," he said. "It was just a little over an hour since we'd left the hospital. Hank couldn't drive as fast as he wanted. Man, that storm shook that little old Firebird something fierce and sometimes we even hydroplaned a little on the thruway, so that made him settle down a little. I guess he wanted to get us all to Cattaraugus still alive.

"'We made it, Johnny. You're home,' Jan whispered to the old man, holding his head in her lap as he was spread out across the back seat.

"'Oh, I know, I know, I can feel it. Nyah-wheh, Nyah-wheh.' Johnny said, and he opened his eyes and I know he could see those wild and tall trees sweeping over the road and dancing in the storm. His eyes closed a minute later and he left this old world.

"We took his body in the house and Jan called whoever it is you call at those times, cops, mortician, I don't know. She was expecting some shit because of her actions, but with the Tribal Council on her side, she's hoping things'll go all right. She told me we had some more important things to do before the coroner got to the house.

"She went into Johnny's bedroom and came back out with some dried tobacco leaves. The three of us stepped outside and, as she told us how, we went to his old fire pit behind the house and got some dry wood from his shed to try and start a fire in the rain.

"I told them there was no way it was going to happen, but he kept working at it, so I tried to shield it. Hank kept on trying to convince me that it would too work. He said The Bug had shown him how they had learned to light rain fires in the war. And as I watched him, he was right. You know, I didn't think he ever spent more than two hours chatting up The Bug, but there it was, that same tepee shaped kindling stack The Bug had shown us, so I started helping him and, by gosh, we had a rain fire blazing in no time.

"Jan stepped on over and passed us each a few of those tobacco leaves and once we had them, we all gave thanks together, laying the leaves in the fire to burn. That fire burned bright even in the downpour. We stood there for a few minutes soaking in the rain and the smoke until the flame blinked out."

"But why you, man? This guy didn't even know you, or Hank for that matter. I still can't believe that *he* was even there," Innis commented after hearing the conclusion of Johnny's departure from the hospital. "Why didn't the guy's family just take him home if he was gonna die, anyway? It was great that you did it and all, but really, don't you think it was their job?"

"Johnny didn't have any family," Jan answered, running her fingers through Floyd's ponytail. She had reached the top of the ridge just as Floyd finished his story. She glanced at the fire and nodded to Floyd.

"This is for my use now," he said, digging in his plastic bag and pulling out some tobacco. "This is the last of Johnny's tobacco, and since I was the only Eel there, I guess I inherited it." He passed the dried leaves out equally among the four of them, giving the Hack his last, as the bearded man just then reached the top of the dike.

"Put them in the fire with me," Floyd said, putting his arm around Jan's shoulder. She looked at him and laid hers on. "Help me give thanks," he said as her leaves took.

"For what?" Innis asked, leaning over and placing his leaves on the flames, regardless.

"For being able to burn these notebooks. For not needing them anymore. I came to knowing I wouldn't have that need anymore while I was at the old man's funeral. Me and Hank had walked in the men's door of the Longhouse together two days after Johnny died. His body had come back from the coroner's and the funeral was going along as it should. We looked at all the skinny benches along the walls, the wood stove at one end and the fireplace at the other, the women's door on the opposite side and wall of the building. You even been in one?" he asked Innis, who shook his head.

"The place hadn't changed any, but it wasn't at all like the last time. This time, I could almost see that invisible line dividing the men's side from the women's, like it had been drawn right there on the walls. Man, that Longhouse was packed. I peeked out one of the windows and could see more people standing outside.

"Just as I sat down, I saw Brian Waterson sitting over on one of the corner benches. I was going to go over and talk to him, you know, to let him know what happened with the milkweed, but he moved his hand just enough to make me stay where I was, and I don't know, I also had this weird feeling that Brian knew all about what had happened with the milkweed, the ghost machine, and everything else in the last few months.

"Later, after one of the Elders had stood up and spoken for a real long time in Seneca, some drummers and singers stood up from the men's side and, almost silent, walked on over to these benches in the middle of the Longhouse. Just as they tapped out their beginning drums, this guy in jeans and an old grungy bright orange hooded sweatshirt stood up and walked over near those benches. He started lifting his feet with their rhythm, you know, like dancing in place. A bunch of others got up and joined him, and as soon as those singers gave their opening notes, he got moving, dancing this invisible orbit around the drummers' bench. And that orbit just grew bigger and bigger," Floyd said, shaping his arms into an ever-expanding circle.

"Jan stood up on the other side of the room and joined that ring of people. She was one of the last to fill in that ring. The folks who came after her began a new ring, surrounding the first, and moving in the opposite direction.

"Someone stopped in front of me, blocking my view, and I looked up, you know, almost expecting to see Johnny standing there, but of course it wasn't. Brian Waterson held his hand open, the same invitation Johnny had

195

given me at that social that seemed a million years ago. He told me in a whisper that I wouldn't ever need another milkweed again.

"I shook my head just a little at his invitation, but as soon as I started, I heard, in this real different, loud voice, almost like it was shouted right into my left ear: 'you must dance when you are approached,' just like that," he shouted in the middle of his story, for effect. "Man, I whipped my head around, but there wasn't anyone sitting there. They had all gone up. Right next to me, Hank was still sitting there, watching, but he didn't look like he had heard any weird shouting. I looked back up to Brian, but he was already in the outer circle.

"I elbowed Hank and stood up and he jumped up right next to me. We stepped in behind Brian and began shuffling. I hate being at the end of the circle and, you know, kept hoping the others would catch up and complete the circle, so no one would see how bad I was dancing. But I listened and moved and with each step, as the beats became more familiar, what everyone else thought didn't even seem to matter anymore, they all kept getting further and further away.

"And then it happened. With each beat of the drum, I felt some new memory explode into my head. It was just like that—these little mini-explosions. Fights in high school, playing with some string for Riff, you know, that cat I used to have, man I loved that cat, graduation parties, birthday parties, that haunted house party down at Connie's place the Halloween I was twelve, snowball fights, kickball games, fireball games, getting my toes caught in the spokes of your bike when I was riding on the handlebars." Innis nodded, remembering that bloody mess, himself.

"Learning how to ride a bike, myself, the swamp in our woods burning, moving into my trailer, diving down here for the first time," he said, pointing out across the water's surface. "Making fall corn husk dolls in those September fields with Mel behind her house, that old summer daycamp at the picnic grove, getting lost in the woods, funerals I've been to, faces I haven't seen clearly in years, I remembered. Man, I even remember the night I discovered jacking off—I thought I had done something wrong with it," he laughed, slightly embarrassed at his revelation.

"From the naming of the first Plastic Fred to the last time I saw Sherman Koslik, I had it all. The drumming slowed but I didn't want it to stop. I glanced over at Hank and man, there were tears sneaking on down his brown cheeks, but you know, Hank didn't even have the least bit of trouble dancing. He was just moving along fine with everyone else in that circle.

"And then I looked down at my own feet and, I couldn't believe this, they were gliding along perfectly, missing no steps in that son of a bitchin' dance I hadn't done in over fifteen years. It was funny, I remembered the lessons from one of those women who met with us in fourth grade once a week to teach us traditional dancing in the school gym after classes were over. Most of the other kids had moccasins, but I didn't, and it was kind of hard to learn in those old stiff Salvation Army shoes. I was what you would call a slow learner in dance and I had a lot of trouble at first, but she kept telling me to just feel the music, to know what it meant to be with that music and with my people. I got it late that afternoon, and as we left that day, the woman, Mina Preene, came up to me specifically and told me I would always have it. I remember her last words perfectly that day. She told me, 'The dance will always take you home'."

"What was the dance?" Innis had finished listening to the story and, for a few minutes, sat looking silently over the water. The sun was going down and shown brilliantly over the reflective surface.

"Eel dance." Floyd smiled. Innis looked at him and nodded. He was not so sure he even could Eel dance; it had been a long time.

"Johnny was the last Eel on Cattaraugus," Jan offered. This explained a lot to Innis. He didn't know much about Longhouse, and was not a very religious man, but he knew that some part of him would also want other Eels around when it was time for him to leave. But there was still a lot unanswered for him. Before he could ask any of it: what if she hadn't met Floyd; what if Floyd hadn't come along; what if Johnny had lived—would Floyd still be lost, she answered everything in a sentence.

"Brian Waterson told Johnny that another Eel would come along in time and that was enough for him," Jan said simply, with the conviction of someone who truly believes what she is saying.

Throughout all of this, Bob Hacker had the look of someone who had no clue why he was even in attendance. Even at the job, though he had certainly helped out, he had mostly just kept an eye on Floyd and covered for him in the bad time. While it seemed he'd been able to follow this story, he clearly couldn't bring himself to believe it. He had lain the tobacco on the fire and had watched it all fly, just the same. Floyd turned directly to him, but addressed all four of them.

"Let's go down to the water's edge," he said, placing the still warm rocks in his plastic bag and carrying the bundle over the boulders. As they slid and climbed among the rocks the few minutes to the bottom, the bag jangled musically. At the edge, Floyd turned to Bob again.

"I know you're probably wondering what the hell this is all about, and I really don't have much of an explanation for you, but I wanted you to be here when I gave this up. Since Innis and Jan here are the only ones who have read my notebooks, this probably won't make a lot of sense to you, but if you wanna know someday, I'll tell you.

"Hack . . . Bob, I mean, I just wanted you to know how much this gift you passed on has meant to me, but I need to give it up now. I'd like you to help me. I don't need it anymore." Floyd pulled the pieces of the ghost machine out of the plastic bag. "It should rest with the other ghosts." He took one of the bladed wheels and whipped it out over the water. They watched it glide over and eventually meet its reflection in the water. Innis would swear it was over the area their family land had been. Bob picked up the other wheel and flung it out over another area, but the breeze changed its arc's direction and it entered the water at about the same area the first had.

The two of them, without speaking, dug out a place among the boulders to place the sphere section of the ghost machine. They covered it with the rocks from Floyd's bag.

"I'm sure if someone needs that ghost machine at some point, they'll find it," Floyd said, beginning the ascent to the top of the dike.

They stood at the top, watching the sun completely disappear behind the dike's far wall. "Look down there," Floyd said in the growing shadows. "Can you tell where those rocks are?" They all looked but the fire smudges had already started to blend with the darkness. "By morning, the water levels will have risen enough to wash those scars away," he continued. "Those rocks will be just like all the others. We don't need them to keep our pasts. We're the only connections we need to get on in this world." They watched the rocks fade into dark obscurity, as the air grew sharp around them.

"We should probably get back to Hank's," Innis said tentatively. He was expecting the usual protests from Floyd, and this was the way to ease them back.

"Yup. Let's go," Floyd answered, turning to the grassy slope of the dike's outer wall. Innis stepped quickly, hoping to get back to the house before Floyd lost his inexplicable attitude toward the idea of going back to Hank's. They reached the bottom and waited for the other two, who were having some difficulty navigating the dike's wall in the fresh dark. Even in boots, Floyd and Innis knew the balance needed to negotiate the steep incline.

They pulled into the driveway a few minutes later. Jan and Bob wondered why the house looked so dark. They couldn't believe that the party was over yet. Innis looked over at Floyd, who seemed not to be surprised in the least at the way the house looked. He knew that the party wasn't over, but he also knew that the light coming from the windows was generated not by incandescent bulbs, but by blazing kerosene lanterns, maybe even kerosene that had been boosted from Nora's tank by their late uncle.

They could hear tentative music coming from inside as they reached the side porch. Floyd stepped in the open door first and, as Innis and the others followed him in, he pointed to the louvered doors that had covered the entrance to the smaller bedroom. They were opened wide and Stan's drawings shone warmly, the Eagle Dancer flickering gently in the orange lantern light.

All the others were crowded in the living room. The four knew, as they moved in through the throng, that the music they heard was coming from an acoustic guitar. The two cousins knew exactly which guitar it was. Innis was eager to see who was playing it, but Floyd seemed to already know.

Bob Hacker walked into a comfortable space in the crowd. Floyd, who had one arm around Jan's shoulder, put his other arm around Innis's as they squeezed through to the front and saw Hank sitting in The Bug's old chair, the only piece of furniture he had kept, and strumming the opening chords to "Jambalayah." Their family was crowded in the near corner on a new couch, some sitting on the arms, others leaning on the back.

"I was wondering when you folks were coming home," Hank said, starting the song in earnest with a war whoop worthy of his father.

"Son of a bitch, In, we just might get rich," Floyd said as the three joined the others in the corner, and Jan Freen became one of the night-time kick-ball players.

August 11, 1992
March 20, 1994
Niagara Falls, New York